Gelato Forever

LYNN JOSEPH

For Cursey

Chapter One

Sunday night is family night with a capital F meaning no one can miss it, not even Dad. It's the only time during the week we all get together. Dad, me, and my four younger sisters.

I slip the printed email from my jeans pocket to the side of Dad's plate. He'll see it as soon as he finishes stacking the beef ribs onto a platter and sits down. The innocent piece of paper taunts me as I finish setting the cutlery on the table.

You're being selfish, Ava. You know you can't go. Shouldn't go. Why bring it up? It'll upset him. It'll upset everyone!

The logical side of my brain argues back. *It's not like I need anyone's permission. I'm twenty-four.*

Yet, my fingers itch to grab the paper before Dad sits down. I slide them under my legs as I take my seat.

"Are we ready, girls?" Dad's deep voice booms from across the room. He's heading to the table. It's now or never. My heart rises to my throat. I lean towards Dad's plate, just about to snatch it up when Bridget speaks loudly by my side.

"Ava, can you grab the muffins, please? I forgot them on the counter."

"What?" I glance over at my sister, who's two years younger than I am. She's my closest friend and the only one who knows what I'm about to spring on Dad and the rest of the family tonight.

"Why can't you get them?" I whisper frantically as Dad approaches, a smile blazing across his brown face. A film of sweat hovers at his temples from grilling outside in the August heat. She frowns at me. "Because I need you to step away from the table right now. Or else."

I give her a quizzical look.

"Muffins?" she says sweetly, tilting her head toward the kitchen. Her smile is fake and annoying, but it does the trick. I walk to the kitchen to retrieve the basket of corn muffins made by one of my sisters from the boxes of Jiffy cornbread mix I see laying on the counter. By the time I've located the butter dish in the fridge and peeled off a roll of paper towels for the messy sauce, Dad is seated and smiling at his daughters one by one.

"News or food first?" he asks.

"Food!" half the table shouts.

"News!" Bridget's voice is louder than the rest. Dad raises his eyebrows.

My feet tap a rhythm on the floor. I want to get the news over with. I can't eat a bite of the delicious ribs, cornbread, and macaroni pie – all the Southern comfort food Dad enjoys despite us telling him he needs to be careful as a Black man in his forties.

"Ava?" Dad asks, his eyes gentle and probing. Like he already knows something is up.

"News?" I swallow hard.

Bridget, who is sitting next to me, kicks me under the table. "What Ava means to say is she has *important* news."

"Bridget, hush."

"She does? You do?" asks Emerald, my youngest sister. She's sixteen and the anxious one. My heart clenches at what my news may do to her. Her big brown eyes stare at me, a worried light flickering in them. "What kind of news?"

"I know! You're finally going on a date." Daisy, the second youngest, says with a laugh. Daisy is seventeen, a total romantic, and convinced we're a remake of the five Bennett sisters in *Pride & Prejudice*.

"Not funny," our middle sister Corrine admonishes. "Ava doesn't need to cave to any social norms." Corrine is nineteen and attends a private college on a full scholarship two hours away, but she's sure to always come back every Sunday for family dinner. I give her props for her commitment to the family. Which makes me feel worse.

"Tell us your news," Corrine says, sitting back in her chair.

Dad claps his hands to get our attention. "Ava, Bridget, Corrine, Daisy, Emerald. Enough." He loves reciting our names out loud in our alphabetical order. We've been called the alphabet sisters throughout middle and high school.

"Let's do news. But you can all eat as we share. And what is this paper next to my plate?" He opens it carefully as if it might explode.

I want to run upstairs. I force myself to sit still with Bridget's hands clasping my own under the table.

I watch Dad's face as he reads the email. None of my sisters are helping themselves to the platters of food spread out on the table. They're all focused on Dad.

"What is it?" Emerald squeaks out.

"Good news or bad?" Daisy's voice drops low.

Corrine whips her head from me to Dad. "Ava, we got you, girl, whatever it is. Are you pregnant?"

I choke on the water I'm sipping. Bridget pounds on my back. "Corrine. *Please.*"

"It's good news," Dad says, lowering the email. He turns to me, his eyes glinting in the overhead lights. Is he crying? No way. Not our big, strong dad who is single-handedly raising his five "beauty queens" as he calls us.

"Your mom would be so proud of you, Ava." He gets up and comes around to my side of the table. He leans over and puts his bulky arms around me. "So proud."

"But I can't go. Can I? Not really."

"Of course, you're going."

A chorus of "go where?" echoes around the room.

I ignore my sisters and focus on Dad. "Don't you need me here? Emerald is only a junior. We're planning to go look at colleges in the fall. Daisy is boy-crazy. Someone's got to rein her in. And Bridget . . ."

"Bridget, nothing. I have a college degree and a bunch of job prospects lined up. I'm not a little girl. Neither are you. Neither are any of us, Ava. We'll manage six months without you. Or however long it takes."

"What's going on," Daisy wails.

"Where's Ava going? I want to go too." Emerald springs out of her chair. She darts around the table to throw her arms around me. "If you go, I go."

I sob and laugh at the same time. I reach up behind my head to hug her back.

Dad takes off his glasses. He cleans them on his shirt. They look foggy from the tears he's trying to wipe away without us noticing.

"Dad, it's okay." I reach out a hand to grasp his. "I don't have to go. It's just an acceptance letter."

He shakes his head. "You worked hard getting your Associate's degree at the community college, while taking care of all of us. It's time for you to follow your dreams. Your mother would have wanted you to go. I didn't know this was what you were dreaming of though." He waves the email around. "This is a genuine surprise." He chuckles.

My sisters are leaning forward, elbows on the table, eyes swinging between me and Dad as if watching a tennis match.

"Now, will you tell us?" begs Daisy. Although Emerald suffers from anxiety and I always do my best to calm her, Daisy is the sister who shares every bit of her life with me. I'm the first one to read all her stories and poems. Who will do that when I go?

If I go. All summer I've lived with this nugget of gold buried under my pillow. It gave me hope. But it also gave me anxiety. Because of what accepting this offer will mean.

I'm not sure I can walk out the door. Part of me feels as if I'll be turning my back on my family. Another part is dragging me to my laptop to purchase my plane ticket, book my apartment, and email my acceptance back.

Bridget stands up and taps her fork against her water glass. The *ping* noise silences everyone's questions. "I would like to congratulate Ava Walker on her new adventure. We all know how amazing Ava's homemade ice creams, sorbets, and gelato are. The refrigerator is filled with her creations."

"So is my belly," Corrine interjects rubbing her midsection, making everyone laugh.

"Well, Ava has been accepted into . . . ."

I stand up. "Thanks, Bridget. I'll take the microphone." If anyone is going to tell the family, it has to be me.

"Girls," I look from sister to sister. I curl and uncurl my fingers into a fist gaining the courage to speak.

"As everyone here knows, I was fourteen when Mom passed. Emerald and Daisy were only six and seven. Corrine was nine. Bridget was twelve. I promised mom we would stick together. That's what she told me. 'Stick together.' And we did. I made sure of it."

Tears brighten Emerald and Daisy's brown eyes. Corrine stares hard at something on the far wall. Bridget rests her chin on her hands and nods at me, urging me on. I don't dare look at Dad.

"I dropped out of every club and activity and focused on getting my schoolwork done and taking care of our family. I'm sorry you all lost your mother. I did my best."

"She was your mother, too." Corrine whispers.

I nod my head. "Yes, she was."

My chin trembles. I can see Mom's dark brown eyes staring at me from the hospital bed, memorizing my face. She told me to talk about her a lot so her babies would know her.

"You guys probably don't know that Mom gave me my first ice cream maker. I was ten. It was a Christmas gift. My favorite gift of all time. Mom and I experimented after school. We tried out recipes for sherbets and yogurts and a lot of ice cream flavors until I got good enough to do it myself. But Mom only liked one flavor. And she asked me to make it every single week.

"Chocolate chip." Dad smiles at me.

"Yup. It was her favorite. One day I said, 'Mom I'm sick of making chocolate chip.' She scolded me. 'Don't say that Ava. Chocolate chips are dark nuggets of happiness.'"

A laugh erupts from Dad. He slaps a hand down on the table. "Sounds like her."

Bridget giggles. My other sisters stare at me, like they are wondering where this is going.

I will them to understand my next words. I hold up the printed email. "Mom may have been kidding. But ice cream made her happy. It made all of you happy. So I thought, what more could I want to do with my life, if not make people happy? Starting with my own family."

"Read it," Daisy says.

"Read it," Emerald echoes.

"Read it," Corrine chimes in.

I open the paper with shaky hands. I'm still not sure this is the right thing to do. I clear my throat. "It's from the Florence Culinary Arts Institute."

"*Florence?* As in Italy?" Corrine whistles. "This is serious."

"Hush," Dad says, "continue."

I read aloud:
Dear Ava Walker,

Congratulations! We are very happy to welcome you to the **Gelato Masters** *course this fall. The course will be taught in English and Italian. An English interpretation service will be provided for all classes. We highly recommend that you enroll in an Italian language class during your time in Italy. Once the fall semester is successfully completed, you may enter the Gelato Winter Festival in December. There is a cash prize and a gelato internship with a top gelateria for three winners. We will follow up with all of the documents you need to obtain a student and work visa for your coursework. Housing information for student rooms and apartments are attached. Again, congratulations, and welcome to the Florence Culinary Arts Institute.*

I put down the piece of paper. "There's a little more but that's the gist of it." I glance around the room. Total silence. I glance from one sister to another. No one moves.

Suddenly, chairs go flying as my sisters rush over to hug me. They pelt questions at me fast and furious like trains run off their tracks.

"When do you leave?"

"Can you teach us how to make gelato when you come back?"

"Will you come back?"

"Are you going to fall in love in Italy like in the movies?"

"Is there really a Gelato University?"

I nod. "Yes, can you believe it? And yes, I'm coming back. And no, I won't have time to fall in love. I'll be busy making gelato."

"Mom would be thrilled for you." Bridget is hugging me so hard I can barely breathe. "I told you they'd love the idea."

Tears roll down my face. Happy tears. "You did."

"Good thing, too, because I already sent in your acceptance email."

"What?"

Bridget nods. "You bet I did. I also got your visa and passport all organized. Those things take time."

"But how?"

"I gave you the documents to sign amongst a bunch of other school documents for the girls." She grins at me, and I laugh.

"Trickster."

"Gelato trickster to you, missy."

Dad sits in his chair at the head of the table watching us high-five and talk over each other. I hold up my hands. "Wait a minute. Will you guys be okay if I leave for an entire semester?"

"Yes!" the entire room shouts at me.

"It could be longer if you win the gelato festival, which you will because yours are the best." Corrine claps.

Dad shakes his head. "Finally. You get to use the education fund your mom left for you." He looks up at the ceiling as if she's floating up there, which maybe she is to him. "You hear that Hazel, love. Ava is going to Gelato University. In Italy."

I grin at him. I can hardly believe it myself. Twenty-four years old and I'm heading off like a pioneer for the first time.

Me, who hasn't had time for a real boyfriend.

Or a real job.

Or a real life.

I'm going to Italy!

Chapter Two

My "To Do" list screams at me as soon as I wake up. Tasks that I thought I had weeks to complete, like getting Emerald and Daisy ready for their junior and senior years of high school, are condensed into days.

Not that my stomach isn't doing leaps of excitement all the time. Just the word *Italy* gives me shivers and I keep whispering it to myself.

"We have to get you ready too," Bridget tells me one day as I'm creating Excel spreadsheets of dinner menus, chores, emergency numbers, and more. She's perched on a stool next to me, helping me organize information to input.

"Me?"

"Yes, you." Corrine enters the kitchen and leans on my workspace. "You can't go to Italy looking like this." She waves her hand up and down my body encased in baggy sweats and an oversized t-shirt. My go-to comfy clothes that serve dual purposes of being interchangeable and covering up messes.

"I'm fine," I mutter, going back to the spreadsheets. Maybe we need to hire a housekeeper. It might be simpler. It certainly would be more hygienic. I shake my head thinking of what weeks of uncleaned sinks and toilets would look like. Ugh! "Besides, there's too much to do. I don't have time to worry about how I look."

Corrine shivers dramatically. She pulls out her phone and aims it at me. Snaps a few pictures then examines her phone, making tsking noises under her breath.

I try not to let her bother me. I have more important things to worry about. And here comes one now.

Daisy rolls up on pink bedazzled roller skates. She's been wearing them everywhere this summer. I glance down at them and back up at Daisy's round face and flushed cheeks.

"You're not planning on roller skating in school are you?" I hate how wishy-washy my voice sounds. If I were her mother, I'd say firmly, "Daisy, you're not wearing roller skates to school." And that would be that. But since I'm her big sister I try to be cool about stuff and not come across like a strict parent.

It doesn't always work. It's hard to be patient and hope my sisters will choose the wiser course. Sometimes, I have to drop the big sister role and be a plain old authoritarian. As in, I tell them what they must do, or else. The "or else" is to take it to the top. Meaning Dad will have to get involved. This roller-skating business may be one of those times.

She shrugs. "It's great exercise. I could ask the principal."

"Okay. Read your school's Rules & Regulations Handbook. If it doesn't say anything about roller-skating, you may ask your principal in a nice email. And remember to give him choices."

"Yes, I know. Give solutions, not problems."

"Exactly. And I want to see it in writing. You can cc me."

"But you'll already be in Italy."

"They get emails in Italy."

"I'll handle it," Bridget swings an arm around Daisy's shoulders. "No need to bother you."

"Fine." Daisy rolls off to the other side of the kitchen and pokes her head into the snack cupboard. "We don't have any more Strawberry Pop Tarts?" she wails.

"Write it on the board." I wiggle my fingers in the direction of the fridge.

Emerald slides in on her socks and leaps her butt onto the counter next to my workspace. I'm now surrounded by the entire crew. I can feel all their eyes on me, and I sigh. "What?"

"Ava, no disrespect, but you look like a—," Emerald sighs heavily and looks sad. "I can't even say it."

"Well, don't then." I turn back to my laptop. "I'm busy."

"When was the last time you did anything to your hair? Or your wardrobe? Or your face? I don't think you even own lipstick." Emerald ticks each of my inadequacies off one by one. As if I don't know them already.

Every time I planned to go shopping for myself, something more important popped up that needed doing. I gave up. As for my hair, who has hours to visit a salon? The only time I take for myself is to plug in my air pods and run three miles each day. If I didn't do that, I'd be crazy by now.

Corrine lifts the scraggly hair I've pulled back and banded tightly into a ponytail. "Nuh-uh, girlfriend. No more excuses. We are getting this sorted out. Sooner rather than later. I made an appointment for you tomorrow at the best hair salon in Portland. I just texted pics of your hair to the stylist, so she knows what she's in for. I told her to turn this into *fabulous*."

"But today, we're taking you shopping," Bridget hops off her stool and checks her phone. "Daddy gave me his credit card and said to buy whatever you need for your trip. We'll start in Portland, but if we have to, we'll drive down to Boston. Ain't nothing stopping us."

My mouth opens and closes like a fish blowing bubbles. "You did what? He did what? How? When?"

All four of them surround me, leading me away from the laptop, moving like a wave pushing me toward the door.

"We don't have time to waste," Daisy says, rolling alongside of me and leading me outside by one arm.

"Right. We have ten years of self-neglect to reverse in two days." Corrine pulls open the front passenger side door of our family's SUV and hustles me in. Bridget jumps into the driver's seat. Emerald, Daisy, and Corrine climb into the backseat.

"I'm too busy for this! I haven't finished organizing the housework, cooking, and after-school activities. I still have Dad's stuff to do."

Bridget reaches over and pats my arm. "Your hard work has paid off. We're all thriving because of you. Now it's your turn."

I slouch down in my seat. "I can't believe you're kidnapping me to go shopping."

"Ava, you do realize that Bridget will be around every day now, and Corrine is a mere two-hour drive away. Plus, Daisy is going to be a senior in high school, and I'll be a junior." Emerald sticks her head between the front seats speaking sternly to me.

I glance back over my shoulder at my baby sister. She's so grown up now. Maybe they don't need me. Maybe it's me who needs them.

"By the way, Dad ordered a matching set of luggage for you." Daisy pipes up. "I picked them out."

My mouth drops open almost to the floor mats. "Let me guess. They're pink and glittery."

"Excuse me! It took me a long time to decide on which set said, '*Look at me, I won't get lost in the crowd, but I'm cautious so don't think about distracting me.*'"

We all laugh. "I can't wait to see what arrives."

"Well, I didn't know your taste. You never buy anything for yourself."

I shrug. "I'll be happy with whatever you pick. Thank you."

"You're welcome."

GELATO FOREVER

At the mall, we head straight to Macy's. Bridget says it will have the most options to choose from.

"You must find your inner goddess," Daisy exclaims, as she flicks through long flowy dresses on a summer sales rack. Exactly the kind of clothes she wears herself when she's not roller skating.

"You mean her inner badass chick," Corrine argues. She's across the aisle looking through the fall line of leather jackets and turtlenecks, which are her style.

Bridget holds up velour sweats and large sunglasses. "You can wear these with sexy tank tops. It's called layering."

"That looks like something a reality star would wear." I shake my head at her. "Not for me."

Emerald dances over with armfuls of Calvin Klein underwear. Bras, panties, and slip dresses that look like a child should be wearing them. "Buy these," she thrusts them into Bridget's arms. "They'll fit her. I checked the sizes on her old rusty bras before we left home."

They all chuckle and I look down. How embarrassing. My baby sister is picking out my bras and panties.

We spend about an hour poking through racks of clothing. I can't help thinking of all the things I could be doing instead. Things I could check off my "To Do" list.

After the mall, we head to a few local boutiques. I try on a deep red coat with red buttons that looks and feels glamorous. Bridget buys it immediately before I change my mind. She won't let me see the price. "It's probably ridiculous. Can we go home now?" I want to forget shopping completely. "I'll never find anything I like that I can afford. I can wear my jeans and sweatshirts."

"*Nooo!*" My sisters shout me down. "No way."

"But where else can we look? Online?" I suggest that hesitantly. I don't like online shopping. The clothes never fit me right. I have a small waist and long legs, but my thighs are beefy. It's better to try everything on in person.

"I know exactly what you need," Emerald says. She pulls out

her phone and directs Bridget to drive to a location outside her usual home to school to mall route.

"What's this?" I ask when we pull up in a neighborhood I don't usually venture to. Music stores, coffee shops, and used book stands dot the sidewalk. There are young people who look like us, meaning with darker skin tones, and I like the vibe already. If I ever had the time to hang out, this is where I'd do it. There's an African clothing shop and a set of African drums in front of an African restaurant. This could be a great location for the gelato store I want to open one day.

Emerald stops in front of a vintage clothing store that looks as if Daisy bedazzled it. CDs tied to colorful pieces of yarn spin around in the light breeze sending mirrored shards of light in every direction.

"Wow. Emerald, this is magical."

"I know. It's the coolest. You'll love it."

"I already love it."

I forget about the ticking clock and start to help my sisters figure out what my style is. We pull out shorts, dresses, sweaters, boots, and more for me to try on.

My "buy" pile quickly grows higher than my "discard" pile. I turn this way and that in front of the three-way mirror admiring curves I didn't realize I had.

When I'm standing in front of the mirror in an especially slinky dress, Bridget exclaims, "You're hotter than all of us put together. You've been hiding your natural beauty under ugly clothes and that damn *To Do* list."

I throw my arms over her shoulders. "I wish Mom was here."

I intend to whisper it, but it comes out loud enough for Emerald, Corrine, and Daisy to hear. They swarm me with hugs and kisses. We're a soggy mess.

"Enough," Bridget pulls away. "Go put this on."

"This?" I anxiously hold up the teeny tiny pair of shorts and the teeny tiny top she dropped into my arms.

"Yes, and hurry back so we can see it. I think this outfit will showcase your figure perfectly."

I doubt it, but I do as she says. When I step out of the dressing room, Daisy wolf whistles at me. Corrine gives me a thumbs up while smacking Daisy for her "disrespectful" whistle.

"Come look at yourself." Bridget drags me toward the mirror.

"This is way too small for me to wear in public." I gasp at the wide expanse of my exposed thighs.

"*Oh la la.*" Emerald fans herself as if it's extra hot in here.

"This is indecent," I murmur.

"Screw your courage to the sticking place, Ava." Emerald pops her hands on her hips and glares at me. "You look hot because you *are* hot. It's time you stopped dressing like a mom in the pickup line after school and start looking your age."

A sweat breaks out on my forehead. "I can't pull this off. I'm not a booty shorts type."

"Your booty says otherwise." Corrine spins me around and pats my butt.

My entire face turns as dark red as a raspberry gelato.

"And this tiny crop top. This is more you, Emerald. Or you Daisy. Not for me. I'm too old."

My sisters shoot down all my protests. They add the outfit to the pile of clothes to buy. I sit down exhausted and overruled. I let them select jeans and flowy, off-the-shoulder tops for travel and exploring. Leggings and tight tee shirts for classes. Cute mini dresses and rompers for fun daytime events. I point out a Denim jacket and practical black sweater, which they ignore. And finally, a selection of sparkly dresses that barely skim my butt for evening events.

"Where would I wear those dresses?" I ask.

"On dates!" Bridget shouts.

"With your Italian hottie." Daisy snickers.

"For when you fall in love." Emerald puts her hands together under her chin and bats her eyelashes at me.

"Italy does have a reputation for being romantic," Corrine adds. "You want to be ready for anything."

I wonder if my sisters realize I've never kissed a boy. I've never been on a date.

Italy may help me get closer to my dream of a gelato store of my own, but Italy is not a miracle worker.

Besides, falling in love is not part of my plan.

I'm afraid I'll disappoint my sisters. None of these dresses will get worn.

Chapter Three

I gather my passport and baggage claim ticket from the airline representative and thank her.

"Ava, isn't that the boy you had a crush on in high school?" Bridget puts her hand to her mouth. "I can't believe it. He's checking into your flight."

"Who?" I'm too busy stuffing everything into my shoulder bag to look up.

"There." Bridget points to a parallel line of people dropping off their luggage. "What's his name again?" She snaps her fingers. "Tyler Donovan." I look over to where she's staring. It *is* him. Tall and lean with muscled arms in a burgundy tee shirt. A Harvard t-shirt.

His dark brown skin glows like he's been landscaping all summer. I've seen pictures on social media of him working with his mom's landscaping company around the Cape Elizabeth area. I can't see his honey-colored eyes from where I'm standing, but I could never forget them. Nope, Tyler Donovan hasn't changed at all.

The last time I saw him was at our high school graduation party. Bridget forced me to attend. I congratulated Tyler then on getting into Harvard. He offered me a shot of a yellow liqueur I'd never heard of and couldn't pronounce.

"Limon who?" I was hovering around the drinks table outside. I went to school with these kids for four years or more, but I didn't know anyone well enough to laugh and joke around the way everyone else was doing.

"It's Italian." He poured the shimmery liquid into a small plastic cup and handed it to me. The way he was holding onto the bottle made me dizzy with appreciation. He'd selected me to share his liqueur with.

I sipped the strong drink and coughed. My eyes watered. "What's it doing here?" In a neighborhood outside Portland, Maine.

"Graduation gift from my older brother. My dream is to go to Italy." His honey eyes shone as he spoke. Like he could see Italy over my shoulder.

"Me, too," I said. It slipped out so fast I didn't have time to stop my lying tongue.

"Really?" He looked into my eyes. I was dazed on the spot.

"We should get together and talk about it. I want to live there one day. Speak Italian, eat delicious ravioli and pizzas. Get a Vespa and zoom around the narrow cobblestone streets. And of course, gobble up as much gelato as possible." He raised the bottle. "Cheers to Italy."

I stared in wonder. This guy knew exactly what he wanted. Down to the food and the kind of ride he'd have in his future. While I was dog paddling around in my life. Taking care of my sisters and our home and making sure everything and everyone survived.

"That's...great," I stammered.

I took another sip of my golden drink. This was the closest I'd ever get to Italy.

"What about you? Why do you want to go to Italy?"

Shoot. *Think, Ava, think.*

He tossed back another shot of his liqueur.

I could slink away. Ignore his question. My mind whirled with exit strategies. I slammed back the rest of the drink in my cup and placed it on the table next to his.

Without asking, he poured more of his gold liquid into both cups, as if he didn't want me to leave. "Well, Ava?"

This was the longest conversation I'd ever had with the most popular boy at our school. Captain of two sports teams, editor of the school paper, and a debate champion. Plus, he was good looking. I hadn't realized he knew my name like that. I was not on his radar at all.

His eyes held mine. The thing with lying is to make it as truthful as possible. The problem was there were no truths about my wanting to go to Italy. I was so far below Italy's radar I might as well be frozen pizza.

"It's a secret. I haven't told anyone yet." That, at least, was true.

Tyler didn't respond. Zeke Cranston, his best friend, and one of the football players grabbed his arm and dragged him away. Bottle and all.

"Who're you talking to, dude?" Zeke muttered as they weaved through the crowd like they were dodging opposing players on the field.

I could just make out Tyler's answer. "That girl wants to go to Italy. Like me."

I heard the laughter as I shrank into the shadows. "I bet she does."

I wasn't sure which hurt more. That Tyler dismissed me as "that girl." Or that Zeke made fun of my dream. Because at that moment, I knew it was my dream too.

What would it be like to fly across the ocean, live for a while in a foreign city, and meet new people? Maybe discover something new about myself, even if it was only that I liked the food?

Italy was an impossible dream. But at least it was something.

"Yeah, that's him," I tell Bridget, pivoting her away from the counter and back into Boston's Logan Airport's immense departure hall. It was surging with folks dragging bags behind them. We could get lost in the shuffle before Tyler saw us.

"This could be fate," Bridget says, as I push her forwards.

"I don't believe in fate." I walk faster, passing Bridget. "Fate means something that's destined to happen. It's pure coincidence that he and I are going to Italy at the same time."

Bridget hurries alongside me as we maneuver towards the family waiting in a designated spot. "Whatever the reason. This is an opportunity to talk to him. Be friendly. Don't play wallflower."

"Right. Should I pretend to be you then?" I joke.

"If you must. I'm awesome. I have enough sparkle to share, sis."

"And not a bit shy, either." I laugh as we locate our family.

"What took you guys so long?" Emerald wails as Bridget and I stop in front of them.

"Stop whining, Em," Daisy says. "We don't want Ava to have her last memory of you being a big baby."

"It's ok," I throw my arms around Emerald and Daisy. "You're always my babies."

Emerald tucks her face against my shoulder. Her long braids tickle my nose. Daisy leans back and eyeballs me up and down. "You look so beautiful. I can't believe you're the same sister who wore raggedy clothes and had raggedy hair last week. No one would recognize you now."

Corrine pushes Daisy aside and grabs me in her arms. "She's right. We're like your fairy god-sisters. We worked our magic on you."

Bridget joins the trio surrounding me. The sweet smell of lotions and creams, hair sprays, and perfume mixes together on me. I feel like Miss Universe when she wins the crown and is swamped by a bunch of gorgeous contestants.

"Don't forget to text us every day," Emerald says, pouting her bold, green-colored lips. "I want to know everything."

"Don't forget to write in your travel journal," Daisy says. Earlier today, she'd given me a gorgeously painted journal for the trip.

"Take lots of photos. I want to see the art and architecture." Corrine says.

"Have fun and make friends," Bridget says. "Especially with you know who."

"Who?" Emerald, Daisy, and Corrine ask.

I groan. "Nobody. Bridget is being facetious."

"No, I'm not."

"Let Ava breathe, please," Dad shouts over the sound of their voices. He gently moves the gang aside to reach me. I'm tall but Dad is much taller. I have to tiptoe to put my arms around his neck. He bends over to bear hug me. It's the safest place in the world.

What the heck am I doing leaving Dad and my sisters here in the United States while I travel so far away from home to follow a dream?

Chapter Four

Bridget was right. Tyler Donovan's on my flight. He's at the boarding gate, pacing in front of the giant windows talking on his cell.

I wonder whom he's talking to that's causing those deep grooves in his forehead. He switches his phone to the other hand and drags his free hand down his face. His gaze swings in my direction. I slide down in my blue vinyl seat next to the boarding lanes.

I don't know why I feel as if I'm stalking him. I'm not interested. He is a boy from my past. Barely. I'm heading into a fantastic future. I don't have time for men. Not even Tyler Donovan.

I open my book and stare at the words in front of my eyes. I re-read the same paragraph twice. The words can't compete with the slideshow in my mind of Tyler's picture-perfect life showcased through his social media posts and stories.

Tyler's beautiful mom and handsome father and brother sailing on a boat in Casco Bay around Portland. His summer jobs landscaping the lawns of wealthy folks on Peaks Island. His dog Pluto riding in his bicycle basket along the Greenbelt. His bronzed Pilates model girlfriend with a name like Tiffany.

No, not like Tiffany. It *is* Tiffany. The daughter of a celebrity who summers on one of Maine's exclusive islands.

Okay, so I more than peep at his Instagram page occasionally. But it's only because I try to keep up with my classmates' lives. I'm not cyber-stalking him. Honest.

The flight starts boarding and I'm grateful to get in line and get seated. Maybe now I can forget about Tyler.

When I get to my row, I glance at my boarding pass and then at my seat twice before sliding in. Wow, Dad did me good. I knew he'd upgraded me to business class, but I wasn't sure what that would mean.

My facial muscles expand into a big smile. I wish I could show Bridget my wide plush comfy seat, with its curved headrest and its footrest and the laptop size screen in front of me, presumably full of movies to watch during the ten-hour flight.

After tucking my bag away by my feet, I throw the pink Hello Kitty blanket, courtesy of Daisy, over my legs and lean back. Heaven! My first flight and it's a piece of cake.

Passengers trudge by lugging bags and backpacks. I want to wave at each person going by. For the next ten hours, we're all neighbors on this shared flight. Instead, I smile and nod my head at the other excited people heading to Italy.

"Hi, excuse me."

Oh my god. Tyler is saying hello. He must remember me.

"Hi," I say, trying to infuse warmth into my shocked tone.

He looks at his phone, then at me. "I'm your seatmate." He cracks the kind of smile you give to a person you'll never see again. A polite, let's just do this, smile.

"Oh," I pull my blanket closer so it's not touching his seat. My mind is screaming, "WTH?"

I watch in a daze as he stores his carry-on luggage overhead.

He sits down and slides his backpack under the seat in front of us. His hand fumbles for something near me and I shrink back.

"I think you're sitting on my seat belt," he says, a tiny spark in his hazel eyes.

"Oh, sorry." I raise my ass up and extract one end of his seat belt. My face burns with embarrassment.

"You should put on yours too." He buckles his seat belt and picks up a stray belt strap. He looks pointedly at my midsection which is covered by the word *Kitty*.

"Thanks." I look around for my other end and take longer than is necessary to buckle myself in. You'd think I'd never driven in a car with seatbelts.

Once I'm buckled in, I stare down at my lap. I hope I don't blurt out, *do you remember me*? *We went to high school together.* Or worse, *I used to be in love with you.* I clamp my lips shut before anything bizarre slips out.

But seriously, what are we going to talk about for ten hours? This is crazy. Fate is crazy.

His cell buzzes. He picks it up, glances at the screen, and groans. "Leave me alone, damn it." He swipes his phone closed and shoves it in the seat pocket in front of him. He leans back with a sigh and shuts his eyes.

Okay, so his life is not as picture-perfect as it appears. It makes me feel a little sorry for him. I turn to look out my window at the trolleys going by carrying boxes and bags. Another plane lines up on the runway in the distance.

A loud growl rumbles below as our plane pulls away from the hangar.

My heart gives a *rat a tat* beat.

I'm going to Italy!

I, Ava Walker, will soon be strolling along the same streets that Michelangelo walked while thinking about sculpting the *David*.

I feel the edges of my mouth sliding up into a smile as I rest my face on my fist against the window.

Suddenly, the plane's engine revs up with a loud screech.

I grab both handrests. My knuckles bulge out from squeezing them so hard.

"Are you okay?"

I turn my head to see Tyler Donovan staring at me with a look of concern.

"It's my first time on a plane," I whisper.

His face softens. "Oh, these noises are fine."

I nod and swallow hard. "I should have read that book my sister gave me. *Flying for Dummies.*"

His laugh sounds like fall leaves crunching underfoot. Deep and full.

He rests a large warm hand on top of my hand. "It'll be okay."

I stare at his hand as if it's a black widow spider.

He notices and yanks it back. "I'm sorry. I didn't mean to offend you. I thought I could...um...help."

"It's ok." I squeeze my eyes shut as the engines rev up louder and louder in a high-pitched wail. Suddenly, the plane hurls itself down the runway like a rocket. I suck in my breath. I feel myself tilting backward as the plane jolts into the sky.

Tyler's hand is near mine and without thinking, I grab it, squeezing it harder than I've squeezed anything before.

Just as I think we're going to fly straight out of the atmosphere and into another galaxy, Tyler says, "I think I know you."

I shake my head. I can't formulate words to admit or deny it.

I feel him staring at me. Will he remember the girl who never spoke in class? Who slipped in and out of our high school doors with one purpose in mind; *Get in and get out.*

He leans forward and peeps into my eyes. "You went to my high school." A huge smile fills his face. As if he's happy to see me.

"I did." I smile weakly, stunned he remembers me.

"You're one of the Alphabet sisters. Let me see, which one?" He cocks an eyebrow and I want to tell him it's me, Ava Walker, with whom he had classes every single year.

I laugh instead. It's nice to be reminded of my family's nickname. One year there were three of us at the school at the same time. I was a senior, Bridget was a junior and Corrine was a freshman. A, B, and C.

"I remember you," his voice rises in excitement. "You were amazing in all our school plays and musicals. Oh, my goodness, Bridget Walker. I can't believe it. Everyone had a crush on you."

Errrrrt. Wrong. The tips of my ears burn up.

But forget my ears. The plane drops through space like it's flying down a skateboard ramp. My stomach drops with it. I stifle a scream.

There it goes again. The aircraft dips and rises like it's on a see-saw now. I'm too busy keeping my stomach from doing somersaults to correct Tyler.

Here we go again!

My stomach gurgles with fear.

"It's okay, Bridget, that's just turbulence. It's normal." Tyler rubs one of my hands between his two large brown hands.

I nod hard and a lot. Like one of those bobbing dog gizmos on a dashboard.

I'm going to be sick.

He thinks I'm Bridget. He's excited to be talking to her. How can I tell him it's plain old me? How can I get this pilot to stop lurching the plane around like a drunk driver?

Chapter Five

Tyler breaks open a carton of cookies and hands me a couple. "Here, eat some of these. You'll feel better. They're ginger snaps. Highly recommended for nausea."

Is he serious? I take a few but hold them in my hand. "Thanks."

He pops a few into his mouth. "Try yours, they're really good."

I take a tiny bite. Then another. The cookie is thin and flavorful. Sweet and a little spicy. The ginger flavor sparks in my mouth.

The plane finally settles down and after awhile, the seat belt lights go off. The pilot makes announcements.

A flight attendant appears offering us beverages of our choice.

"What're you having, Bridget?" Tyler looks at me with a sweet smile. He leans over and whispers, "They have real espresso on board."

"I'd love an espresso," I say to the attendant.

"It's my favorite thing to order on this airline," he says. But it doesn't sound snotty. Just informative. I wonder if I'll ever be so casual about flying internationally.

The flight attendant hands us our hot drinks and winks at me, "You guys make a cute couple."

Before I can correct him, he's gone down the aisle with his cart.

"Awkward," I say.

Tyler shakes his head. "Maybe it's fate. I tried talking to you a few times in high school, but you ignored me."

I realize it's Bridget he's talking about but I'm curious. "I did?"

"You avoided me."

"Oh." I sip my espresso and think back to Bridget in high school. She was beautiful of course and always busy with extracurricular activities. She never told me that Tyler Donovan was interested in her. A feeling of homesickness drenches me. My sister knew about my own crush on Tyler. She must have been protecting my feelings. I have to tell him I'm not her.

Tyler is talking and I'm missing it.

'What?" I ask.

"I was just saying that the ginger snaps are even better if you dunk them into the espresso. The flavors are amazing together."

"Really?" I tilt my head to take in all six feet of his dark handsome physique. I can play along just for the flight. I can be Bridget until we land and see what happens. I mean it's not as if I'll be seeing him again once I get to Florence.

"Okay." I try what he suggested.

When I taste the combination of coffee with ginger my toes tingle. It's how I feel whenever I discover a brand-new ice cream flavor. "Tyler, these flavors are amazing."

"Close your eyes."

"What?"

"Do you trust me?"

"I hardly know you."

He laughs. It's a happy playful laugh. So different from how he sounded in the boarding area or when his phone beeped earlier.

"Just close your eyes, ok."

I do as he says. I slap one hand over my closed eyes in case I'm tempted to peep. I hear him ruffling around in his backpack.

"Taste this." Tyler's fingers hover near my mouth. "You have to open your mouth."

I open my mouth and he places something on my tongue.

"Now, chew."

I close my mouth and chew. Delicious aromas and flavors burst through my entire being. A thrill runs up and down my spine. I'm not sure if it's how close he is to me or if I'm tasting something I've never tasted before in my life.

"It tastes like chocolate."

"Right."

I shake my head left and right. "But it's not. What is this?" I'm dying to open my eyes.

"You can look."

I drop my hand. He's smiling at me, and I smile back. It's like we're playing a game. I can't remember the last time I played a game. For sure, it wasn't with a handsome man.

He's holding a piece of brownie in his hand. I raise my eyebrows at him.

"Black sapote brownie. I made it myself," he says with pride.

"Is this an *edible*?" I squeak.

"Hahahahahaha," his loud laugh causes our neighbors to look over at us.

"Sorry," I say to the couple in the next row.

"Shhhhh!" I whisper to Tyler. "Well?"

When he stops laughing, he holds up the brownie as if it's Ming treasure. "Black sapote is a fruit that tastes just like chocolate pudding. It's native to Central America. It's hard to get. But I love it. I tasted it when I was on a study abroad there."

I pinch off another piece of his precious brownie and chew it slowly, trying to dissect the flavors. Chocolate but with a beautiful delicate flavor. Almost like honey.

I look over at Tyler with my eyes wide open. This could be it. This could be the secret ingredient to a winning gelato flavor I invent. "Can you get me some of the real fruit?"

"I don't know Bridget. It's hard to find outside of Central America. But I could try. Why do you want it?"

"You want to hear about why I'm going to Italy?" I ask.

He nods and turns his entire body towards mine.

I tell him about my love of ice cream. And how that grew into a fascination with its incredibly perfect cousin, gelato.

"And now, I'm going to learn all the ins and outs of making artisan gelato from gelato's homeland, Italy. Do you know there are Gelato Festivals every year? To create brand new flavors? It's an entire art form."

"Seriously?" Tyler's mouth hangs open. His hazel eyes are huge saucers. "That is so cool. So original. You're the first person I've met whose study abroad sounds better than mine."

I snort. "I doubt it. What're you doing in Italy?"

"It's going to sound boring." He looks down, then back up at me. I see a hesitation in his eyes. This isn't the Tyler Donovan I remember from high school. Back then he was so confident. So self-assured. What happened to him, I wonder?

"Tell me," I say. "I want to know." And I do. I've had a lot of experience trying to get Daisy and Emerald to talk about themselves after Mom died. This is far from that experience, but the reluctance to talk about themselves and what they were feeling reminds me of Tyler now.

"Well," he shrugs. "I'm getting my master's in International Relations. At the University of Florence."

I knew the guy was smart. But wow! "That's not boring, that's amazing. Your family must be so proud of you!" I mean I'm sitting here feeling proud of him and I barely know him.

Frown lines appear on his forehead. His mouth turns down. He sits back in his seat facing straight ahead. "Yes, they're proud.

But not everyone was happy about my choice to go to school in *Italy*. So...." He raises up his palms and an air of dejection surrounds us.

It's my turn to frown. Who wouldn't like his choice? But I can't ask him that. It's too personal.

I look around at our little corner of the airplane to find something else to talk about. It's cozy with our side-by-side reclining seats. Our two trays tilted down with cookies and brownie crumbs, and empty espresso cups sprawled on them. My pink blanket and his backpack open at our feet. It's as if we made this shared space ours in the short time we've been on board.

I settle back but leave my hand next to his on the joint hand rest. To my surprise, our silence is not awkward or uncomfortable. It's kind of nice.

After a little while, Tyler sighs heavily. "Sorry to kill the vibe."

"No, not at all." *We had a vibe?* I do my best to hold back the smile trying to escape my lips. I can't grin like a teenager with a crush. *Geez, Ava, get a grip.*

"Where are you going to study gelato?" Tyler asks. "I hope it's near Florence."

I make a face at him. I'm feeling giddy. About our vibe and all. I can't wait to tell Bridget that Tyler Donovan and I talked on the flight over.

"Bridget?" He interrupts my wandering thoughts.

"Oh. My family calls it Gelato University. But it's a three-month course at a culinary school. And, yes, it's in Florence."

He shakes a fist in the air in a celebratory gesture. "You're going to love Florence. And how amazing for you. I'm impressed. Do you speak any Italian?"

I shake my head. "No, not yet. The courses have an English interpretation. But I need to sign up for an Italian language course. I want to do an internship afterward with a master *gelatiere*."

"What's that?"

"A Gelato Master. But I have to learn Italian first. I'm not great with languages. I can barely remember my Spanish from high school."

"I thought you took French? You spoke fluent French in that play your Junior year."

I swallow quickly. "Look how much I forgot? I can't even remember which language I studied." I roll my eyes at my fakery.

You're not Ava. You're Bridget. Think like Bridget.

"I teach Italian to study abroad students," Tyler says.

"Really? You're fluent?"

He smiles. "Been studying Italian since high school. My brother said it was a waste of time. But what does he know?" He says that last part bitterly.

Before I can analyze it, he continues, "It's a part-time teaching job I got through my university. If you want to, you can sign up for my course. It's not expensive and it's held in a classroom in the middle of Florence, so it's easy to get to."

We stare at each other. My heart hammers in my chest. Was Bridget right? Is this possibly a second chance at a love that passed me by in high school?

I stare at him for too long. He draws back. "What's wrong?"

I shake my head. "Nothing. I was just wondering if you still like Bri… um…*me* the way you did in high school?"

"Honestly, I never got a chance to know you very well."

I look deeply into his eyes to see if he's legit. The last thing I want is to blindside him or Bridget from a potential relationship. If either of them is interested, that is.

His smile lights up his hazel eyes.

I inhale deeply. His closeness makes me feel fluttery inside. Like a butterfly escaping its cocoon and flying madly in circles.

I cross my legs under me. He pulls up the Hello Kitty blanket and tucks it around me. Like he's making me as safe as possible. Our eyes lock and I catch my breath.

I have a flashback to when we were freshmen in high school. It was right after my mom died. I had missed two weeks of school and it was my first day back.

I was in English class. My sweater had fallen off the back of my chair and I hadn't noticed. Tyler tapped me on my shoulder and handed it to me.

"I'm really sorry." He seemed to be talking about the sweater. But I knew he was talking about me losing my mom. None of the other kids had said a word to me. As if death was contagious.

Our eyes had locked then, too. I don't know what he saw in mine. But I remember what I saw in his. The same thing I'm seeing now.

Tyler Donovan is kind, compassionate, and very sure of himself.

Chapter Six

At the Florence airport, Tyler and I say our goodbyes. We exchanged contact information on the plane. He told me he only uses text and phone because he swore off social media this summer for reasons he didn't want to go into. I let it slide. I wasn't going to ask why I hadn't seen any new photos of him in the past month or two.

Anyway, since I don't know anyone else in Florence, I'm glad to have his number.

But I'll only use it in case of an emergency. Honestly, I can't hang out with him. He's in love with Bridget. And how long can I pretend to be her for Christ's sake? Plus, I'm anxious to immerse myself in this amazing city and its world of gelatos. I don't want a guy, even a cute one like Tyler Donovan, distracting me from my goals.

As I Uber to my apartment's address, I look around at my new city for the next three or more months.

My body is in shock from the long flight and trying to operate six hours ahead of its internal time clock. If this is jet lag, I'm not a fan. The most important thing now is to get settled in and try not to feel homesick.

When I step out of the Uber, my legs wobble. I press my heels down and take stock of the situation. The Uber left me in front of a set of four wide concrete steps leading up to massive, green double doors with lion-head knockers. It looks like something from a fantasy.

Luckily, the lockbox opens easily and I'm soon inside. The studio is tiny but perfect.

An iron balcony with room enough for one, or two if we squish together, opens onto the back of the street. I glimpse the Arno River between the ancient stone buildings, only one block away.

After everything is put away, I look around at my new home. Something is missing. I eye the empty shelves where groceries will go. I peep at the bedside nooks where I should have photos of the family.

I can't believe my sisters didn't think of that when they were helping me pack. Maybe they thought I didn't need any.

I glance at my phone. It's barely 8 a.m. their time. I can't call and interrupt their morning routines.

There's only one thing left to do. I must head back out. Otherwise, I'll collapse on the bed. I will snuggle under the embroidered coverlet and fall asleep for the next 24 hours. And I'd never recover from my jet lag.

Tyler warned me to stay awake until a normal bedtime. That means I must force myself to stay awake until 9 p.m. tonight. I look at my phone again. Seven hours?! This is going to be hard. What can I do for seven hours?

I open my contacts list. I stare at Tyler Donovan's name and number. My fingers hover over the screen. I kind of miss him. Between our flight and changeover in Rome, we spent over fourteen hours together. Most of it was side by side. I wonder what he's doing right now?

Not like you can call him on the first day, Ava. It would look desperate. Stalkerish.

I shake my head to get visions of Tyler's smooth brown muscles out of my mind.

I open my Maps app instead. I search for the closest supermarket. I'm used to doing the shopping back home. This is a no-brainer. Maybe if I do something normal like grocery shopping, I won't feel so alone. Or so eager to call a man I shouldn't.

Nothing in the nearby Italian supermarket reminds me of home. The store doesn't offer push carts, just small hand baskets. No one seems to shop for an entire week, like we do back home. It's all small portions. One onion. One garlic. One tomato.

Then, I have to figure out how to weigh and put a price sticker on my own produce. Like whoa! The honor system here is impressive!

By the time I reach the floor coolers full of homemade, uncooked pasta next to shelves of olive oil and cheap, good wine, my basket is too heavy to carry. I push it along with one foot as I study the assortment of goodies. I'm shocked at how inexpensive they are compared to back home. Especially the wines. Fancy bottles of Pinot Grigio are only three euros. Bridget loves this wine. She'd be in heaven here.

It is Italy, after all, I remind myself. Wine and olive oil are not imported. They're grown here.

I snap photos of the bottles to send to Bridget and Corrine. Olive oil is like God's gold to them.

The most difficult shopping comes when I get to the basic toiletries like shampoo, conditioner, and body wash. I can't figure out which one is which or whether I've picked up all of one thing and none of another.

I'm seriously stuck. The labels are in Italian. Even brands that look familiar are labeled in Italian.

I try asking women wandering through the tiny aisle, but they only speak Italian.

I'm almost in tears. I examine one product and then another over and over. As if the answers will magically appear or my brain will learn Italian by osmosis.

Maybe it's because I'm exhausted. Maybe it's because I feel alone in this new city where I can't speak the language. Or maybe it's because I miss him and I'm looking for an excuse (probably the latter), but I press Tyler's number.

He answers on the second ring.

"Bridget, are you okay?" He sounds winded. Like he ran for the phone.

My entire body sighs with relief. I can't believe how happy I am to hear his voice.

"I'm sorry, are you busy?"

"No. What's wrong? You sound funny?"

"Umm...this will sound dumb." I describe my dilemma with the indiscernible beauty supplies. I do my best not to cry in frustration.

"No worries, turn on your video and show them to me."

"Really?"

"Yes, it's not a problem. You'd be surprised at the disasters I encountered when I first came to Italy."

I smile to myself. I can't imagine Tyler encountering any difficulties he couldn't handle. "Please don't think I'm silly. I'm usually extremely competent." If he only knew how much.

"I don't think you're silly. I'm glad you called. I can't have you representing us Americans with lotion in your locks. Or shampoo on your skin."

I laugh out loud. His raucous laughter joins mine. I forget about feeling alone.

I snap photos of the different products and send them to him.

He sorts them out for me by sending back each one separately with its translation underneath.

"Oh, silly me, I could have used Google translator myself."

"And not call me? No way. I'm much better than Google."

Hotter, too, I can't help thinking. *Shame on you, Ava.* Objectifying this man. But inside I'm kind of giggling.

"Don't forget, my Italian class starts on Monday. I can get you in. I've already checked. Just say the word. It looks like you could use it."

"Yes."

"Yes, you could use it? Or yes, you want me to sign you up?"

I stare at the bottles in my basket. I bite my lip. Shake my head. *Don't do it, Ava. This can only lead to trouble.*

I ignore the voice and blurt, "Yes, sign me up. I'm competing for a gelato internship after my course. I might as well start learning Italian as soon as possible."

"Great," he says. He sounds like he's happy I'll be learning Italian from him.

"How much is it?" I ask, squinching up my face as I pray it's not too expensive and I can afford it on my savings.

"I've got one condition."

"What is it?" My heart hammers in my chest.

"You can take my class for free."

"What?" I screech so loudly people look over at me. I lower my voice. "No, I want to pay you."

"Wait, Bridget."

I cringe at my sister's name. "Yes?"

"You can take the class for free if you promise that I can taste all your gelato creations. You know how much I love desserts. And you'll need someone to test your flavors on. I'm happy to volunteer myself."

I snicker. "Are you serious? It could make you sick!"

"I like to live dangerously."

"Deal," I say, "If you can help me learn Italian so I can get an internship, I'll try out my gelato flavors on you."

"Sounds like a win-win."

"Your international relations skills are working already," I tease.

"I'll text you the details. Are you okay now? Do you need anything else?"

I can't tell him I wish he was here next to me making me laugh and feel safe in Florence the way he made me feel safe and happy on our long flight.

"I'm good. Thanks."

"You got this. I used to think you were a total extrovert. But you're not, are you? You're quieter than I remember."

I'm not sure how to answer that question. So, I say, "Things change."

He chuckles. "I guess they do. See you Monday. Call me for anything else."

I hang up quickly before he can point out more differences between me and my talented younger sister. I could confess the truth. But then he'd disappear. It's not as if he would like the *real* me.

Chapter Seven

I fill two large shopping bags with truffle pasta, Tuscan extra virgin olive oil, almond biscotti, beauty products, and wine and walk the short distance to my studio.

I love my neighborhood. It's located outside the colonial tourist zone. I purposely chose the "wrong" side of the Ponte Vecchio bridge, to be away from the tourists and to live like a local.

A medieval arched tunnel leads to the narrow street where my building is located. It's more like a cobblestone path than a street. It slopes upwards following a curve. Doorways line the roadway on either side.

Residents, old and young, sit on their steps in the early September sunshine. Some hang out their windows. Lace curtains flutter in a barely-there breeze. Tables, stoves, books shelves, and large crucifixes or paintings of Jesus are visible from the outside.

As I trudge up the little hill with my groceries, neighbors smile and wave hello. Some call out, "Ciao," and I say it back, the Italian sound new on my tongue.

An older man gets up and takes one of my bags to help me to my front door. I smile at his crinkled blue eyes and craggy face. "Grazie," I say.

"Signor Moretti," he says, pointing to his chest.

I smile. "Ava Walker."

"Benvenuta."

"Grazie," I say again, relying on my few Italian words.

He shows me a meter box on the side of my building. He opens it up and points at a switch swaddled in duct tape. Mr. Helpful is yammering and pointing at the switch. I can't understand a word of his rapid Italian, but I get the gist of his pantomime, which is that if the power goes out, I must come outside and turn it on.

I really need to start my Italian lessons sooner rather than later. And find a headlamp!

I show him I understand by shutting my eyes and giving the switch a pretend flip, then opening my eyes wide.

The man smiles, his gums are missing at least three teeth. "*Sì, sì.*" He claps. Other people join in. The green doors open right into my studio. There's not much privacy around here.

Everyone seems to be curious about me, their new neighbor. I hear some of them whisper, *Americana*. I'm the only Black person on the entire street. That could feel weird, but it doesn't. The vibe is super friendly and welcoming.

I end my first day in Florence by wandering up my street towards the Bardini Gardens. Bridget video calls me during my walk. All my sisters peer at the phone screen throwing questions at me like game show contestants.

"How was your flight?"

"Was it scary?"

"Have you met any Italian hotties?"

"Have you met any royalty?"

"Did you eat any gelato yet?"

"What about pizza?"

"Hold up guys, let Ava talk," Bridget shushes the posse. "Give us the highlights," she adds.

"Wow, this hill is no joke," I huff into the phone.

"Enough about the hill, tell us if you met any cute guys yet!" Emerald raises her eyebrows at me dramatically.

I hold up my hand to silence them as I finish my uphill trek. I stop walking when I get to the gardens.

I hold my phone high so they can see the flower archways, the stone statues dotting the greenery, and the stunning view of Florence with green hills in the distance. I didn't know I'd find such beautiful and tranquil gardens near my apartment. I feel so blessed. Florence is magical.

There's a lot of *oohing* and *ahhing* coming from my phone.

"I sat next to Tyler Donovan on the plane and now we're friends," I say it quickly like it's a pill I must swallow and get it over with.

"Oh, my God!" Bridget swoons. "I called it. Knew it. You guys are fated to be together. A second chance romance."

"I doubt it," I say. "I haven't had a *first chance* romance."

Laughter rings out from the phone. I laugh along with them.

I continue walking through the gardens and sharing the scenery with my sisters via our video call. I'll have plenty of time to wander by myself, enjoy the blooms and artwork, the smells of fresh-cut grass and lilies, and feel the late afternoon sunlight on my face.

A café sits off to my left, with outdoor sofas and wrought iron tables and chairs that look like an Italian postcard.

"The menu offers gelato," I tell my sisters. "I'll have to call you back."

"Ciao," the server says when I get to the counter.

"Ciao." I glance at the offerings, but I already know what I'm going to order.

"Pistachio, please." It's an Italian staple. I watch as the server scoops up my gelato and swirls it onto a sugar cone. A picture-perfect confection. I almost don't want to bite into it.

"Thanks," I say as I pay with my new Euros.

"Grazie," the server says. He gives me a smile and a wink. Is he flirting with me?

I smile back. No wink. "Grazie." I practice stretching out the *zzzz* the way he did it.

I go outside and sit on the grass. I close my eyes and lick my way around my cone. I almost die with pleasure. My first gelato in Italy and it's as delicious as I expected. Creamy and light. Flavorful and smooth.

I finish and go back inside to order another one.

The server gives me a questioning look. I point to the gelato laid out like pretty colored ribbons in their individual tubs.

"More?"

I turn up my palms with a Cheshire cat smile on my face. "I'm American. We love seconds. And super-sizes."

He laughs. "Americans love the gelato."

I shrug in a guilty, not guilty way, and point to the Stracciatella tub. Another Italian classic. Full milk, heavy cream, sugar, and chocolate. No eggs. When made right it is the perfect dessert. The right choice for the end of today.

Chapter Eight

The Florence Culinary Arts School is not far from the wedding cake looking Duomo, which is Florence's main cathedral. For the record, Firenze has many "main" cathedrals. Each one contains more history than the entire city of Portland. But the Duomo is the queen of cathedrals.

My gelato course starts off with a big bang. Literally. I'm so embarrassed I want to leave before it gets started.

It's my sisters' fault. Of course it is.

We Facetimed last night for an hour. They selected my clothing for my first day of class. They checked the weather. Hot and sunny with blue Tuscan skies. And 72 degrees.

"You've got to look cute," Daisy insisted. "Dress to impress."

"I want to look professional. I want to be taken seriously. This is going to be my life."

"You can look good and be serious. I do it all the time." Bridget rolled her eyes at me over the phone.

"Let's compromise," I said.

Emerald chose the outfit.

Daisy picked out the shoes.

"You call this a compromise?" I screeched.

But they insisted.

Now I'm wearing a sundress, a light sweater over my shoulders and high, sexy wedge heels. It's the heels that do me in.

I'm walking to my designated counter space in the gelato lab. Who knew there'd be a gelato lab? I'm so excited looking around the cavernous white room with its long steel tables and individual sinks that I don't look at where I'm walking.

My foot catches on the edge of one metal table leg.

I grab onto the table to steady myself. I drop my metal bowls. Three shiny bowls I was given when I picked up my canvas bag of equipment at the check in desk.

My bowls crash onto the floor. The sound is deafening in this sterile room.

The bowls spin in wild circles on the floor like rogue planets trying to escape the galaxy. I grab at them, but they're slippery suckers. Plus, I can't chase them in my heels. This floor is so clean it's sparkling with wax. I'll end up next to the bowls if I'm not careful.

"Here, let me help you." I look up to see a young man in a long white coat. It has double brass buttons all the way up the front, to his collar. His black hair is combed back neatly. His eyes are a hypnotic dark blue. His smile is misplaced in the mini chaos.

"Oh my," I breathe.

"Are you okay?" He picks up the bowls and tucks them under one arm. "We'll get you another set. Sorry about that."

He reaches out a hand to assist me to my designated counter space.

Turns out the young man is our lab instructor. On closer inspection, he's not *that* young. Maybe thirty-five or forty.

"I'm sorry." I feel my face heating up. It's turning bright red under my brown skin. I'm going to kill Daisy.

He assures me that this happens to at least one student in every session. "Bowls drop all the time," he winks at me. "It's the universe's way of reminding us that we're not in charge. We must let go, to let happen."

What? Is there a double meaning in his heavily accented English. *Let go, to let happen?*

"Okay, thank you," I say, as he retrieves a new set of bowls from a cabinet and hands them to me. The other students watch us as if we're a soap opera in the making. I duck my head in shame. *Really, girl, this is your first impression on the people you'll be working and studying with for the next three months? Not to mention your first impression on your teacher?*

The instructor walks to the front of the classroom. He crosses his arms on his chest and looks at us one by one. I look up under my lashes.

"Who has made gelato before?" he asks in Italian first. Then in English.

I breathe out with relief. I've made it a bunch of times.

I raise my hand. Around the room, most of the students raise theirs, too. Only two people don't raise their hands.

"Does ice cream count?" asks one of them.

"No. Gelato is a different beast from ice cream."

The girl groans.

"It doesn't matter," says Mr. Dark Blue eyes. "I prefer that *none* of you have made gelato before. Because now we must unlearn all the bad habits you developed. Correct all the mistakes you've made in trying to create the art that is gelato."

Whoa! Who made *him* the Gelato King?

"My name is Marco Andreolli. Not to be confused with the footballer by the same name. I have won the Gelato competition three years in a row. My flavors have been developed by companies all over the world. I am certified as a gelato master in every country. I have my own gelato brand in Italy and Japan. Welcome to Gelato 101."

I whistle in my head. Ok, Gelato King it is.

He smiles at me as if he can hear my mental commentary. As if he knows I'm out of my league here. I thought all my ice cream and gelato-making experiences would be a benefit to me. But it's a liability.

"Open up your canvas bags, please. Take out your uniforms and let's get started. You may address me as Chef Marco."

More like *Gelato Master Marco*, I think as I pull out the long white coat that we're supposed to wear every day. It covers me from neck to knee. The cute outfit my sisters selected is hidden from view. I'm wearing the most unflattering cover-up possible. Yet, I'm thrilled.

I button it up wishing I could snap a selfie to send back home. That'll show my sisters they need to stop trying to control my life from across the ocean. Tomorrow I'll wear comfy jeans with a t-shirt and sneakers. Like most of the other students.

I glance around the room as Chef Marco calls out our names one by one. We have to say a little something about ourselves and why we're taking this course. He encourages each of us to share our individual paths to this moment.

I wring my hands together trying to listen to my fellow students and think about my own answer at the same time. The students are diverse in every way, from ethnicity to life experiences. I forget about myself and listen to their stories.

One woman, who is turning sixty years old in two months, wants to start a new career. She retired from being a nurse after forty years. Her name is Matilda and she's from New Zealand. Her plan is to go back home and open her own gelateria. We applaud her.

A Southeast Asian man from Singapore tells us he wants to expand his family's novelty sweet business with homemade gelatos. His older brother is inheriting the business, but he wants to contribute to its success in his own way. His name is Tam and he bounces on his feet as he speaks. We applaud him.

A woman who looks to be in her early thirties, and is covered in piercings and neck tattoos, is from Toulouse, France. Her name is Lisle. She's taking the course to go back home and open a gelato business with her autistic brother so he'll have a place to work. We applaud her.

A young man from Germany named Patrick says he's tried regular university, he's tried public service, and he's even tried joining the church but nothing has stuck. He's hoping his love for gelato will give him the career he's searching for. We cheer him on.

I can't believe how heartwarming everyone's stories are. This is much more than a classroom of students. It's a gathering of like-minded spirits.

When Chef Marco calls out, "Ava Walker!" I feel tears pricking the back of my eyelids. I can't give them a generic story after everyone else shared so willingly.

I turn to the roomful of near strangers and tell them about my mom teaching me how to make ice cream. How when she was sick, I would stay up late cranking the ice cream maker and creating new flavors for her to taste. It was our special thing.

"Since she died, this is how I feel most connected to her. I want to learn how to make artisanal gelato to honor her. To open my own gelateria one day. To make my mom proud."

Everyone claps. Matilda says, "I'm sure she's already proud of you, Ava."

I wipe my eyes. "Thank you."

I sit back down and the girl next to me pats my back. Her name is Gisela. She's from Ecuador. About my age. Her plan is to open a gelato bar on the Galapagos Islands. We all cheer and say we want to go there to eat gelato with the tortoises. She and I smile at each other.

"You want to be my lab partner?" she asks.

I nod happily. "I promise I'm not as clumsy as I seem. I'll try not to drop any more bowls."

She shakes her head as if to say, that's ok. Her long shiny brown braid swings with her head movements. It's as thick as a heavy rope.

The introductions end with laughter and smiles. I look

around the room. What started out for me as awkward and embarrassing now feels like a little home away from home.

Chef Marco explains what we'll be learning in this course. The study of sugars, balancing principles, formulation of basic mixtures, formulation of fruit sorbets, and gelato-making theory we'll apply to recipes.

"I didn't know we could *study* sugar, but ok, I'm here for it," Gisela whispers.

I stifle a laugh. "Me too."

Then, Chef puts up a recipe on the giant screen in front of the room.

Amore per il cioccolato.

"Today, we're skipping all the lessons and going straight into practice. We're going to make this recipe. It's sink or swim time, students." He laughs a wicked laugh and I'm waiting for him to rub his hands together. He doesn't, but the smile is everything.

"We're starting with a flavor that means love. Chocolate love."

I repeat the words to myself. *Amore per il cioccolato.* Is it crazy that Tyler Donovan's smiling face comes to mind?

Yes. Because I'm learning how to make gelato. I'm not falling in love in Italy. And I must concentrate. This is the most exciting thing I've ever done in my life. I can't let some guy from my high school who doesn't even remember me get in the way.

Chapter Nine

It's less than a ten-minute walk from the Culinary School to the address Tyler texted me this afternoon. His exact words were: *Can't wait to see you. Here's the address for where we're meeting. I signed you up for my Italian Interactive class. Hope that's ok.*

I've no idea what an Italian Interactive class is, but his "can't wait to see you" sounds promising.

On my way there, Bridget sends a text.

I know you'd want an update so here goes. First day back for Emerald and Daisy. I dropped them off. Tomorrow, I'll let Daisy drive to school. She's complaining I'm treating them like babies.

I laugh out loud. *Sounds about right. Remind Daisy to take her glasses. You know she pretends she can see perfectly.*

Already did. What's going on in Italy? You met any cute guys yet?

My gelato master is cute.

Really? My kind of cute or your kind of cute?

I laugh again. *What does that mean?*

I like them tall, brawny, and boisterous. You like them serious and sexy.

Wow. She's not wrong there.

How do you know that? I've never dated anyone before.

I saw the way you followed Tyler Donovan's every move in high school.

Not true.

True.

Well, I'm going to his class right now. He's my Italian language teacher.

WTH! How did that happen? Never mind, it doesn't matter. Ava, this is your chance.

My chance?

Yes. The universe has given you a second chance. I told you that already! You didn't talk to him before. But now you can...be...the teacher's pet. Two winking emojis appear.

I send back a laughing emoji. *You're silly.*

I tap my finger on the screen hesitating to send my next message.

Did you like him in high school?

I press send and hold my breath. I've stopped walking. I'm in the middle of a tiny sidewalk in front of an ancient stone building waiting to read my sister's next words. I watch the three little dots moving up and down. My heart moves with them.

I bite my lip and stare hard at my phone screen. It won't matter. I tell myself. Whether she liked him or didn't. Because I'm not here to fall in love with anyone. Least of all Tyler Donovan. I resume walking. My GPS says I'm almost there.

Bridget's message appears. It's too long to read quickly so I stop walking again.

My eyes flicker over the entire message. I force myself to stop and read each word.

Everyone liked Tyler Donovan in high school. I saw him at parties and dances. He even came to some of the cast parties. But I didn't like him the way you did. One time he tried to ask me out. I told him he should talk to you.

I cover my face with one hand. No, she didn't. How embarrassing.

What did he say? Why did you do that?
Because I was tired of you being Ms. Invisible.
I was busy.
Right, busy being invisible.
What did he say? When you told him to talk to me?
I wait. Is she going to respond?
Well?
He said it was impossible to talk to you.
My heart thrums loudly.
What does that mean?

When she doesn't text back, I decide to call her. Her phone rings and rings.

She's still there. Why doesn't she answer the phone?
Bridget? I text her.
Sorry, I was thinking about how to say this.
What?
Ava, no one could talk to you back then. Even me. You had a "you against the world" mentality. It was intense. It was scary. And it blocked us all out. Tyler, too.

I stare at Bridget's words for so long that people trying to pass bump into me. As if I'm part of the street. Like a lamppost or a door. Like I'm not even standing here. I suck in my breath.

Out of nowhere, a red-hot fury engulfs me. How dare they walk into me? How dare she say this? Our mother had died. What was I supposed to do?

I had responsibilities dumped on me. I didn't have time to hang out and party. This is so unfair. *They* are so unfair. I glare at the passers-by.

When I catch my breath, I move with heavy legs up the steps to the building. All this time I believed I was doing the right thing by taking care of everyone. Giving up my life for them.

Even now, I'm doing this gelato course for them. Because going back home to open a gelato store is *the* dream, not just my dream. To stay close to my dad and sisters. I don't have any other plans for my life. It's always been about my family.

Bridget sends another text. *Sorry if I hurt your feelings. Maybe it's time for you to step out of the shadows and live your life. It seems like you ran into Tyler Donovan for a reason. And not just to learn Italian.* She adds two hearts next to her words. To soften the blow, I guess.

The blow of telling me I was...self-absorbed...and unapproachable?

Any plan I had about telling Tyler the truth...that I'm Ava, not Bridget...flies out the window. It takes a long time for a bird to change its feathers. All I'm going to change for now is my name. And I had photos of Bridget's passport and driver's license on my phone for safekeeping, enabling me to sign up for Tyler's Italian class as Bridget Walker. Easy Peasy.

Chapter Ten

As soon as I see Tyler standing in front of the classroom, all thoughts of birds and feathers and sisters go out of my head. My entire body feels like someone's flipped a switch sending a jolt of energy and excitement through me.

He gazes around the room and his eyes settle on me. I smile down at him from my seat in the third row up.

"The thing that's special about this language class is that it'll be interactive. We will meet three times a week for the next ten weeks. But only some of our classes will be inside. Florence is too amazing for us to ignore. Even if this classroom is located inside a 15th-century palace." He opens his arms wide.

I glance around at the arched windows and intricate carvings adorning the windowsills. Yup, it all looks 15th century to me. At least, based on other styles I'd seen in Florence this past weekend.

A flurry of movements and whispering erupts as our semester schedule is passed around. When I get my copy, I read it over twice. I can't believe what I'm seeing.

It's a syllabus outlining all the places Tyler and I talked about when we were on the plane.

He'd asked me what I wanted to do and see in Florence.

"A lot of things. Everything."

"But do you have some definite things you can't miss?"

"Of course." I didn't tell him I'd been researching Italy for years. Ever since our graduation party.

"Like what?"

I closed my eyes and ticked off on my fingers each treasure I wanted to see. Everything I wanted to do. It was a long list.

I'm looking at that list now. From the Uffizi Gallery to the bike ride along the Arno River. From viewing the *David* in the Accademia Gallery to tasting the best gelatos in the top three gelaterias.

"We're going to eat gelato in this class?" A student asks incredulously.

"I was wondering the same thing," another says.

Hands start flying up in the air.

Tyler calls on each person and answers their questions patiently.

"Yes, we're going to these locations. We'll have student passes."

"Yes, you can skateboard with us while we ride the bikes."

"Yes, we're going to speak Italian in a museum, and a karaoke bar."

Kids whistle around the room. I suppress a laugh.

I remember telling Tyler that I wanted to go to *Red Door*, the American college student hangout in Florence for burgers and fries and milkshakes. It has a famous karaoke section.

"How does it work though?" I ask, after raising my hand. "How will we learn to speak and understand Italian if we're doing all these fun things?"

I seem to be the only one concerned about the learning aspect of the course. As fun as this looks, I need to be able to speak

Italian by the end of my three months so I can be ready if...*when* I qualify for one of the coveted gelato internships.

"How does this work? That's the question?" He sits on his desk, arms stretched out behind him. Ripped triceps poke through his t-shirt. The kind of muscles you see in magazines or on Instagram models.

They remind me of one evening in high school. He didn't see me pull up in my car. I was waiting for Bridget to finish her play rehearsal. He pulled off his sweat-soaked jersey and wiped the back of his neck with it. His dark muscles gleamed under the streetlamps. I think my jaw hit the steering wheel.

"Is that your question Ms. Walker?" He swings one leg and stares up at me.

I nod my head. I wish we could be back in our seats 30,000 feet in the sky. Whispering our ideas to each other while everyone around us slept.

"Yes, uhm...*sir*." I clear my throat. Is that a smirk on his face?

"Here's how it's going to work. Each week, I'll send you by email, a module of vocabulary words to learn that pertain to the places we're visiting or the activities we're doing. Practice saying them. Then, during our field trips, we'll speak Italian. Or as much as we can, increasing our vocabulary every week. In class, I'll explain the nuances of the Italian language from Dante to Machiavelli. Any more questions?"

No one raises a hand. We're all nodding and examining the list of places again.

"Are we going to get credit for this course?" a voice asks hesitantly. "I want to take this. It's innovative and exciting. But I need the college credit."

A murmur goes around the room.

Tyler nods at the student. He stands up. "We're all getting credit for this course. Even me."

The students laugh. I join in.

"How are *you* getting credit?" asks a young woman in a kente head wrap.

Tyler brazenly looks at me.

Heads swing to see what or whom he's staring at and I slide down in my seat.

Bridget can't be right again. Am I going to be the teacher's pet? Or is Tyler one of those overly friendly people who are happy to run into someone from high school and make a big deal out of it?

There are folks like that. Super personable. He's one of them. I can't go mistaking his camaraderie for romantic interest. It could be a platonic friendship he's offering.

"Well, Mr. Donovan, I guess we'll be starting this class learning how to say, *Te amore*." The woman in the head wrap puts two fingers to her eyes and then points them at him. Like she's saying, *I'm watching you mister*.

"I think you mean, *Ti amo*," Tyler corrects her.

Everyone laughs. This time I work hard not to let my brown face turn a candy apple red.

I cross my legs, one over the other, and pull down my tiny dress. I don't have my chef's uniform to block the long expanse of bare legs I'm exhibiting, thanks to my sisters. Maybe their plan to break me out of my shell is working. It may be working too well on Tyler.

But this isn't high school. I can't revert to being a love-struck teen with goo-goo eyes for Mr. Hot and Popular. That's what he was voted in our senior yearbook. His dashing smile and sparkling eyes looked out of many pages.

I should know. I've flipped through that book and stared at his photos over and over again.

Chapter Eleven

"I'm not sure what's more disturbing. That I'm drinking alcohol on a 'school night' or that I'm drinking it with my teacher." I throw him a sassy look. Well, sassy for me. Which means I tried to wink.

About an hour ago we'd left class together. Tyler had waited for me to gather up my notebook and backpack.

"We can't pretend we don't know each other," he'd said. "Let's go grab a pizza or something. I'm starving."

I was, too. I hadn't eaten since lunch. "Okay, but let's wait until everyone in our class leaves. I don't want people thinking I'm getting special treatment."

"You *are* getting special treatment." He said it confidently. "So, get used to it."

He steered me out of the room, down the front steps of the building, and into the street. Which is where things went wonky.

"Whoa!" I stepped closer to Tyler. "Where'd all these folks come from?"

He tucked my arm under his and walked toward the intersection. "It's dinner time."

"But Florence has so many places to eat. Why's everyone in this spot?"

He pointed to the building across the street that looked like a giant warehouse. "That's the place to go for an aperitivo and some of the best pizza in Firenze. The Mercato Centrale."

I took a deep breath. "Okay, let's do it."

He laughed. "You don't have to say it like we're going to war."

I quirked an eyebrow at him. "I feel like I am."

"If that's how you feel on our first date then I'm in trouble."

I stopped walking. "Date?"

He shrugged. "Date, hang out, whatever you want to call it. We're in our twenties. No need to get freaked out by a word."

He was right. I was making a big deal out of a little word. But that four-letter word held so many confusing messages.

"As long as there's gelato involved," I said, trying to be lighthearted and carefree. Which anyone who knows me knows I'm not. Those are words that would never be used to describe me.

"Seven o'clock in Florence is not the time to be outside on the streets," he said as we made our way into the market along with a horde of people. "You could get trampled by the tourists heading for dinner."

Tyler held on tightly to my arm and led us away from the people. We climbed a flight of stairs that opened out into a gigantic food court. Everywhere I looked people swarmed like ants on a mission at the colorful food stalls. The buzz of different accents and music and activity was real.

Focus on one thing, I told myself. That way I won't get disoriented. I let go of Tyler's arm and clasped his hand instead. He smiled down at our joined hands.

"It's more practical," I hissed.

"Sure." He squeezed my hand. "Never knew you to be nervous around a lot of people, Bridge."

I ignored his remark. Instead, I focused on the food stalls.

There were huts with giant cheese wheels. Huts with seafood. My nose was confused by the competing scents of freshly brewed espresso, spicy shrimp, and dark chocolate confections.

Tyler bought lavender and rose water chocolate and gave it to me. A flavor I've never tasted before.

"Welcome to Florence."

"Why do I get the idea you have a sweet tooth?"

He shrugged and kept tugging me along beside him.

Like the supermarket, there were bottles of wine, olive oils, and homemade pasta for sale. But here, you could ask the vendors questions about their goods. So, you'd know exactly what you're buying and how to cook or serve it.

The combination of smells triggered memories of Mom's garlic-laced meals. She could make a mean pasta bolognese.

"I love it all." Tyler's face looks like a five-year-old's on Christmas morning.

We're sitting side by side on stools at a high wooden table eating fresh mozzarella.

"What's not to love? I've never even heard of a cheese bar. We need these in the States."

We order several kinds of fresh mozzarella and other cheeses to taste with the artisanal bread. I'm munching on olives like they're going out of style.

"Is Italy everything you'd hoped it would be?" I ask in between bites.

He sips his sunset-colored drink made of prosecco, orange juice, and Aperol liqueur. It's sparkly and fun and...more than a bit intoxicating. I feel my shoulders sliding down in a relaxed manner. My legs stop shaking nervously. My hands loosen their hold on the stem of my glass. I could get used to this after-school/after-work ritual. Aperol Spritz is the go-to Italian drink. I'm already planning on taking back some bottles for Dad.

"I love it," he says, bemused. "But nowhere is perfect. Not even Italy. The country has issues to resolve like any other country. But it's got a good heart."

"Like people," I murmur.

I turn completely around on my stool and view the layout of the market floor. "Look at all these new ingredients." My eyes feel like they're on fire from staring at one bustling stall after another. "I bet I can find new ingredients for gelato creations in this room. And I don't mean generic flavors. I mean things like truffle and seaweed. Aperol and prosecco. The Italians must already have gelato flavors like that, though."

"We can do gelato research." Tyler spins a piece of cheese around in his hands. "I'm down!"

"Can I get you guys anything else?" Our server speaks better English than I do.

Tyler responds in Italian. Is that rude? Is he leaving me out? He sees me staring at him and shakes his head. "Sorry. It's a reflex to speak Italian here."

"That's okay. I need to learn it sooner rather than later. Especially if I want to ask the vendors questions about their products to locate the best and freshest ingredients possible."

Tyler chews and nods. He takes a sip of his drink and sighs. "It's a beautiful language, too. Problem is that Italy is basically the only country where you'll speak it. In that sense, it's not a practical language like Spanish, French, or Mandarin."

"That's okay, I plan on using it a lot while I'm here."

Tyler's lips turn up into one of his yearbook smiles. It's a smile for me. What with the alcohol and newness of the place I've forgotten to channel Bridget.

I give him back my real partially shy, awkward smile. Baby steps.

Chapter Twelve

"I must confess. I had an ulterior motive for bringing you here."

I knew it was too good to be true. I lean back. "How so?"

"With my master's thesis." He looks up at the high ceiling. "It's about food."

I frown. "Aren't you studying International Relations? Politics and law and stuff like that?"

He picks up my hands. Our cheesy fingers slide against each other. "Food politics."

"For real?" I think for a minute. I don't want to come across as ignorant on the topic. But I *am* ignorant of the topic. "Can you explain?"

"One of the reasons I brought you here," he sweeps his arms outward, "is because I'm researching food markets like these in Italy."

I bite into my gooey mozzarella. "Mmmm, go on." I point to

my full mouth. I twirl my fingers in the universal language of keep going.

He laughs. "Delicious, right?"

I nod hard.

"Food markets are healthy for humans in more ways than one."

I swallow. "How? I mean, healthier options from local vendors, right?"

"Yes. Supporting local farms is important not just to eat better, but to make it affordable for everyone to eat healthier food. Think of how expensive your supermarket's organic produce is. Many people can't afford that. Plus, there's also the social dynamic." Tyler's on a roll and his excitement about his topic is palpable. It's got my attention.

"Go on," I say. "I want to hear more."

"This food market for instance has been around since the 1800s. Local Florentines came...still come...here every day to buy the items they need to make their daily meals. They interact socially. Learn new recipes. Ask questions. Be neighborly and build a community. Large generic supermarkets with their weird overhead lighting, lack of interaction, and hurry up and pay systems fail to support communities. It's purely commercial and corporate."

"So, you're researching these food markets to..." I reach over and pluck lint off his shirt. I yank back my hand. What the hell. I hope he didn't notice.

"To make a case for superpower countries to learn from the hundreds of years of history where food gathering is still a meeting point for people. It sharpens our social skills. In our own country, the government favors big industrial producers rather than the small hard-working producers of nutritious seasonal products. We've never had food scarcity. We don't understand the importance of supporting local farmers."

"I love your thesis. How can I help?" I wipe my hands on a napkin.

"I'm going to write a book."

My eyes open wide. "A book?"

"Yes, that's why I want to stay longer in Italy. Be closer to the many food markets across Europe. I'm going to turn my thesis into a book. Then I'll consult with governments on the importance of food markets and, *hopefully*, make a difference."

Tyler should have been voted *Most Likely to Change the World*.

"Your plans are amazing. I had no idea you thought like that."

He twisted up his mouth. "You thought I was a dumb jock?"

"No, of course not. You got into Harvard. You were our class Salutatorian."

"Our class? You were one year behind me."

I stare at him blankly. Damn! My leg shakes horribly under the table. This is my chance to tell him the truth. He's explained his life dream to me. The least I can do is tell him whom he's talking to. Tell him I'm Ava.

But I can't. It's the way he's staring at me. Like he wants to share so much more. And I want to hear it all. I love listening to him talk about ideas. I don't want to lose this as soon as it's starting.

"I keep forgetting we were one year apart. I saw you so often." I cringe inwardly at my lie.

He smiles a dimpled smile. "That's okay." He touches my arm. "We're here now."

We sit in silence for a few minutes, sipping our drinks and looking around at the Florentines enjoying their after-work aperitivo.

"You make me look at gelato differently," I confess. "All my talk about fancy ingredients, when you want to help people."

"Bridget, it's you who made me decide that food markets would be the perfect topic. I was considering a few different ideas before we met on the flight."

Hearing him call me Bridget makes me wince more now than ever.

"Me, why?"

"The way you talked about gelato. The fresh natural ingredients you want to put in your flavors. It's all tied to local producers. And you talked about how gelato makes people happy. You're right. Gelato does that. Everything you want to do is the same thing I want. I want to give people the theory and reasons it works for society. You want to put it directly in their hands to enjoy."

I sit up straighter. "I never thought of it like that."

It makes sense why we're here together now. This isn't a date. This is research. I suck down the last of my Aperol Spritz. What can I say? I'm honored to be his muse. But I'm disappointed it's nothing more. Even though I said I don't have time for a relationship. I can see what dating Tyler Donovan would be like.

I sigh. It'd be pretty amazing. As amazing as the gelato we learned how to make in class today.

"You ok, Bridge?" He leans forward and peeps at me under the cover of my afro. He does that a lot. Makes eye contact with me. "You don't mind if I call you Bridge, do you?"

I fling my hand up in the air. Maybe it's the alcohol talking, or I feel like I've nothing to lose. "Call me whatever you want Tyler Donovan. Be my guest."

A frown filters across his brow.

This time I don't want to smooth it out. I don't want to touch him.

Or maybe I want to touch him too much. God, I'm so confused. I need to talk to someone. But I can't tell Bridget. Even though she's my sister and best friend. She'd tell me to straighten this mess out right away.

For the first time in my life, I'm going to choose another route.

Chapter Thirteen

"The man who invented gelato was from right here in Florence, Italy. He was an architect, a stage designer, a military engineer, a mechanic, a painter, and a cook, amongst other things. He was a true Renaissance man." Marco Andreolli, is devastatingly swoon-worthy as he struts around the room. He talks with his hands as much as with his words.

"Bernardo Buontalenti designed forts, villas, palaces, and gardens. He invented gelato in the late 1500s, basically about 500 years ago."

Chef Marco stops in front of the screen on the wall depicting a portrait of the father of gelato.

"The Grand Duke Cosimo l de' Medici asked Buontalenti to take charge of a banquet for visiting Spanish dignitaries. Being so multi-talented, Buontalenti created a new dessert that impressed everyone. It went global. Without the use of TikTok or Instagram." He turns and smiles at his little joke.

Laughter breaks out in the classroom.

"What were the ingredients? Does anyone know?"

Chef Marco taps his fingers together as he walks.

"He should be on a book cover," my lab partner Gisela whispers.

"Yes," I whisper back. "For a steamy romance."

"Imagine what's under that long white coat of his." She giggles behind her hand. I giggle, too. I feel like I'm sixteen. Except I never got to feel like this at sixteen.

"Anybody?"

I raise my hand. "Yes, Ava." Our gorgeous Gelato Master points in my direction. I stand up and recite the recipe I know by heart from our first-class reading assignment.

"Mr. Buontalenti made his sorbet with ice, some salt to lower the temperature, fresh lemon juice, sugar, egg, honey, milk, and a drop of wine. He also flavored it with bergamot, whatever that is, and orange."

"Very good, Ava. Bergamot is a citrus fruit grown in the Mediterranean. It's the size of an orange but looks like a lime. So, it's a yellowish green color. It's the key ingredient in Earl Grey tea. It gives Earl Grey its aromatic flavor."

"Oh, *that's* bergamot," I say out loud. "I always knew Earl Grey had a special blend, but I never paid attention to what it was."

I turn to see if I'm the only person who didn't know what bergamot was. Everyone's scribbling in their recipe book, so I guess not.

"Thank you, sir." I stress the sir. I sit back down. Gisela leans over and whispers, "Would you date him?"

"Me?" I ask, shocked. "Why me?"

"One of us should. I'll be 25 on my next birthday and I still haven't found the man I want."

I was going to say, "me either," but that's not true. Instead, I say, "I'll be 25 on my next birthday too."

She smiles. "When's your birthday?"

"May 4th."

"We're almost twins. I'm May 6th."

We're both looking at each other in delight. At our close birthday connections. Or maybe because we're making a friend in this new city.

"Does anyone know what's in the gelato flavor named after Mr. Buontalenti? I'll give you a hint. It's basic and it's not."

Chef Marco goes to the whiteboard. "Go ahead. Anybody."

"Eggs and sugar," Matilda shouts from the back.

He writes "eggs" and "sugar" on the board.

"Milk," yells someone else. Chef Marco adds "milk."

"Heavy cream," Gisela says.

Marco adds that to his list. He turns around. "Ava?"

I have no idea what's in this gelato. I've never had it. I can't believe I've never tried the flavor named after the genius who invented gelato. I have so much to learn.

"Take a guess," Marco tells me.

"Bergamot?" I throw it out there.

He smiles. "Good guess."

I sink back down and turn to Gisela. "As soon as we get out of here today, let's get some of that Buontalenti gelato." She nods. "*Claro que sí.*"

"It's a secret ingredient," Marco writes on the board. He underlines the word "secret" like five times.

He goes to his desk and pulls out an elaborately designed bottle. He twists open the cap and walks over to me and Gisela. "Smell."

We inhale the aromatic scent. "Nice," Gisela says.

"Fragrant, yummy." I could inhale that all day.

He continues walking. He gives every student a sniff of his magic bottle.

Matilda shouts out, "Amaretto."

Marco laughs. "Finally. The secret ingredient in Buontalenti gelato is a liqueur. Usually, it is Amaretto. Italian Amaretto only, please. But I'd like each of you to pick a different secret ingredient. Tomorrow, I'll be bringing a lot of liqueurs to class."

An excited buzz ripples through the class.

"If you have a special one of your own that you'd like to try, you may bring that to class. We're going to create our own variation of Buontalenti gelato. The lesson will be on adapting gelato recipes with new ingredients."

I immediately think of Aperol. The drink I shared with Tyler last night. As I gather up my materials to leave, I wonder if my choice of a secret ingredient has to do with Tyler or because I think it'll make a good gelato.

I can't go mixing up my professional life with my personal one. That would be a recipe for disaster.

Chapter Fourteen

"Tell us everything!" It's Friday evening. My four sisters are sitting around the dining table back home. It's almost midnight my time. Gisela texted me an hour ago to ask if I wanted to go to the karaoke bar. But I'm in my studio apartment having a virtual dinner with the family.

Dad's face pops into view. "Sweetie, we don't expect you to do this every week. Please don't spend every Friday night talking to us. You're in Italy, baby."

"I won't, Dad. I wanted to see everyone all together though. I miss you guys."

Dad reaches out to touch my video image. It makes me smile that he thinks he can touch me.

"Enough of the mushy stuff," Corrine pulls the screen away from Dad. "Give us the scoop." She laughs. "Get it? *Scoop*?"

I groan. "Yes, I get it."

"Tell us about your first week in Italy. We want all the details."

Bridget grins in the background. "I *may* have told them you're dating Tyler Donovan."

A chorus of "*ohhhs,*" and "no, you didn't tell us," come from Emerald and Daisy.

Corrine grins at me. "I remember him. He's hot. Or he *was*. Is he still looking like a snack?"

"Enough with the food puns." Bridget rolls her eyes at Corrine. "Let Ava talk."

I put my fingers to my lips and shake my head at them. "Don't talk about this in front of Dad," I whisper.

"He already knows." Bridget bounces her head into the frame.

"You told Dad?"

Bridget shrugs. "Why not?"

"Because. We're not dating. I'm sort of helping him research his thesis on food markets in Italy. And he's teaching me Italian conversation. It's all very platonic. No romance. No dating. Stop making it more than it is."

"Defensive much?" Daisy asks.

I roll my eyes at her. "Not defensive. Setting the record straight."

My sisters' faces fill up the screen.

"Are there any other guys you're interested in?" Emerald asks, her brown eyes wide and sincere. "We want you to have fun."

"Yes," Daisy nods. "Get a tattoo or something."

"What?" Dad bellows in the background. "No tattoos."

They laugh and shush him.

"I meant she should do things on her bucket list."

"Thanks, Daisy." I smile at my little sister. "I will do some amazing things, I promise. Next week I'll have a lot more to tell you."

"How's your gelato class going?" Bridget asks. "And the Gelato Master?"

I fiddle with the space bar on my laptop. I told Bridget that Marco is a gorgeous Italian man. But I don't want Dad to think I'm wasting my time and money flirting with my teacher.

"It's fantastic. We're making gelato with our own secret ingredients on Monday. It will be fun to try something brand new."

"You should go out and try something brand new right now," Daisy says grouchily. "Live a little so I can enjoy Italy vicariously through you."

"Or live *a lot*!" adds Corrine.

"Do it for us." Emerald sighs. "We miss you, Ava."

"I miss you, too. And I'll do more stuff to tell you about. I promise."

After we hang up, I lay back on my bed and stare at the ceiling. It's midnight. I'm not tired. I'm not sleepy. I'm in Italy. I need to cross things off my bucket list as Daisy suggested.

Problem is, I've never had a bucket list. I've never imagined doing anything outside the box I lived in. Going to Italy is the most original idea I've ever had. And it wasn't even my idea. I stole it from Tyler. But now that I'm here, it's kind of a shame to stop at this.

I whip out the notepad I keep in my backpack for jotting down recipe ideas. At the very top I write, *Ava Walker's Bucket List*. Underneath that I write, *Things to do in Italy*.

I tap my pen on the pad. I write:

1. *Win the Gelato competition at the end of the semester.*
2. *Make a new friend.*
3. *Learn to speak Italian fluently. Or as best as I can.*
4. *Go on a gelato tour around Tuscany. Taste as much gelato as possible*!

My pen hovers over the page for a minute. I feel the words forming in my mind. My brain directs my fingers to write them down.

5. *Kiss a man for the first time and fall in love.*

I stare at those words in the silence of my studio. I can't believe I dared to write that. The more I stare at the words, the more they taunt me. Who would I kiss? Who wants to kiss me? Should I have a fling? An Italian affair? A one-night stand?

I'm probably the only woman who is 24 and has never been kissed. I'm like Drew Barrymore's character in the movie, *Never*

Been Kissed. Except I don't feel sad or lonely or unpopular. I just feel un-kissed.

There's nothing I can do to remedy that right now, but...I look at the time. Ten minutes after the Cinderella hour. I open my text messages and send off a quick text to Gisela. In minutes my phone pings.

Gisela writes: *Get over here asap! It's a manomania.*

I remember that English is her second language. *A monomania, you mean? Which means partial insanity.*

I know that! This is a MANomania!

I chuckle and start getting dressed. A sparkly dress hanging in the back of my closet catches my eye. I yank it off its hanger and look it up and down.

Maybe my sisters knew what they were doing after all. I slip into the short dress and grab a shawl to wrap around my shoulders. The September night is cool and clear.

Up in the sky, a full moon follows me across the Ponte Vecchio bridge. I am not alone. My heels click clack loudly, but no one can hear them because the streets are filled with revelers.

Everywhere I look, people are laughing, talking, and drinking. They're sitting on curbs outside bars. They're leaning against walls. They're waving hello to me and offering me drinks as I step by.

A feeling of possibility and excitement fills the air. Or maybe it's filling me. I'm one with the moon as I reach the big red doors to the karaoke club and walk in.

It feels like I've turned a page. As if I'm entering more than a club. For the first time, I feel as if I'm starring in my own adult life story.

Chapter Fifteen

Drake is singing *you know how sticky it gets* as I push my way through the crowds of partygoers. Mostly college students and locals in their early twenties. The bar has two margarita machines flowing nonstop. A reddish haze swirls in the air making me feel as if I'm entering a devil's lair. I clutch my bag criss-cross over my body.

My excitement at trying something new is waning fast. I text Gisela. She tells me to walk through the club to the next room where the karaoke is happening. Drake lovers bump and grind on me. I start pushing bodies aside. I could use body armor in here. The DJ switches to Michael Jackson. Everyone's shout-singing, *you wanna be starting something*. I feel doomed. I'm never going to make it through to the other side.

Just when I'm ready to give up and turn around, I feel a strong hand tugging on me. The arm slides around my waist and I'm looking up into Tyler Donovan's dark handsome face. His dimpled smile gleams at me.

"You lost?" He shouts in my ear.

I can only nod. What are the chances I'd run into him here? "I'm looking for my friends from my gelato class. They're supposed to be in the karaoke room."

He points towards the next room. "Over there."

I nod my head again. There's no opportunity for bantering in this melee. I hold on tightly to the back of Tyler's shirt and let him steer me towards a corridor which leads to a large room filled with more people and different music. The Karaoke Room. Thank God.

I let out a huge sigh of relief. My heart is racing but not from Tyler's arm encircled around my waist. Although that usually would be enough to make me blush and sweat.

It's these crowds. The spinning lights and strong bass booming all the way through to my bones unnerve me. Like I'm standing in the middle of an amusement park where everyone loves the rides except me.

Tyler seems to understand how I feel. He's kept his hand on my back and is leading me toward Gisela who is standing up and waving in our direction. I'm not one to play damsel in distress but it feels comforting to have Tyler by my side. Especially since I'm used to being the comforter for everyone else.

I squeeze his arm and mouth a silent "thank you." He encircles my shoulders with one muscular arm. I look into his dark eyes. I see the humor there. And warmth but also a glint of something dangerous. As if he's ready to fight off anyone who gets too close to us.

I lean into his hug for one brief second and nestle my head into his neck. It feels so safe. His entire body stills for a second. This weird vibe whizzes through my body. I step forward. I can't be catching feelings. Not here. Not now. And definitely not with Tyler Donovan, the hottest guy I've ever laid eyes on since before high school.

Chapter Sixteen

"You made it," Gisela grabs my arms. I nod happily. "Thanks for inviting me."

Gisela makes room at the table where many of the other gelato students are gathered. Even 60-year-old Matilda from New Zealand.

They clap for me when I sit. I wave and slide down the bench next to Gisela. I turn around to see where Tyler is, but he's disappeared into the crowd.

"Who was that masked man?" Gisela jokes.

"Just a friend," I shout over the music.

She gives me a look that says, *who're you kidding?* Thankfully, she leaves it alone. I want to have fun and not worry about my feelings for Tyler Donovan.

"What're you drinking?" Gisela signals for the server.

Half-full pitchers of beer sit on the table. "Do they make Aperol Spritzes here?" I ask hesitantly.

"I wish," Matilda shouts.

One of the guys says, "It's beer or margaritas, princess."

"Okay. I'll try a beer."

"Bridget!"

Oh no! Tyler Donovan is back. He's carrying a brightly colored drink that looks like the Aperol Spritz we were drinking last night.

"I thought they didn't make those here," I say fast, stalling so he wouldn't shout out my sister's name again. I can't explain here. Not to him. Not to them. I take the drink he's offering with shaky hands.

"Not usually. It was a favor."

I wonder for a hot second why bartenders here, who are all women, would owe Tyler a favor. But I'm busy trying to stop this train wreck of my identity crisis from happening. I push thoughts of Tyler with one of the cute bartenders far from my mind.

Focus Ava, get him away from here. He cannot meet your friends.

Tyler smiles at the people at my table. It looks like he's about to introduce himself.

"Hey, let's go sing." I jump up from the bench.

"Really?" Tyler frowns. "Now?"

"Yes, now." I steer him away from the table before he can call me "Bridget" again.

Gisela follows us. She tugs my arm and whispers, "Are you okay? Why is this man calling you Bridget? Are you sure he's a friend? How long have you known him?"

Boy, she's more of a mother hen than I am. But I appreciate her looking out for me. "Thanks, but honestly I've known him a long time."

Although that's not true. I barely knew him six years ago. And I ran into him again one week ago. He could be a serial murderer for all I know. I've seen those Netflix series where the nicest guy turns out to be the most dangerous.

"Bridget is a nickname from high school," I whisper in her ear.

"Okay," she nods. "I'm right over there. In case you need me."

I smile at her. "Thank you. I'll be right back." Why am I lying to Gisela, who may be the new friend I want...and need?

Tyler leads me over to the karaoke stage. Three kids are up singing their hearts out to a Prince song.

He stops near the DJ booth, on the side farthest from the giant speakers.

"You look amazing." His eyes are bloodshot. He spins me around. "I love this dress. It reminds me of old-school Jennifer Lopez. *Sizzling.*"

"Tyler, are you ok?" There's something manic about the way he's acting. "Are you drunk?"

"No, I'm fine. Couldn't be better." His tone shifts downward.

"What is it? What's wrong?"

He waves a hand in the air above his head. "Nothing." The sides of his mouth droop. "My ex-girlfriend called me."

"Oh! That's a bad thing?"

He shakes and nods his head at the same time. "It's a terrible thing. She wants to get back together."

Oh boy. Plot twist. I wait for him to say something more, but he doesn't. He wipes his eyes. "Anyway? What are we singing?" He's looking at me as if I'm his last hope. "It'll make me feel better."

I freeze. Singing was only a ruse to get him away from the table. But now it looks like he wants to sing for real. "I'm not very good," I admit.

"Of course, you're good. You were the star of the musical every year. You have the best voice. Let's pick a great song."

"Uhm...my voice. It's sore. I think I'm getting sick." God, I must tell him the truth. How long can I let this charade go on? What do I have to lose? What do I have to gain?

He leans back and looks at me from arms' length. "You're not sick. But if you don't want to sing with me it's okay. I understand."

He looks so sad.

"I can't, honest. I'm sorry I suggested it. I forgot."

He shakes his head. "It's funny how we think we know someone. And then we realize we don't know them at all."

What the heck is he talking about? The faraway look in his eyes tells me he's thinking of someone else.

"You're not the girl I thought you were in high school. Just like my ex isn't the girl I thought she was."

My heart feels like it's being sliced in two. It's not Tyler's fault he doesn't know me. An aching feeling fills my chest. Like I'm adding pain to this wonderful guy who has been nothing but nice to me. Always.

"Let's go back." Tyler takes my hand to walk into the crowd.

"Wait."

He stops walking. He rubs his hand down his face and sighs. "It's okay, Bridge. We don't have to sing." But I'm not listening to his words. My brain is spinning with scenarios.

I could get up on stage and pretend to be Bridget and sing a song with him. To cheer him up.

I could be the old Ava who refuses to sing at all, go back to my table, and try to fit in.

Or I could be the new and improved Ava. The one who'll kick butts with her gelato creations. The girl who can show Tyler Donovan what he missed out on. The girl who's been inside me hiding for all these years. The one I'm here to discover.

Don't think, just do. Isn't that what my sisters have been telling me?

I turn fully towards Tyler and give him the best version of a flirty smile that I think would make Jennifer Lopez and Bridget Walker proud.

"You want to sing? Fine. I'm picking the song." I sashay off to look at the list on the DJ's iPad.

"Yes, ma'am." I hear Tyler's comeback a beat late. As if he had to think about it.

"Come on," I twirl my hand in the air in what I hope is a diva-like manner. "You'd better know how to rap. Because we're going to shake this place up."

Chapter Seventeen

You don't know what you're capable of until you're standing on a karaoke stage in a foreign country singing your favorite dance song next to the boy, now a man, you've loved for years.

Especially when people you don't know sing along, and cheer for you, and yell for more.

I feel as if a hardened shell that encased me for the last ten years is cracking open.

On a stage.

It's exhilarating.

It's frightening.

We wind up the audience with our rendition of *Let's Get it Started in Here* by the Black Eyed Peas. I don't recognize this girl. I'm belting lyrics like I was born for the stage.

Tyler catches my vibe and man can he rap. He's gripping his microphone and we're killing it. We throw up our hands in the air. We jump up and down on the stage. The crowd goes wild.

People surge from the other room into the karaoke room until it's even more packed than before.

Sweat drips down my forehead and into my eyes. I'm not stopping. The "audience" calls for more. The DJ looks at us and we look at each other.

"Another one? I'm up for it?" Sweat pours down Tyler's face.

"Sure." I spin one finger in the air. *Let's do it.*

Beyonce and Jay-Z's *Crazy in Love* come on next.

"You asked for this?" Tyler grins at me.

I shrug. I'm not telling. I didn't, but it's perfect. I know Beyonce's lyrics without having to read the words. But it's when Tyler raps Jay-Z's part that I stop and stare at this guy. My heart is cracking wide open. I almost forget to sing Beyonce's line about how she's been pretending, playing herself. That line resonates with me.

This has got to be one of the happiest nights of my life. I didn't even know I could feel this excitement. Tyler's dimples shine through when he turns to smile at me, waiting for me to sing.

I cradle the microphone and sing about not being myself lately. And how I don't care. How his love has got the best of me.

I'm truth telling through Beyonce's music.

The words are spot on. I feel crazy in love. At least right now. At this moment. Or maybe I've always felt like this for Tyler Donovan. I just never expected that he'd notice me. Or be into me.

The song ends. A thundering applause greets us. I notice Gisela has been videotaping us. I'll have proof to share with my sisters. Because no one would believe this.

Phones have been held high throughout the entire two songs.

Tyler and I hold hands and bow together. I slip my microphone back onto the stand and run for the steps. Tyler is laughing hard. He's ahead of me. He catches me as I trip and almost fall down the last steps.

He sets me down. I'm spinning around in my short dress so fast that the room feels like a house of mirrors.

I stop and look at Tyler's hazel eyes glowing at me. I lean forward. Without giving it a second thought, I press my lips on his. Hard. The way I think you're supposed to kiss a man you like.

Because the truth is, I really like Tyler Donovan. I like him much more than I ever imagined I would. Even when I had that crush on him for years. It felt nothing like this.

This is flesh, blood, and bone real.

Lo and behold, Tyler slips his hands around my waist and pulls me closer. My hips line up against his hips. My heart beats against his heart. He tilts his head sideways to capture my lips with his delicious mouth. All thoughts fall away as I sigh his name under my breath.

Chapter Eighteen

I've heard people talk about this feeling. I've read books about this giddy mind-blowing excitement. I've seen movies where time seems to stop. Everything is rainbows and butterflies.

But never have I imagined it was real. I figured it was a fantasy. An exaggeration. It is not.

I wake up Saturday morning to my phone ringing and a voice asking, "Please tell me you're free today."

"I'm free today."

"How would you like to go exploring?"

I leap out of bed so quickly that my feet tangle up in the covers. I fall hard and my chin hits the floor. "Ouch!" I cry.

"What's wrong?"

"I fell out of bed."

I hear a stifled laugh. "It's not funny."

"Sorry. I was just thinking that you're falling for me already."

"Ha ha ha."

"And I like it."

I can't wipe the silly grin off my face if I wanted to. "What time?"

"An hour? I'm renting a car. But I can't drive it into the colonial zone."

"I'm not in the colonial zone. I'm across the Ponte Vecchio bridge."

"Smart girl."

"Thanks, I did my research."

"Okay, text me your address or drop a pin where you'll be in an hour, and I'll meet you."

"Where're we going? What should I wear?"

"Be ready for anything."

"Nice!"

"And Bridget?"

I groan inwardly. Stop calling me that! But I say, "Yes?"

"We'll be speaking Italian. I hope you remember all that we learned this past week."

"Oh no," I groan out loud this time. "I haven't studied. Or practiced much."

"I guess it'll be a quiet trip then. On your end."

"We'll see about that."

He laughs and we hang up.

I race around washing up, taking a quick shower, fluffing out my hair, and choosing my clothes. It's a warm fall day.

I go with sexy hipster jeans and a cute crop top. I toss a sweater in my bag and some snacks for the road.

I slide cherry lip gloss on my lips and darken my lashes with mascara. A bit of sun block in case we're doing anything outdoorsy, and I'm ready.

This feeling of anticipation thrilling through my veins reminds me of our flight taking off. Not the bumpy turbulence that came after we were airborne. But the race down the runway and the swoosh of lift off.

I still have ten minutes, so I stroll down to the gelato restaurant at the edge of the Ponte Vecchio bridge. The name of it is *Ponte Vecchio Gelato Bar*. But it serves all kinds of drinks and snacks and of course, an array of gelati. I call it the Gelato Bar in my head, imagining it as my neighborhood hang out.

It's always packed with locals and tourists sitting outdoors eating gelato and drinking coffee.

I squeeze my way into the restaurant and order two cappuccinos to go. From what I recall of our airplane trip, Tyler could drink caffeine all day.

"Need help?" A young man offers to hold my drinks as I pay.

"Sure."

"I wish this other coffee was for me." His tone is flirty.

I look up from swiping my debit card. "Excuse me?"

He shrugs. "You're gorgeous."

I'm so taken aback I stand there with a dumb expression on my face. This has never happened to me before. No one has ever called me gorgeous. Is he kidding?

He looks me up and down. "You look surprised."

I take my drinks back and hurry outside. Crazy tourist.

A car horn beeps madly. A round red car zooms up next to me and a window rolls down.

"Your chariot, milady." Tyler looks way too large for this tomato-sized vehicle that resembles a mini chariot from Cinderella. He jumps out to open my door.

"Would you be one of the fair mice groomsmen driving the chariot?"

Horns blare behind us. He holds up one hand to shush them.

Rude!" He says and jumps back in. "Buckle up, princess."

I slide our drinks into cup holders and buckle my seat belt.

Tyler's sexy dimples pop out when he turns toward me. "Ciao."

"Ciao," I say back.

He reaches over and squeezes my knee. "Grazie per il caffè."

Blood rushes through me making my knee tingle. My poor knee. So innocent in all of this.

He clears his throat.

"Prego." I struggle to remember the word for 'you're welcome.' He's so distracting. Wearing a cashmere v-neck sweater, his strong clavicles showing, I could swoon. Like a Jane Austen heroine.

Ava get a grip. No swooning allowed.

"Eccellente," Tyler says, interrupting my thoughts of what he might look like without a shirt on. He's solidly built. Muscles rippling under the snug sweater.

How would it feel to put my arms around his solid back? How would it feel to kiss him again?

I'm longing to feel his lips on mine. Taste his tongue. Feel his body pressed up against mine in every possible way.

I sneak a peek at him out of the corner of my eye. One kiss last night was not enough. I want more. I *need* more.

Tuscany's undulating green hills are breathtaking. As are the tall, dark green cypress trees dotting the landscape like exact replicas of the ones in Vincent Van Gogh's paintings.

Tyler steers us expertly past small towns and cities. We pass Bologna. We pass signs that lead toward Venice. I squeal out loud.

"I want to go to Venice!" I don't think I've ever squealed before. But the sun is shining. The sky is the brightest blue. And a sign saying Venice is not far away feels unreal.

Tyler grabs my hand and squeezes it. "We'll go there another weekend. Today there's something I want to show you. I think you'll love it."

"More than Venice? I don't know. We're talking about gondolas, canals, San Marco cathedral, and the Rialto Bridge. What could be better than that?"

What I don't say, but what I'm thinking is, "There's going to be another weekend trip?" The butterflies in my stomach are hugging each other in a giant group hug. I don't have to suck up every single moment of joy today. We're going to do this again.

A voice in my head whispers, "*One day at a time, Ava.*"

It's true. I can't get too excited. Sometimes plans don't work out. People disappoint you. Sometimes they disappear from your life.

But the way Tyler's looking at me, I doubt he's going to disappoint me. He's eyeing me as if I'm chocolate and espresso all wrapped up in one. It makes me laugh.

He raises a brow. "Smooches, are you laughing at me?"

"Smooches?"

"Yes," he says. "You kissed me first. I can call you 'smooches.'"

"That's a horrible nickname."

"But it's accurate."

"You didn't object."

"I didn't have time. You leaped on me."

I fiddle with an earring. Sliding it back and forth through the hole in my earlobe.

"For the record," he says. "I'm glad you took the leap. I wasn't sure how to do it."

"You? Come on. You are...*you*." I stop fiddling and stare at the most popular guy in high school, and maybe at his college, too. He's certainly popular in Firenze.

He shakes his head. "You make me nervous."

"Seriously?" If only he knew how nervous he makes me.

I stop talking and glance out my window watching the road disappear under our tires.

I'm twenty-four and have never felt this fluttering in my stomach. So many things I haven't done. But is it right to feel these new feelings under false pretenses? I already know the answer to that.

One look at the man driving and my heart sinks at the idea that whatever is growing between us may be over before it ever really starts.

Chapter Nineteen

Tyler Donovan is a true romantic. I'd never have guessed it. But when he takes the exit toward Verona, the city of Romeo & Juliet, my heart swells with excitement.

I expected someplace touristy. Venice or Milan or Rome. Even Siena or Pisa.

Not Verona. It wasn't a city I expected to see on my trip to Italy. But now that we're almost there, I know it's the perfect place for Tyler and I to explore.

Especially after the incredible drive we've had. We've been driving for two and a half hours. We stopped once to grab more coffee and use the restroom.

The drive took us past vineyards big and small. The trees were bursting with grapes. He told me it'll be harvest season soon, near the end of September and beginning of October.

I'm glad I saw what the vineyards look like with all those bunches of grapes hanging from vines waiting to be picked.

Between the verdant green fields and the neat, organized vineyards passing by outside the windows, Tyler and I shared our favorites.

Favorite movie: Mine is *To All the Boys I've Loved Before* (I had to watch it a hundred times with Daisy and Emerald); his is *Black Panther*.

Favorite book: Mine is *Practical Magic* by Alice Hoffman (because sisters!); his is *Captain Corelli's Mandolin* by Louis de Bernières.

Favorite food: Mine is crêpes; his is anything Italian (duh!).

Favorite drink: Mine is espresso; his is espresso.

Favorite snack: Mine is Pirouline wafers; his is ginger snaps.

"What about gelato?" He exclaimed. "I thought that would be your favorite snack."

I shook my head vigorously. "Gelato is not a 'snack.' It's an art form. It's life in ice crystals."

He laughed. "That's how I feel about brownies. Nothing tops delicious rich, chocolatey brownies."

I told him the story of my mother calling chocolate chips dark nuggets of happiness.

I meant it as a fun, happy story. By the end of it though, I was choking up.

It'll never get easier to talk about her casually. I miss her so much. Every single day I want to tell her something about the gelato I'm creating. Or about Tyler. About Italy.

I can see her crooked smile and hear her sing-song voice telling me to stop worrying and have fun.

"You're thinking about her right now, aren't you?" Tyler asked.

I nodded silently.

His big smile slowly disappeared. "I remember when your mother died."

My breath caught in my throat.

"I tried to talk to your sister. She was in my class."

I stared at his profile as he drove. How could he not know that I'm that same girl? Am I so different now from when I was in high school? I mean I look different. I dress differently. But my personality. Was I such an invisible creature back then?

"What happened when you spoke to Ava?" I had to use my name. I needed to see if it would trigger any memories.

He bit his lip and sighed. "She ignored me."

"She did?" I remember the time he gave me my sweater, but not him speaking to me and me ignoring him.

Is that what Bridget meant when she said I shut everyone out?

"Maybe she couldn't talk to anyone about how she felt. It was a horrible time. It was the worst thing that ever happened to me. To us. It was very hard to talk about."

He shifted in his seat to look at me. I looked down fast. He's going to know it's me. I can't catch his eyes. Mine are going to tear up and I'll confess everything right here and now and ruin our day.

I know I must tell him. I have to find the right time. But this isn't it.

His hand gripped mine and I put my other hand on top of his.

"I am so sorry you had to go through that."

I swallow. "Thank you."

He drove with one hand in mine for a long time. As weird as this may seem, his comforting me now feels as if we're making it right. This was what I needed back then. But I was fourteen. How could I have known he could make anything right?

And honestly, back then nothing would have helped. Not even Tyler Donovan.

Some things in life are meant for you to go through alone. You pray and hope you get to the other side. The secret is to keep moving. Keep pushing.

I'm here now.

Chapter Twenty

"Angels invented gelato. It wasn't that Buontalenti dude. Only angels can make anything this heavenly."

Tyler can't agree or disagree because his mouth is full.

I press my lips down on the cold, aromatic, smooth-as-butter dessert in a cone I'm holding. It's so incredibly flavorful you can smell the ingredients.

My gelato has milk and cream and pears. It also has Amarone. The famous wine of this region. I don't mind not talking. Eating gelato requires all my senses. I wasn't expecting to be enjoying my third gelato of the day, but this was the sole reason for our trip, according to Tyler.

After he located a parking spot for our tiny tomato car, we strolled along the Adige River, checking out the sites of Verona. That's when Tyler informed me that he brought us to Verona for one reason only. "Gelato."

"You drove almost three hours for gelato?"

He nodded his head.

"So, it has nothing to do with Juliet's balcony. Or the wall of letters to Juliet. Or the locks that lovers lock to the bridge and gates around Verona to seal their love forever?"

He frowned. "People do that?"

"Yes. Verona is the city of lovers."

"I think that's Paris."

My turn to frown. "I'm pretty sure it's Verona."

"Maybe Verona is the city of star-crossed lovers." He snaps his fingers. "That's it. I mean all the letters to Juliet are asking her to fix their love problems, right?" For one imperceptible second, his face clouds over. Like he's struck by an idea he hates.

"What's wrong? You look upset."

He shakes his head. "No, I'm not."

He's not being 100% truthful. But I can't call him on it. Not when I am 100% lying.

I do the only thing I can think of. I change the subject. "So, you're saying that the reason you brought us here was to eat gelato?"

"Not just *any* gelato."

That's how we ended up at one of the best gelato shops *in the world*. The owner is a gelato master who won third place in the World Cup International Gelato Festival last year. It features gelato artisans from around the world. Like the Gelato Festival in Florence in December. Except bigger!

This gelato master uses all local ingredients from farms and vineyards around Trento, the area that Verona sits in.

Tyler tries one made with beer, peanuts, and salt.

"You can make gelato from beer? That's crazy."

How will I find my own unique ingredients to create flavors no one's ever heard of when gelato masters in Verona are making beer gelato? How can I master this art form in three months?

"This sucks," I mumble.

"What?" Tyler is still licking his way around his cone.

"I'll never be as good as these guys."

"You won't."

I snort. "Thanks."

He shakes his head at me. "You're not going to be as good as these guys. You'll be better."

"How can you say that?"

"Because you've got something they don't have."

I pause. What the hell do I have, I wonder.

"Duh!" He grabs me around my waist. "You've got me, baby. I'll be your inspiration."

I give him the classic side eye. "Right."

"No, seriously." He stops talking to gobble the rest of his gelato.

"I appreciate the confidence. And the support. But unfortunately, I'm not going to make a '*Tyler*' gelato." I scoff.

"I'd make a yummy flavor."

I bark out a laugh. "You've eaten way too much sugar."

"Probably, but I think you should make your gelato from your favorite things."

"Which are?"

He shrugs. "You tell me." The way his voice dips low, his words are loaded with meaning.

Chapter Twenty-One

After we're stuffed with gelato, we have no choice but to explore Verona. If only to walk off the calories.

Verona is smaller than Florence. To my eyes anyway. The streets are prettier and there aren't as many tourists. The best part is the decorated balconies jutting out from every building.

Some are adorned with waterfalls of plants and fragrant flowing flowers. Some have tiny mirrors around the edges reflecting the sun.

Some balconies feature gorgeous mosaics. Some are covered with gingerbread trim.

Many are framed with Moorish arches. I wonder which came first—Shakespeare's famous balcony scene or all these amazing balconies.

Tyler and I walk side by side not touching. The desire to touch him is intense though. A strong force pulls me toward him. If he doesn't hold my hand soon, I'm going to attack him again. I have to be cool the way Bridget would be.

We finally reach Juliet's home. Red and pink locks cover every bit of space on a gate below her balcony. Love letters and notes are taped haphazardly all over the walls of the courtyard. Even the archway leading to the courtyard is transformed into a receptacle for notes by the broken-hearted.

Tyler and I sit on the old stone wall watching couples of all shapes and sizes, genders and ages buying Romeo & Juliet locks and whispering their devotions to each other before clicking closed their special lock on whatever tiny space they can find on the gate.

At a certain point, it becomes awkward. It's not as if *we're* going to buy a padlock and commit ourselves to each other by locking it to Juliet's gate. But the questions of whether we should or whether one of us wants to hang in the air.

I jump down from the wall before it gets more awkward. "Let's keep walking around, shall we?"

He jumps down too. He hasn't spoken much since we got to Juliet's home.

I don't want to ask him what's wrong. I've already asked him that once for the day. I don't want to be one of those women who constantly asks the guy she likes what's wrong. It seems desperate and needy.

But I do have a question for him. "You know we talked about all our favorites in the car ride. But we didn't talk about . . ." Oh shoot, how do I put this?

"About what?"

I glance around at our surroundings for inspiration. We're in a large open-air market square. More like a large rectangle lined with shops and beautiful buildings. All the tables and stalls have red and white tents. The love theme exists everywhere in Verona.

"Look, we've landed on your planet. An outdoor food market."

Tyler looks around and laughs. He takes out his phone and snaps a bunch of photographs.

"Let's take one together," he suggests.

A passer-by asks if we want a photo taken together and Tyler says yes, handing the man the phone.

Tyler positions us in front of the market next to a huge red heart. He slides an arm around my waist. "Is that okay?"

"Definitely," I smile back.

The man takes the photo and we look at it together.

"You guys make a cute couple," he says before walking away. He's not the first to say that to us.

I look at Tyler to see what he thinks of that comment.

He snaps a photo of me looking at him. "You're so beautiful."

I feel my face turning as red as the heart I'm standing next to. "Thanks."

"Inside and out. I always imagined you as a fun party girl. Not this mysterious, kind-hearted soul."

My heart stops for a second. This is Tyler Donovan telling me I'm beautiful? And kind-hearted? In a sincere, adoring voice.

"I always thought you'd be a fun party guy too. The popular dude with the pretty girls around him. But you're much more." I step toward him and kiss him right on his lips. I step back. Before I get far, he pulls me close.

I melt into his arms. I've been waiting for this moment the entire day. Since his phone call this morning.

His lips are moist and firm. He presses them firmly against my lips.

Fireworks are going off in my head and heart.

I've lost all sense of time and place. I clasp my arms around his neck, pulling him even closer to me.

If we were anywhere but Verona, this would be inappropriate. But no one cares.

Everyone here is part of a couple. Everyone here wants a forever kind of true love. Everyone understands.

And even if I'm not sure what I'm doing. Even though making out with a man in public is the last thing I'd imagine doing anywhere in the world. Somehow, here, with Tyler, it all feels perfectly right. As if we've come full circle. From high school to Verona.

Chapter Twenty-Two

Sunday night's video conference call with my family is a dessert fest.

Which means I'm eating sugar at 10 pm my time. They're indulging at 4 p.m. Eastern Time.

When they appear on my laptop screen, Daisy is sprinkling coconut flakes on her bowl of ice cream.

Emerald is spinning an architectural wonder on top of her fudge brownie with a can of whipped cream.

Corrine tosses a few rainbow sprinkles across what looks like a homemade waffle.

And dear Bridget is smoothing Nutella and fig jam into a crepe. So much I could see it from my side of the ocean.

It is a cornucopia of sugary wonders. Think of every kind of topping for ice cream, that's us.

As for me, I ran down to the Gelato Bar at the end of my tiny street and bought the flavor of the day before they closed at 9 p.m. I've been keeping it cold in my fridge waiting for this call.

Now as I dip into the pistachio gelato I close my eyes to absorb every bit of its flavor.

"What're you eating?" Emerald asks through the screen.

"Pistachio gelato, a trademark flavor for Italy." I show her my bowl of gelato.

"She screws up her nose. "Why is it so boring looking? It's not bright green like the nuts. It looks like a drab olive."

"Yup," I point my spoon at her. "Good eye. Great gelato is not about how it looks."

"It is to me," Daisy pipes in with a sweet smile on her chubby face.

"If your gelato is brightly colored, like some of those flaming greens, yellows, and pinks you see in shops, then it's not as authentic or homemade as it should or can be."

"Ohhhh! We're getting a gelato lesson from the master." Daisy giggles.

I swat at her face on the screen. "I'm not a master. That's common knowledge."

"Not to us peasants." Daisy forks a piece of brownie into her mouth and chews.

"Pistachio is the hardest flavor to make. It's the flavor you should order to find out if your gelato shop is the real deal. Whether they're making it from scratch or using a mix."

"Really? I didn't know that." Corrine steps forward, licking a spoonful of sprinkles.

Emerald pushes Corrine and Daisy aside. "Tell us more. Why's your pistachio so weird looking?"

"Yes, tell us," Corrine interrupts. "I want to know what I'm eating. I'm all about the natural ingredients and authentic experience."

"Says the woman with rainbow sprinkles stuck to her lips." I laugh.

"Word."

I laugh happily. They haven't changed. But maybe I have. A little bit.

"In the artisanal gelato shops, you don't get to see the gelato that you order beforehand. They keep them in stainless steel containers with covers. It's all about how it tastes, not the color. Of course, tourists think otherwise. The prettier the mounds of gelato in the glass cases, the more they buy."

"Beauty is everything," says Bridget. "Speaking of which, you're looking different."

"Me? How?"

She puts a hand to her chin. "I don't know."

"Like you're in *lurve*," Daisy giggles.

Emerald hoots. "Are you in love, Ava? Is he cute?"

At that moment, my phone pings. I look down from the laptop screen. Who's texting me so late? A smile splits my face when I see a message from Tyler.

He's sent me a photo of us in Verona. Next to the giant red heart. *Thinking of you.*

"Look at that smile. You're definitely in love." Corrine smacks her hands together. "Who is he? Is it Tyler?"

"Nope," I answer a little too fast.

I wish I could tell them every detail of my road trip to Verona. Share these new feelings I have for Tyler Donovan. But I can't. Not yet.

It sounds crazy, but until I straighten out the truth and discover if he likes me for me, I'd better keep quiet about it all. I don't want to get Daisy's or Emerald's hopes up.

Or mine!

Knowing that Tyler is thinking of me right now makes me feel as high as a kite. Like I'm spinning on a mountain top, arms wide open, the world below all blue and green and covered in flowers.

I press my fingers to my lips to stop bursting out a goofy big smile again.

"Yo, sis,"

"Yes?"

Bridget wags her finger at me. "You're not telling us something."

"Maybe it's nobody's business."

Four shocked faces pop into the four corners of my screen to stare at me.

I almost laugh out loud. Except I'm dead serious.

"Since when have you gotten so feisty?" Bridget asks.

Corrine, Daisy, and Emerald all nod their heads. They're quiet, waiting for me to say something.

I pick up my spoon and collect a mouthful of gelato on the edge of it. I raise it to my mouth. "Cheers, guys."

They don't answer.

It's the first time I've kept anything from them. For the past ten years, I've given them my all. I've listened to their problems, cheered on their goals, and applauded their accomplishments. I haven't really even had anything to keep from them to begin with.

I felt that I owed them a mother and an older sister. And I delivered that.

Part of me wants to throw off that cape now. And embrace this new and exciting adventure without having to get their approval, consent, or advice.

The other part of me, seeing the confused looks on their faces, wants to gather them all into a big hug. Tell them I'm not going anywhere. That I'm right here and always will be.

Bridget picks up the tablet and walks away from the family. A series of "boos" follow her.

"Are you using condoms? Can you get on birth control? Are you being careful?"

"Bridget!"

"Don't Bridget me. You're an innocent. The world is full of wolves who want to blow your house down. If you know what I mean."

I can't help but laugh at my younger sister. "There's no wolf."

Bridget sighs. "But there's a house, Ava. And yours is built of good intentions. Much easier to invade than one made of straw."

I look at Bridget's face. Her long-lashed, glitter-tinted

eyelashes. Her grim smile. Her eyes, which are usually sparkling and bright, are downcast.

"Please don't worry about me."

"Well, I am. Just as you would worry about me if I was alone in a foreign country."

I press a hand to my chest. "I can't imagine letting you go away alone."

"Exactly. We're thrilled to see you do what you love. But don't shut us out."

I blanch. "I'm not doing that." Images of me and Tyler singing our favorite Beyonce and Jay-Z song in front of a room full of people flash through my mind.

Followed by images of me and Tyler kissing in the middle of a courtyard in Verona, the most romantic city I've ever seen. None of this I've shared with my sisters.

Bridget leans close to the screen. "We're here for you. Don't think we don't realize all that you gave up for us."

Tears fill my eyes. "I didn't sacrifice anything. I was happy to do it all."

Bridget doesn't say a word. The seconds tick away, one by one, on the virtual clock on my dashboard.

"Be careful," she finally says. "Ask whomever you're seeing a lot of questions. Don't assume anything. Guys aren't going to volunteer information. They're not like us."

I stay silent. Afraid to speak and spill my guts. Tell her everything about Tyler and the charade I'm playing with him. Pretending to be her.

"Share some wins with us," Bridget adds. "Especially for our younger sisters' benefit. You've no idea how much they miss you."

I nod slowly. "I miss them, too. I miss all of you. How's Dad?"

She whispers. "I think he's seeing someone. He disappears at weird times. He's always checking his phone. And sometimes I catch him whispering on a call."

"No way!" I gasp. "Dad's never dated. He says he's got enough beauty queens around him at home."

"Yeah, well I think it's your fault. Going off to do your thing triggered something in him."

I smile. "I'm glad Dad's getting out there."

"Like you?" Bridget arches an eyebrow at me. "Don't try to hide it. Promise you'll tell me soon. I'm dying to hear about the sexy man who's putting that smile on your face."

"Oh, Bridge, it's not like that."

"*Pffff*. It's always like that."

We end the conversation with promises to talk in a few days.

I hang up and sit on my bed staring at the photograph of me and Tyler. I zoom in on it. I can see every detail of his brown face.

The tiny growth of hair on his chin. The thick curls in his hair. But especially the way his lips curl up in a sexy smile. Lips that I can't wait to kiss again.

The only dark cloud in all of this is that I wonder whom he sees when he looks at our photo. Which Walker sister is he thinking of tonight?

Chapter Twenty-Three

By my third week as a resident of Firenze, I'd developed a sound routine.

I wake up early with my neighbors. The water rushing through pipes and radios blaring Italian news are better alarm clocks than my iPhone.

As I leave home, I wave to my neighbors who are already out and about taking in garbage cans, sweeping their steps, or plucking leaves out of their window boxes and planters. On some mornings, Mr. Moretti, the older man who carried my groceries on the first day, hands me a paper bag with fruit or a bunch of wildflowers, or his wife's freshly baked rolls

"Grazie," I tell him. But as the days go by, I add more Italian words.

"Come va?"

He breaks into a smile and says, "Bene."

It's not a lot of Italian on my part so far, but with Tyler's instruction, I'm learning.

Not to be outdone by the Morettis, one evening, Mrs. Rossi,

my next-door neighbor, gifts me an entire loaf of freshly baked bread.

In half English/half Italian, she tells me the "pane" is to make me more "grassa." She grasps her midsection and squeezes out a handful of clothed flesh.

"Grazie," I tell her, thankful for all the gifts my neighbors give me. Even if it's to make me fat.

My upstairs neighbor, Nick Cruse, from New York walks with me across the bridge on his way to his art class a few days a week. We discuss the booming art scene in other cities like Dakar and Mexico City.

I dress in jeans or leggings and a t-shirt for gelato class. I pack a cute outfit to change into for my Italian classes.

At first, I told myself it was because I had to wash off all that milk, cream, and sugar from my face and arms after hours of whipping up gelato. But I admit, it's partly because of Tyler. Our after-class dinners and drinks have become a regular thing I look forward to on the three days of the week we have Italian class.

After waving goodbye to my neighbors, I stop at the Gelato Bar at the corner where I buy my morning cappuccino. The baristas greet me with a cheery, "Buongiorno."

Then, it's straight across the medieval stone bridge where vendors are opening their jewelry shops for the day and down Via por Santa Maria.

I window shop at Desigual and H&M before turning right to cut across the spectacular Piazza della Signoria, where myths and history converge.

Who can tire of seeing the famous Italian sculptures that adorn the giant square? Or the Palazzo Vecchio, which in Italian means "old palace."

I nod at bronzed Perseus holding high Medusa's head. Marvel at the complex sculpture of Hercules and the centaur in battle.

I give a mental military salute to colossal King Neptune as he presides over his ornate fountain complete with marble horses and tritons.

Five quick blocks north and I'm in front of the colossal Duomo and Bell Tower, Florence's trademark sites. The iconic 15th-century, red-tiled dome is featured on all the book covers or movie posters of Florence.

I catch my breath in the Piazza di San Giovanni, then speed off toward the Culinary Institute, which sits smack dab next to the grand library designed by Michelangelo. It's impossible to go anywhere in Florence without running into artistry woven with melodramatic historical events.

All twelve of the students in my gelato class have become friends. It's hard not to as we're constantly working together to master the base mix of milk, cream, and sugar, then choosing the flavor to add in.

We mix the base ingredients according to a 40/60 formula. Forty percent solids (sugar and eggs) to sixty percent liquids (milk and cream).

We pasteurize the base mixture to remove bacteria. Then, we add the flavor of our choosing. Flavors are determined by whatever fresh ingredients we want to add.

Making gelato is about science formulas, fresh ingredients, and excellent taste buds. It requires patience, during the pasteurizing and freezing processes. It requires intense focus, during the measuring and observation. It requires a diverse imagination. A weird trifecta of attributes.

Some of us are more science-oriented. Some are more imaginative. The supreme gelato master must have all these abilities.

After we set our gelato in the freezer unit, we hope and pray it will come out creamy, smooth, and airy. And of course, flavorful.

It's during the waiting periods that we chat and get to know each other better. Lisle shares stories about her brother, Ben, back in France. Patrick talks about his large German family. His brothers are all professional doctors and lawyers, but he wants to make gelato and is considered the black sheep. Tam is quiet, but he likes to dance so we play music and he records his TikTok videos while we watch. He's made us all sign up for TikTok. He's the only one most of us follow, but it's fun to cheer him on.

I sit next to Gisela and learn about Ecuador's amazing ecosystems from the Amazon rainforests to the South Pacific coast beaches.

Gisela is trying to create a different dark chocolate gelato using Ecuadorian chocolate. She calls it "Zamora" gelato. She brought the chocolate with her from her country.

She holds up the dark bars. "It's from cacao farmers in the Amazon basin. Beans to bars."

She breaks off a piece for me to taste.

"That's incredible, Gisela. So rich and raw and...." I search for the right word to describe the unique tingle on my tongue.

"Rainforest-y?" She laughs.

I laugh with her. "I was going to say, 'fruity.'"

"Do you know Ecuador is the native origin of cacao? The earliest known use of cacao by humans is from 3300 B.C. in Ecuador. We *are* chocolate!"

I stare at her in fascination. "I had no idea."

She beams. "The cacao beans were made into a ceremonial drink to serve the gods."

"That must be why it's called 'food of the gods!'" I take another tiny bite and savor the rich chocolatey, fruity flavor.

"You should give a mini-lesson about it in one of our classes. Chocolate is one of the most popular gelato flavors."

"You think anyone else would be interested?"

I nod vigorously. "I don't know about anyone else, but...for me, the history and background make the ingredient...more meaningful...adds to the creation." I think about Tyler's fascination with understanding the history of food markets and their significance to communities. "It's good to know how things started. Like we're not here out of the blue."

She pops a piece of the chocolate into her mouth. "Okay, I'll ask Chef Marco."

I wonder if she knows about black sapote, the fruit that tastes like chocolate pudding that is not widely grown.

I don't get to ask her because Gisela shakes her head. "What am I saying? I can't get up in front of everyone. My English is not 100%."

"If I can get up on a stage and sing in front of all of you, you can teach us about chocolate. And you speak perfect English."

"You had help. Very cute help." She gets up to go check our freezer units.

"About another hour," she says when she returns to her seat.

I've managed to control my emotions by then. I hope all the giddiness I feel inside isn't shining through me like the sun through sheer curtains.

"No comment?" Gisela is relentless.

"He's handsome. But don't change the subject. You can do this. I'm sure there's a lot to learn about cocoa."

"Okay, I will." Gisela knocks her arm against mine. "Back to you. There's a romance brewing between you and Tyler?"

I fidget with my utensils. There're only so many times I can wipe down my mixing spoons.

"I take your silence as a yes." Her laughter is fun and hearty, and I join her.

"You're worse than my sisters," I complain.

Gisela and I eat lunch together every day with the rest of our classmates. We pick a cafe near the school. There are so many, we try a new one every day.

The standing joke is whether we want pizza . . . *or pizza*.

Some days I order a salad. Just to be healthy. Because sadly, my three-times-a-week early morning run along the Arno River has fizzled down to twice a week now.

After lunch, we head back to class for the tasting and scoring of our gelato.

Everyone must share their creation and we take turns guessing the flavor ingredients and the formula. Basically, the recipe.

We comment on the gelato as if we're discussing fine wine. We each have a scorepad where we rate the gelato and make little comments, then pass them to the maker.

It's nerve-racking when your gelato is being evaluated. So far, Matilda and I get the highest scores. But you never know how it'll turn out. I hold my breath every single time as I anticipate my classmates' marks.

Chef Marco gives his comments last. He tells us what we did right. How we can improve and where we went wrong.

I didn't expect to be making this much gelato. But, I'm madly in love with my growing recipe book, infatuated with my pasteurization machine, and giddy when the gelato I create, curls its way out of the freezer unit.

I feel as if I'm doing what I'm meant to be doing in my life. As if my purpose has found me, and I it.

To add falling in love with Tyler Donovan on top of all that... well, fingers crossed. My life is damn near perfect. For the first time ever.

Chapter Twenty-Four

Who goes to a cemetery on a date?
In Florence?
If it's tombs you want to see, you can visit the Santa Croce Basilica and marvel at the resting places of Michelangelo, Galileo, and even Niccolo Machiavelli.

But *nooooo*!

Tyler takes me to a real cemetery with a wildflower garden in the middle of a traffic circle, at Piazzale Donatello.

The sun is setting, and the sky is a glorious pink and purple. It seems like an ideal time for a romantic walk across one of the many stone bridges, not a visit to a cemetery.

I don't even like going to the cemetery where Mom is buried back home, so why would I want to go to this one? But Tyler wants to show me something important.

So, here we are.

The cemetery isn't visible—it's in the middle of a crazy busy roundabout, up steps and behind a wide-open gate, but no one would know about it unless you googled and went searching for it.

The fact that it's completely empty with not a tourist in sight should tell you everything. We had to make a mad dash across traffic, tempting fate, to get to it.

Once inside the cemetery gates, we sign into a Visitor Book and step through to another world.

Tyler's wearing a big smile as he greets a tiny older woman coming out of a side door.

"That's the cemetery's library," Tyler says.

"Library?"

He nods and with a flourish like he's presenting a prize, he says, "This is the English Cemetery. Many famous non-Italian writers, artists, and opponents of slavery are buried here. This library contains their works or books about them. This is the custodian of the cemetery and library, a true scholar and activist."

I put out my hand to shake the woman's hand. She is small and looks to be over 75 years old. Her blue eyes are piercing and bright; her manner is sure and welcoming.

"I'll give her the unofficial tour," Tyler says.

She nods, "Stop back on your way out."

As soon as we walk past the entrance into the actual cemetery with its garden of flowering bushes and plants, I see why Tyler likes it here.

In the middle of chaotic, touristic Florence, here is an oasis of simple beauty and quiet. And it's full of history.

A gravel walkway leads up a hill with monuments and tombstones set on either side. Cypress trees abound. It's beautiful in a sad and solemn way.

I stop at the tomb of American writer, Elizabeth Barrett Browning to pay my respects.

I follow Tyler as he crunches his way on pebbles and rocks toward another gravestone. He stoops down and clears debris on the stone. "This here is the tomb of Theodore Parker."

That name means nothing to me. "Who is he?" I whisper, not wanting to insult the man laid to rest near my feet.

"Parker was a Unitarian minister and a major opponent of slavery from Massachusetts. He led the Boston movement against the Fugitive Slave Act. Lincoln and Dr. Martin Luther King, Jr. used Parker's words in their own famous speeches. He was pretty damn badass."

"I didn't know that. I'm embarrassed to say I've never heard of him."

"Me either. Not until I came here by chance one day. The custodian you just met gave me the history of the famous people buried here. Of them all, he's my favorite."

I look at Tyler's animated face. We've never talked about anything serious like this before. But we both sat in the same history classes back home and none of this was ever covered in those classes.

"You had to come to Florence to learn about Mr. Parker, huh?"

He sighs. "Yes."

"Why is his gravestone broken and falling over? It seems a shame for someone so important."

"It was damaged in a storm a few years ago," Tyler says. "But imagine, the great Frederick Douglass came straight to this cemetery from the train as soon as he arrived in Florence. This is where he stood. To pay his respects to Theodore Parker."

"Seriously?"

Tyler nods, "I come regularly to pay my respects too. It's the least we can do for this man who forcefully advocated for abolishing slavery. He was the one who said, 'The arc of the moral universe is long, but it bends towards justice.' And he was the one who first preached a *government of the people, by the people, for the people.*' Lincoln and King used Parker's words and ideas in their own battles for justice."

I bend down to read the inscription on Mr. Parker's tombstone. I recite it aloud:

HIS NAME IS ENGRAVED IN MARBLE, HIS VIRTUES IN THE HEARTS OF THOSE HE HELPED TO FREE FROM SLAVERY AND SUPERSTITION.

I look up at the sky. The pink and purple clouds have skipped across the sky and are replaced by a descending darkness. A raindrop hits my arm with a plop. I want to say thank you to Theodore Parker in some small way.

I gather up wildflowers growing nearby and place them on his broken gravestone.

"We need to get this fixed," I tell Tyler.

"I asked about it," he says. "The cemetery is run by private donations, and they don't have enough funds to fix it yet."

I stand up and dust off my hands. A surge of energy I haven't felt in a long time stiffens my spine. I look Tyler square in his eyes.

"Fixing up the tomb of a dead man may seem insignificant in the scheme of things, but it's the right thing to do. I'll talk to the custodian. See how I can help."

Tyler nods, surprise lighting in his eyes. "Okay."

"The man inspired Frederick Douglass, Abraham Lincoln, and Dr. Martin Luther King, Jr. Who else might be inspired once they know about him?" I ask.

He doesn't answer because rain is coming fast and we're scurrying back down in the footsteps of Frederick Douglass.

Is it weird I feel like I'm being reborn in a cemetery?

Chapter Twenty-Five

My days become so busy I barely remember I'm supposed to be Bridget when I'm with Tyler.

I forget to answer when he calls me by her name. I don't try to act like Bridget on our dates. And now, I'm too busy helping to organize fundraising events with the custodian of the English Cemetery to be anyone but myself.

Having read Frederick Douglass' account of Theodore Parker in his book, *The Life and Times of Frederick Douglass*, I'm more determined than ever to fix Mr. Parker's tombstone and bring his name and deeds to light.

It's Tyler's idea for us to take a break and venture out into the Tuscany countryside before the weather changes and it's too cold to enjoy.

We haven't left Florence since our trip to Verona, which feels so long ago, so I'm ready for another adventure. And once again, Tyler rents a tiny car. This one is blue.

"Our blueberry," I gasp, holding both hands to my cheeks.

I scoot inside and cross one leg over the other, pulling my

furry wrap close. The weather has turned chilly with October breezes blowing colored leaves off the trees. There's more than a nip in the air with increased rain, shorter days, and fewer tourists.

"Where're we off to?" I ask.

"I said it was a surprise."

"Yes, you said that yesterday. But now we're heading out. And...?"

He fixed the mirror and pushed the gear shift forward. "And it's still a surprise."

"Does it involve gelato?"

"Duh!"

I grin happily at him. "Good."

"Woman, you're going to make me fat."

I reach over and pat his knee. "Don't worry. I won't leave you if you get fat from eating all my gelato creations."

His turn to grin at me. "You promise?"

I nod. "Absolutely."

Our words feel so easy and free. As if falling in love allows you to be more open, less guarded. I almost want to tell him about the whole Bridget impersonation thing so we can get past it and truly be ourselves. But I feel as if we're past the point where I can bring it up and not wreck everything.

Maybe there'll never be a right time. Maybe Bridget and I will have to do a sister switcheroo. Like in the movies where twins exchange places. We look enough alike.

These crazy thoughts float in and out of my head as we drive out of Florence's giant defense walls and into the hilly countryside.

"What are you thinking about?" Tyler asks as we climb away from the city.

"Us," I say, honestly.

"Oh, what about us?" He's excited about this topic. He looks like he would rub his hands together in glee if he wasn't holding onto the steering wheel.

I can't bring up the Bridget thing. Or what will happen between us when it's time for me to leave Italy.

I can't even tell him I'd like to explore a deeper relationship with him. I definitely can't do that while he thinks I'm my sister!

On the other hand, it's Tyler I want. It's always been Tyler.

"I was wondering about your other relationships," I say in an offhand manner. "Before dating me. Have you been in love before?" God, I have no idea where that came from.

His face changes radically. The sunny smile dies on his face. Replaced by a frown, eyebrows inching downward in a scary manner.

"Why?"

"I...uhm...just something I was wondering about."

He doesn't answer. His eyes stare straight ahead like he's reading road signs, looking for clues. Finally, he says in a low voice. "Is it important?"

"I guess...unless...is there something you don't want me to... know?" My voice slides downward until it disappears completely on the last word.

How can I ask him personal questions about his past when I'm not forthcoming?

But his facial expression and obvious reluctance to talk about his past relationships seem sketchy. What *is* he hiding from me? Says the pot to the kettle. Both of which would be me in this scenario.

The air in the small car fills with tension. Mostly mine it seems. He's fiddling with the radio knobs.

I bite my lip and stare out the window. I've never experienced this feeling before. I can't tell what it is. It feels like a combination of a burning spear piercing my heart and a door slamming in my face.

Either one is bad by itself. Together, it's tearing my insides into shreds.

How do people in relationships deal with this scary feeling of uncertainty mixed with deep longing?

There's a 40/60 ratio going on in my body, just like in a gelato base. I just don't know which part is 40 and which is 60.

Are we breaking up? My heart thunders in my chest. He has the same dark look on his face as he did back at the boarding gate for our flight. When he was on the phone call.

That's when it hits me.

"Do you...have a girlfriend...or something...back home?" I clutch the dashboard in front of me. To ease any shocking news.

How did I not think of that? How did I let myself imagine Tyler Donovan was free and available and falling for me? Has all the excitement of Italy gone to my head?

My insides feel as if they're being crushed by a giant cement mixer. If this is being in love, I never want this feeling.

Chapter Twenty-Six

I prop one hand on the window and lean my head on it. Tyler hasn't spoken a word for miles. The radio plays Italian songs in between bouts of static.

I've never felt so alone in my life. Even when I was at my saddest, I didn't feel alone. I always had my sisters.

Sitting next to Tyler, who's not talking to me, and with the big scary unanswered question hovering between us, I'm an astronaut spinning in space, completely untethered.

The large expanse of blue sky and rolling green hills do nothing for me. Rustic homes, cute cattle, and even bunnies dot the roadside. But I don't care about any of it.

Part of me wishes I'd kept my big mouth shut. I'm not sure how to come back from this. Should I ignore the question and move on? But why would I pretend to not care about the very important detail of him having a girlfriend? (Putting aside the fact that I'm keeping a very important detail from him).

Am I wrong to want an answer?

"Oh Mom, what should I do?" I haven't asked myself that

question in a long time. I used to ask myself that every day in the beginning.

I remember the day I found out about her cancer. I'd walked into her and Dad's bedroom she'd decorated in cheery colors of yellow and red like a field of poppies.

She was sitting at her old-fashioned wooden dressing table adjusting a perky newsboy cap on her head. She'd been wearing them a lot lately, saying she was having a bad hair day.

"Another bad hair day?" I asked.

How we didn't realize our mother was having chemo and radiation treatment right under our noses is a wonder. It's a testament to our parents' desire to shield us from pain.

But that day, I saw something besides the cap on her head. On the floor around her were tufts of kinky brown curls. She didn't seem to know they were on the floor.

"Mom, your hair! What's wrong with it?" I had scooted onto the floor and picked up pieces of her curls, trying to hand them to her. I'm not sure what I thought she could do with it.

"Did you cut your hair?" I asked.

Mom looked at me, solemnly. I know now that she was debating what to say in her head. Much like I'm debating what to do about me and Tyler in my head.

"My beautiful daughter," she said. Her voice cracked up. I felt tears filling up in my eyes.

"Promise me that you will take care of yourself before you take care of others. Promise."

I stared at her strangely. What was she saying? What kind of promise was that?

"I mean it," she said fiercely. "You come first. You are important."

I nodded and agreed and promised to do whatever she asked of me. But I didn't understand.

Years later I realized Mom was insisting because *she* had put off medical check-ups and other preventative measures feeling too busy taking care of us to worry about herself.

As far as I knew, Mom had never put herself first.

Now, as I stare out the window at beautiful Italy passing by, I think, Mom would love it here. She would love the way the trees explode with colors and the way the tiny villages pop up everywhere with stalwart bridges and walls of stone.

She would love the food and gelato. Most of all, Mom would have loved the Italian churches with their frescoes and scent of burning candles, perfuming the sacred spaces with possibilities.

"Ava, you are special, you have to believe it." It's like Mom is talking to me right here. Her voice is a song I forgot the words to but they're coming back in bits and pieces.

"I'll always be by your side." More of Mom's lost lyrics. "Don't take a back seat in your own life. Take the steering wheel. You won't regret it."

I remember that one. In her last year of life, I wrote all her words of advice down in my journal, and I know them by heart. Even if sometimes I forget to consider them.

Maybe this is one of those times I need to speak up and put myself first. I glance over at Tyler's profile. He looks younger than he did back in high school. He's biting his lip, which he used to do when he was nervous the teacher would call on him.

Tyler spins the car expertly around one of Italy's many roundabouts and plunges us into a dark tunnel. When we emerge, we're on a road overlooking a valley of vineyards. A big sign welcomes us to the Chianti region.

"Whoa!" I exclaim as I lean forward in my seat, swiveling my eyes in every direction trying to capture it all. I'm not sure if I should be celebrating our destination or cringing that from now on, I will associate wine with heartbreak.

"We can talk when we park the car," he says gruffly. "I didn't forget what you asked. I need to explain."

The way he says the word, "explain" shatters my heart. I almost want to say, "Oh never mind, we're just having a fun time. It's not important." Or worse, tell him it's over and I don't need to hear anymore.

But all I say is, "Okay," and I lean back in my seat and try not to sigh aloud.

I'm not naturally patient. It's something I work on every day as I wait for my gelato to freeze, but I'm not great at it.

Just like I wasn't great at waiting for Mom to get better. As soon as I found out she had breast cancer, I went into full-speed recovery mode. Reading everything, doing anything I could to help her get better, and refusing to accept the prognosis.

"Doctors are wrong a lot," I told her and Dad while googling holistic remedies to counter the Westernized medicine failures.

My body was pumped up with hope and adrenaline every single day. I was a bubble of energy growing bigger and bigger with plans and remedies. I sent my parents magazine articles, podcasts, and YouTube interviews with medical experts in other countries. The whole works.

Until the day I had to face the truth.

Nothing I was doing was going to work. Nothing was going to fix my Mom and make her better.

On one of her last days with us, I sat by her bed in the hospital holding her hand. She couldn't talk. I tried to be brave and strong like Dad asked, but I could see in her eyes she felt sorry for me.

Because of all my hope dying. My bubble of ideas busting wide open. And my plans zeroing out.

I was fourteen when I discovered nothing in life is guaranteed. I swore never to plan on anything again.

Now, sitting here next to Tyler Donovan in Italy, the same boy I dared not to want too much because I couldn't deal with any more uncertainty or loss or whatever life wanted to throw at me, I realize I have not come very far at all.

Chapter Twenty-Seven

The cafe is an extension of a family's vineyard. Black wrought iron chairs sit around tiny tables for two in the middle of paved stones and buckets of flowers.

Below the outdoor tables and chairs, workers wind their way along paths cutting grapes with clippers and placing them in huge red crates. When a tractor pulls up, the workers place the full crates into the back of it and return to clipping the fruit.

I wish I was here under better circumstances because there's so much I want to point out and exclaim over. Like the fact we're watching a harvest, or the amazing smells coming from the cafe, and the possibility of making a wine gelato with these grapes.

A woman bustles out to take our orders. She speaks halting English but Tyler charms her with fluent Italian.

It's early October and the harvest is late this year, she tells us in Italian which Tyler translates for me. She stands there for a moment looking over the crew of workers and I wonder if she wishes she were down there working side by side with them to ensure the best grapes are picked.

Along with our espressos, she brings us a plate of snacks. "Buon appetito," she says with a smile. Cheese puffs, tiny sandwiches, and mini eclairs crowd the plate. I forget in Italy, there are almost always free snacks with your wine or coffee. "I could get used to this tradition."

I glance at the handsome man sitting across from me, his hands on the table clasped together as if in prayer.

"Sorry, what did you say?" He looks lost in thought.

"It's not important," I answer, flinging a hand above my head to chase away a curious bee.

He shakes his head. "It *is* important."

Clearly, he's not talking about snacks.

"Right," I say. *Get back on track, Ava.* I sit up taller.

His beautiful hazel eyes cloud over. When he opens his mouth to speak, he takes a huge breath. As if whatever he's going to say requires extra oxygen.

"I'm sorry I never told you I had a girlfriend. A serious relationship for two years, actually."

"Two years," I repeat like a parrot.

"It's because...well, I was trying to forget all about it."

God, could my heart hammer any louder? His words are making me sick. I want to throw up the snacks I've been munching on. I knew food was a bad idea!

I set my espresso cup down before I drop it. My hands are shaking so much I tuck them under my legs. But my legs are shaking too. I suddenly feel very cold.

I turn my gaze toward the vineyard. The workers are singing along to American hip-hop blaring from a speaker.

My brain registers Fifty Cent's song, *In da Club*. Maybe it's one of the worker's birthdays.

"Are you listening?" Tyler reaches over and touches my hand. I pull it back so fast you'd think he stabbed me with a knife.

I blink at him. "What? I'm sorry."

He tilts his head and stares at me with a look in his eyes I recognize from years ago. A look of sadness mixed with something else.

I never knew what that something else was. My own eyes drill into his now, searching the depths for the answer. What *was* the expression in Tyler's eyes from high school the few times he spoke to me?

I assumed it was pity, like everyone else's.

But it wasn't. It was empathy. I see it in his eyes now.

"Bridget?" His voice wavers over my sister's name.

I drop my face in my hands, devastated for the girl in high school who was drowning in her grief and couldn't see the boy she liked trying to share her pain.

Chapter Twenty-Eight

"Her name is Tiffany Washington. We dated through my last two years of college in Boston."

I've returned from the bathroom where I cried for at least ten minutes and now I'm back with a washed face and a slice of bourbon cake courtesy of the kind homeowner.

I nod at Tyler as I fork comfort cake into my mouth.

I recall seeing pictures of him and Tiffany on his social media. But I hadn't seen any photos of her or anyone on his page in a while.

I'm hung up on the word "dated." Past tense. "What happened?" I ask.

"I returned home from Italy in June. I was so excited to see her and I thought she felt the same way. We were planning a camping trip to New Hampshire. Just the two of us for a week. The day before we were to leave, I came home from work and she was at my house." He fiddles with his napkin, his voice dropping low.

I nod gently. I can feel where this is going. I almost tell him to stop.

He covers his mouth with one hand. "She cheated on me," he blurts.

Even though I'd guessed, it still was shocking. Who would cheat on him?

"That must have been awful," I say softly.

"It was kind of my fault," he says stiffly as if he's been taking the blame for a while and getting weary of it. "She didn't want me to come to Italy after I graduated. I said we could do long distance."

"Oh." I shove more cake into my mouth.

"It wasn't hard for me. I was busy with school and discovering Italy. I thought we'd visit each other. She'd come here. I'd go home for the holidays." He looks at me, pleading with me to understand his side of it.

I nod, like *go on*.

"That isn't even the worst part."

I wait, holding my breath.

His voice drops so low I can barely hear him.

"It was with my *brother*. That's why she was at my house. They didn't expect me to come home and they were having one for the road. At least that's what Everly said. The bastard."

"What the hell?" My hand rushes to my throat. "Oh no. Oh God, no." Images of my four sisters flash through my head. I can't imagine a worse betrayal ever. *Ever!*

"Tyler, I'm so sorry." Nobody should ever have to discover their brother or sister is capable of cheating on them.

He nods. "Thank you."

We sit silently. My mind fights not to dwell on the awfulness of the scenario he's painted for me. I know his brother. He graduated two years ahead of us. He was tall and handsome like Tyler. But not at all nice.

"I'm going to get more espresso." I jump out of my seat and

walk across the dusty courtyard into the cool darkness of the cafe. I order two more espressos and grab a bag of chips. What I'm really doing is buying time. My mind is fighting with itself. I feel sorry for Tyler. But I wonder how this affects him. He can't trust anyone after that. Not for a long time. What happened to him is huge. A double betrayal!!

Back outside, Tyler is standing looking out over the vineyard. I hand him the bag of chips.

"Thanks," he says, splitting open the bag. He puts a chip in his mouth and chews. He seems a million miles away. I can't comprehend this level of duplicity so I stay quiet.

Finally, he starts speaking. "She keeps calling me wanting us to get back together. I tell her I'm not ready to talk about anything like that. But she's persistent."

That must be who he was talking to on the phone at the airport.

"She says love is about forgiveness."

I stuff chips into my mouth and chew. She has a point. No, wait. How can I think that? She slept with Everly. I always knew Everly was jealous of Tyler. Since high school when Everly was a junior and we were freshmen.

Everly would throw out comments in the hallways when Tyler walked by with one of his many friends who are girls. Everly called Tyler a "prissy boy" saying only they would play football and be one of the girls too.

Tyler was plain nice. Everyone liked him. On the other hand, Everly was manipulative and sneaky. His only friends were people he could boss around.

But Ava, you should encourage forgiveness. What would Mom do?

Tyler shakes his head, his brows scrunched up and his eyes staring ghostlike over the fields. "Even if I forgive her, how could I forget it? I'll have to see Everly. I would have to see them together at family events. I can't handle that. She says I can because I'm the strong one and she's weak. She says I have to save our relationship because I jeopardized it by moving so far away."

Whoa. This woman sounds like a manipulator. She and Everly have a lot in common.

If I learned anything from my sisters, it's how to spot one of those two-faced people with ulterior motives. Between our weekly Bachelor show nights and Bridget and Corrine's boyfriend dramas, I've learned a thing or two.

But I don't think it's my place to offer up my opinion. This isn't about me. Tyler needs a friend to listen and I must do that for him.

Two fresh espressos arrive. We sip our drinks and listen to the hum of the tractor and the sound of Fifty Cent telling it as it is.

"I don't think I could trust her again. You know?" Tyler says suddenly.

I nod slowly. "Yes, it would be very difficult."

I can't believe how calm I sound when just ten minutes ago my guts were throwing themselves against the walls of my body, making a Jackson Pollock scene inside me.

Tyler looks over and smiles. Not one of his big, dimpled smiles. A tiny smile that says, *I'm trying here*.

"How long ago did it happen?" I ask tentatively.

"I found out in June. But it happened last semester. And it was not a one-time thing. It was a whole affair for three months."

"Ouch!"

"Yes, you see why it's hard to talk about. Everything she said to me I dissect and wonder, was she with him when she was saying that?"

"Oh definitely. I'd be doing the same thing. I can't imagine how you feel. It seems so painful."

"It was a nightmare." He stops. "But you went through a far more painful experience when you were younger. With your mom."

I shake my head. "No. My mom dying wasn't anyone's fault. She didn't betray me. It was a..."

What, Ava, what was it?

He's waiting for me to finish. I sip my espresso. "It was heartbreaking in a completely different way." I finally manage and he nods.

"I remember it well. I felt so sorry for all of you girls. Especially Ava."

My head snaps up. "What? Why?"

"It completely changed her."

I'm shocked. "How do you know that?" I blurt.

He frowns. "It was obvious. When we started high school, she was running for President of the Student Council. As a freshman! It was unheard of. She had this platform. What was it?" He scrunches up his nose.

At the same time, we both say, "*Bring Back Bread!*"

"Yes," he smiles. "That was it. She wanted the cafeteria to bring back bread for our hamburgers and hotdogs. The PTA had forced the school to stop serving bread to fight obesity."

I laugh. "Yeah, they were serving thin cardboard crackers that tasted like plastic."

"How do you know that? You were still in middle school."

I sit back. "She talked about it." I flip over my cloth napkin and roll it into a long sausage. *Change the subject, Ava.* But I can't. I want to know what else he remembers about me.

"Yeah, she wouldn't shut up about how unfair it was. Bring back bread." He laughs. "Trust me she had a real following."

"She did. Funny you remember that."

"Remember it. She inspired me to look at food differently. She had these charts and graphs of how important grains were. It was serious."

"You're kidding, right?"

He shakes his head. "Nope. Ava Walker was a force. An inspiration. Before your Mom got sick, I thought she was going to take over the school singlehandedly. Well, the PTA anyway."

It's strange hearing him talk about that long-ago girl. Before

Mom got sick, I thought I could change anything. Make things right.

Tyler clears his throat. "I'm sorry. I don't mean to bring up sad memories."

"Oh no, it's interesting hearing about . . . her from someone on the outside."

"It was sad to watch from the outside. I tried to help. Bring her the homework assignments, or give her class notes, but she never paid any attention to me."

I sit silently. I can't recall the things he's saying in any specific detail. Just vague memories. That time is a blank for me.

He continues. "You wanted to know how she changed?"

I nod. I don't trust myself to speak.

"When your mom got sick Ava withdrew from the election. Withdrew from everything. Didn't talk to anyone. Just disappeared completely. Like she wasn't even there. The feisty, opinionated girl became an invisible girl." His voice drops. "I suppose grief can do that to a person."

I feel tears pricking the corners of my eyes. For the first time, I'm peeking into my past. To that girl whose entire world had imploded. I didn't realize anyone noticed. Especially not Tyler.

Tyler grabs my hand off the table. "Let's change the subject. Let's talk about us."

"Us?"

"Yes. When I'm with you, I forget about my terrible summer. Since our very first conversation on the plane. You've been like a breath of fresh air. I know that's cliché. But it's true. I don't think about the bomb my brother and girlfriend—*ex-girlfriend*—dropped on me. It's as if you carry a pure space around you. I get to enter it and it's a whole new world."

The swift change in the topic makes my mind whirl. I take a deep breath. *Ok, focus, Ava. He's saying you make him forget about his ex.*

I find that a little hard to swallow. "Does that mean you're compartmentalizing?" I can't help but ask. "Ignoring reality?"

He shakes his head. "It's impossible to forget. But I can't change it. I don't dwell on it."

"That's very Zen of you."

"Yeah," he smiles weakly. "I wish I had a few extra siblings in my back pocket now that I've lost one."

"You can borrow one of mine. I have plenty." *But not Bridget!*

The owner of the cafe brings over a bunch of newly-picked grapes to our table.

"Grazie," we both say.

"Wow, this is real farm-to-table goodies," Tyler says to me.

I'm too busy stuffing grapes in my mouth to respond. The juices explode on my tongue. I've never tasted grapes warm from the sun and fresh off the vines.

We eat in companionable silence.

I'm dying to ask Tyler where does all of this leave us? What is our situation? As if he's reading my mind, his face gets serious. "I like you a lot, Bridget Walker."

My heart drops to my toes. Did he have to use my sister's name at this moment?

"I think we have an amazing future ahead."

I stare into his dark eyes. I want to kiss him. Feel his lips on mine. Slide my arms around his neck and curl into his broad chest.

"As long as you don't lie to me, we're good. Better than good. I can't handle another betrayal." His eyes stare deeply into mine begging me to understand.

I lick my lips. This is a disaster. I'm a horrible person. I'm going to have to confess or end it.

Once he finds out I've lied to him the entire time he's known me, it'll all be over.

I make a quick decision to tell him today on the drive home after we've had a chance to shake off the horrible memories of his ex. I pray he has the heart to understand why I did it. And to forgive me.

Chapter Twenty-Nine

Tyler insists we continue our day, put the drama behind us, and celebrate a fresh beginning to our relationship.

He drives for another twenty minutes then parks the car on a narrow country road behind automobiles, trucks, and even a couple of horses. "Ta-da!"

"What is it?" I look around as our feet crunch over crisp fallen leaves and our arms brush tree branches hanging across the road forming an arch of flowers.

"You'll see."

We pass more cars and horses and cute old-time buggies. I'm clueless as to where we're headed literally and metaphorically.

Finally, we push through a low-hanging bower of leaves and a wide expanse of billowy grass opens up before us. A true-to-life meadow just like in picture books. I almost expect a talking rabbit to pop up.

"This is magical."

"We aren't there yet. This isn't the surprise."

"Oh, right I don't see any gelato."

This makes him laugh and I feel our day spinning in an entirely new direction. Maybe I do make him forget all about the horrible summer he had. Maybe I *can* figure out a way to get past the whole impersonating Bridget fiasco.

Through the meadow, over a stone bridge, and past a large pond with swans. It can't get any more picturebook pretty.

"This is ridiculously beautiful, Tyler."

He beams at me. "Just wait."

"Now I know what people mean when they say it's the journey, not the destination that matters."

"Oh, you'll love *this* destination."

Ten more minutes of walking past birch trees and willows, pointing out one turtle, two rabbits, and three furry dogs, and finally, we're there.

A large banner is strewn across what looks like a medieval wall.

"*Welcome to Festa del Vino at Panzano in Chianti!*"

"A wine festival?" My eyes open wide. "I've never been to a *wine* festival before."

"You can't live in the Tuscany region and *not* go to a wine festival."

"For sure," I agree. "Where do we start?" I feel like Alice in Wonderland dropped into an unbelievable world. "What town is this?"

"This is officially a hamlet, not a town. It's Panzano."

A modern square with shops and restaurants leads to quaint roads and low stone medieval arches. "You better watch your head," I tell Tyler as we stroll through the hamlet.

"I almost expect a knight or monk to come out any minute. To fight for my hand or something. I'll have to give him my...*handkerchief*." I yank the silk scarf from my neck and wave it around.

Tyler plucks the cloth from my hand and does a sweeping bow. "At your service, madam."

I giggle. "Where's your horse?"

A woman with a large straw hat and bag pushes between us. She's dragging the hand of a man in glasses reading the program for the wine festival. "Are you kids going in or not?" She bellows at us.

We step aside quickly.

"American," I whisper to Tyler.

"Pushy American," he snickers.

We get in line to buy tasting tickets. The festival is small enough that we can walk around it twice and stop at every booth to try as many different vintages from as many different vineyards as we can manage.

It's not easy. I'm trying to chug more water than wine, but hydration is losing big time.

The wine is delicious. Fruity, crisp, tangy, full of cherry notes and earthy aromas. At least those are the words I pick up as I listen and learn.

Frankly, I don't learn much. I mostly drink and compliment the wine growers and ask if their wines can be used to flavor gelato.

I get a few strange looks.

As the sun heads westward, a band begins to play. Italian love songs at first, with a lead singer crooning like he's Harry Styles.

Then surprisingly, or not surprisingly given I heard Fifty Cent in a Tuscany field today, the band swings into Top 40 hits.

People are dancing and wine is being drunk by all. It is a merry festive evening and I'm in the middle of it, holding Tyler's hand.

I may be slightly tipsy. In fact, I may be more than slightly tipsy. Because I don't care that we're in the middle of a hamlet surrounded by a dancing, singing crowd, where wine is flowing and stars are glittering in the darkening sky above. My eyes are on one person.

I lean into him, look up from under my lowered eyelashes, and whisper, "I think I love you."

I slap my hand over my mouth and burst into hysterical giggles.

The look in Tyler's eyes is not helping.
Either he's really happy. Or he's tipsier than I am.
"I think I love you back."

Chapter Thirty

After hanging around drinking coffee, and helping to clean up the medieval square, Tyler and I drive back to Florence, tired, happy and I think madly in love with each other.

This is no time to confess I am not who he thinks I am. As much as I want to tell him the truth, my tongue can't form the words. I feel one hundred percent smitten. As if I got handed the final rose at the end of all the rose ceremonies. I can't throw it away now.

Besides, he's leaving the next day for a week in Sicily to conduct research on food markets for his thesis. I'll use the time apart to figure out a solution to my dilemma.

It's hard to say goodbye when he drives up my tiny street to drop me off.

Since it's so late at night, he can drive without getting stuck in the crazy traffic of cars, bikes, and sightseers by the Ponte Vecchio bridge.

We kiss each other over and over. One for good luck, one for having a great week. One for we'll talk every day. One for whatever else we missed.

It's a caravan of kisses and I'm tingling all over. He holds my face tenderly between his hands and whispers, "I meant what I said earlier."

I nod, my insides melting from his nearness.

After the car disappears up the hill, I stand on my steps breathing in the cool night air.

A smile forms on my lips. I run my fingers over them. They're sore from Tyler's deep kisses. It almost feels like the cold burn from eating icy gelato.

I could get used to feeling this. Tyler's kisses. What a great name for a gelato flavor. I laugh happily as I let myself inside the door and go straight to bed.

My next week is so busy I wouldn't have had time to hang out with Tyler even if he were here. Chef Marco has stopped being laid back and fun and has turned into a dictator.

He's urging us to consider what we'll create for the Gelato Festival in December and insists we learn how to recognize the freshest ingredients.

He takes us on a field trip to a fruit and veggie market behind the Santa Croce Basilica. We follow him as he weaves in between the produce handlers like a maniac on a mission.

"This!" He shouts. "This is a fresh pomegranate." He yanks open the round fruit and red seeds spill out all over the ground.

"And this is what a lemon should look like." He throws two lemons into the air and catches them; he gives them a squeeze and tosses one to Gisela and one to another student.

"Inhale the aromas. They should smell like Sicily."

I giggle with Gisela. "What does Sicily smell like?"

Chef Marco hears me. "Sicily smells like lemons! Over 90% of Italy's lemons come from Sicily."

Gisela and I exchange looks. Our teacher has gone mad.

Marco spins around in circles, tossing out fruit for us to catch as he shouts out their names. He's like a game show host tossing out prizes.

"Amarena cherries!"

"Oranges of Ribera!"

"Sicilian prickly pears!" I catch a prickly pear. It's quite ugly but I love it because it makes me feel closer to Tyler in Sicily.

"Sicilian red oranges!"

"Wow! Sicily grows a lot of fruits," I whisper to Gisela.

She nods as she catches another lemon. This one is from the Amalfi Coast.

It's a smorgasbord of fruits.

After each of the twelve students is holding at least one fruit —I'm holding cherries and a pear—we head back to the lab.

"We're going to create new flavors today, without any recipes," he says.

Everyone looks confused.

"What?"

"Yes, whatever you're holding is the flavor you're making today. If it's pomegranate, then you make pomegranate gelato. If it's Amarena cherries, then you make something with that. Etc. etc."

"But I have two fruits." I hold up my cherries and pear.

"You're in luck. You get to figure out how to combine two completely different flavors into a delicious frozen dessert."

"Why me?"

Marco gives me a stern look. "Because you're ready for it."

I look around the room. Matilda also has two fruits. As does Lisle and a Welsh man named Dylan.

"It's because you're so good at this," Gisela whispers to me.

I blush. "Feels more like a punishment."

My first two batches are a disaster.

Chef Marco puts a fresh pear on my desk and grins at me. "Try again."

I end up staying later than everyone else. All the students leave for the day. Chef Marco hands me the keys. "You can lock up and put the key in the mailbox outside my office. Don't leave until you've made me something I can eat."

I gulp. "Okay."

Tyler texts me and I tell him I can't chat. "Too busy whipping up a cherry pear gelato."

He sends back emoji kisses.

I go back through my class notes on our lessons on ratios. Coming up with the right ratio of ingredients is the key. Sounds simple but it feels impossible right now.

My third batch tastes too bitter. It's heavy on the cherries.

I cut back on the cherries for my fourth batch. I sit and stare at my bowls. I look around the lab. I feel as if I'm missing something. Something important.

And that's when it hits me. I need to make a sorbet. In Italy sorbets and gelato go hand in hand. We've had several classes on making sorbets, but I never choose to make them. Probably because I don't like sorbet as much as I love gelato. But I see now that Chef Marco is forcing me to think outside my usual boxes.

Once I figure that out, it's smooth sailing. I wish I could figure out my major romantic problem as easily.

With an immersion blender, I stir together the fruit and strain it several times to get out the seeds. Then I add simple syrup and taste it. It's almost perfect.

I poke around on Marco's giant shelves. I find what I'm looking for. I squeeze some drops of lime into the mixture. Bingo! It's perfect.

I put it to freeze, clean up and fold my apron and lock up the lab. As I walk down the hallway to find Chef Marco's office, there's a bounce in my step.

I *am* pretty good at making gelato. And sorbets. Maybe I have a chance at winning the gelato competition. And getting that internship to work with an Italian Gelateria before opening my own back home.

The words "back home" reverberate in my head.

I've always wanted a gelateria so the Walker sisters can stick together. Each of us can contribute our personal talents to the venture. But where would that leave me and Tyler?

Even if we get past the present issue of my lying to him, how will we deal with long-distance or any other life decisions that are sure to arise because our trajectories are so different?

As I let myself into my dark apartment, a familiar sense of uncertainty and dread of an unpredictable future overcomes me.

But this time, the fear is that love doesn't conquer all. No matter what the books and movies want you to believe.

Chapter Thirty-One

I learned a long time ago that the best thing to do is to shut down the pain and keep moving. It's the only way.

At the end of class on Friday, Chef Marco sends us the link to sign-up for the Gelato Festival. Not everyone wants to spend an additional three months in Italy, but for those of us that do, filling out the form is an exciting first step.

"Remember, this is your chance to create something that represents you and what you love most. Make it unique to yourself. You get to name the gelato and tell the story of how it came to be. Don't let me down."

"What do you think you'll make?" Gisela asks me as we gather our recipe books and aprons to leave for the weekend. We both filled out the form to enter.

I think of the black sapote brownie Tyler gave me on the plane. But where the heck would I find a South American fruit in Italy?

"I'm not sure," I tell Gisela honestly. "He said to make what we love. I've never had a favorite flavor. I always make whatever my mom and sisters liked."

She nods. "The guy who won the Gelato Festival last year created a gelato with a handmade rose water base."

"I know. I need something I love as much as he must love roses."

Gisela smiles. "I can think of one person that might qualify." She winks at me.

"I don't think so anymore," I mumble.

"What happened?"

Outside, dusk covers Florence in a pale mauve glow. "Kind of a long story." I shrug.

I'm glad she doesn't press me. I suppose the biggest difference between friends and sisters is that friends aren't pushy.

Everywhere people are walking briskly, hurrying to get to a warm bar or restaurant. With no Italian lessons all week, I walk with Gisela to a nearby hangout where most of our class is gathered going over today's recipes and eating more gelato, if that's even possible.

We fall into a discussion about the competition as soon as we're seated. Everyone is pointing at me and Matilda. Saying we're the ones to beat.

"No," I shake my head. "It's wide open. Gisela here has a secret weapon." I nudge my friend.

Gisela laughs. "It's not a secret. You all tasted my chocolate from Ecuador. It's what I love and it's what I plan on making."

Matilda chimes up. "I suppose I better do something with kiwifruit, mates."

We all laugh. Patrick, who is from Germany, says he will investigate making sauerkraut gelato.

"Eww!" Gisela groans. "That's disgusting."

He throws an arm around the back of her chair and leans forward, "Not what she said last night."

"Oh my God!" I stutter looking from one guilty-looking face to the other. "For real?"

Gisela blushes harder as Patrick kisses her on the cheek. "I'm a lucky guy. I already won."

"This class!" I laugh for the first time all week. "Love is on our brains."

"It *is* Italy," another student pipes up.

Yeah, but is it true love? Or is it Italy, I wonder.

"Full got me knackered trying to keep up with you all," Matilda groans.

"Matilda, don't try it. We saw you flirting with Chef Marco." Patrick ambushes her.

"Moi!" Matilda opens her eyes wide and bats her long lashes. "Not me. I'm here for the food and wine and gelato only."

I wish I could say the same thing.

Making my way home after eating pasta and drinking two glasses of wine I shared with Gisela, I notice a group of American students walking and singing loudly in front of me. It seems so easy to be happy and carefree in Italy. Part of me wishes I could be like that. Then I remember I was like that last weekend with Tyler. And it felt perfect.

I miss him more than I expected.

The truth is Tyler has brought something to my life I never had before. I wish I could put a name to it. If I could, I'd figure out a way to make it into a gelato flavor and it'd be my favorite.

Chapter Thirty-Two

Saturday is the first day I have all to myself. As much as I enjoy my gelato classes, hanging out with my new friends, and road trips with Tyler, an unplanned day in Florence by myself feels like the first day of summer vacation when any and everything is possible.

My phone buzzes as if to remind me I'm not alone.

It's Tyler's morning greeting of kisses and hugs. I send back my morning message of flowers and hearts.

He texts back emojis for me to guess what his plan is for today. Lots of fruits, veggies, meats, and cheeses. I laugh out loud. More farmers' markets for him. I swear he's more food obsessed than I am.

You're making me hungry. I text.

What're you up to today?

I think for a moment. Then I text back an emoji of a scooter.

You're renting a scooter? He texts.

I send one smiley emoji and one with scared round eyes.

I've never ridden one but I saw cute pink ones to rent near my apartment and have longed to try it. I am not telling my sisters or dad becaue they would be worried. This is something I am doing solely for me.

I'm going to ride it all over Florence. I might even go to the cemetery again. I text Tyler.

Nice! Please tell Theodore Parker I said hello.

I assure him I will. Zooming around the medieval city is everyone's idea of a fun day. Cleaning around gravestones, probably not.

I hurry up and get dressed, excited to get the mini-lesson on riding a scooter before I set out.

In no time, I am pushing a cute pink helmet down over my hair and adjusting the side mirrors on my rental scooter.

My first stop is a bakery facing the river where I park the scooter and order an espresso and two slices of pumpkin bread.

I sit outside in the sunshine, enjoying my snack and people-watching. The scooter sparkles in the morning sun. I'm proud I dared to rent it. It's not something the old Ava would have done before traveling to Italy.

I make it to the cemetery in one piece, after dodging honking taxis and cars on the traffic roundabout. The cemetery custodian welcomes me. I hand her the extra slice of pumpkin bread, still warm from the baker's ovens.

"You came back," she says happily, blue eyes twinkling. "Come into the library." She ushers me into a room lined with books, a long wooden table in the center covered with more books, papers, blueprints, and magazines. A laptop sits open at one end of the table.

"I'm writing my blog," she says.

I sit down and get right to the point. "I want to do more to help out. Now that the fundraiser for Theodore Parker's gravestone is going well, and we've almost reached our goal...is there anything else I can do?"

She nods. "There's always more to do." She jumps up and scans her bookcases. She returns with papers and hands them to me. "Do you want to join the cemetery board to participate in fundraising decisions and how the money is spent?"

"Seriously?"

She nods. "It's the best way."

She hands me a notebook and asks me to write down my name, address, email, and phone number. "We have online meetings."

"Okay," I stand up and give her back the notebook. "Thank you. I'm proud to be a member."

She smiles in a kind but professional manner. "Okay, let me tell you what we need help with."

I sit back down and for the next half hour, I do nothing but listen.

This former nun, medieval scholar, and cemetery custodian with her intelligent eyes and sharp features tells me story after story about the ongoing persecution of the minority Roma people in Italy, whom most refer to by the derogatory term "gypsies."

I feel my blood roiling with the injustices for the marginalized poverty-stricken group. Some of the atrocities sound similar to what Black Americans are still experiencing in my own country.

"I want to help." I find myself saying.

"You will. You're now part of our board. You'll be included in our meetings."

I give a small laugh. "Do you sign up everyone?"

She shakes her head. "No, my dear, only the ones who volunteer. And I can see you want to make a difference."

By the time I leave the English Cemetery, I've not only cleaned up around Theodore Parker's grave, but with the custodian, I've created two online fundraisers to pay Roma workers to landscape the cemetery.

"Writing my blogs about literature, politics, and other intellectual pursuits is great. The real work is helping the bodies, minds, and spirits of the men, women, and children who need us here and now."

I clasp my hands together and lean my chin on them. "You're right." Then, without me realizing it, I agree to come twice a week to tutor Roma children in basic English.

"You're good at this," I tease.

"We meet here in the afternoons. Come when you can."

It's not much. But it's a start for me.

The same spark I felt when I was fourteen and wanted to raise my voice loud enough to change the status quo, is back. This time, I'm ready to fight for a lot more than bread.

Chapter Thirty-Three

"How's it going, kiddo?"

I almost cry at hearing the cheerful sing-song tone of Dad's voice. More cheerful than usual in fact and I wonder about his new dating life.

"I'm great, Daddy. How's everything with you?"

He leans close to the screen. "Why? What have you heard?"

I burst out laughing. "Oh, nothing."

"Right! I know your sisters. Nosy posies."

"Honestly, Dad, all I know is you're going out a lot."

He smiles and his brown eyes crinkle up in the corners. "Fake news!"

I giggle. "Okay, who are you *fake* dating then?"

"No comment." He pretends he's turning a key on his lips and throwing it over his shoulder.

Before I can say anything else, all four of my sisters bum-rush Dad from behind and grab the tablet out of his hands. It's Sunday afternoon and they're all there as usual, even Corrine who's back from her dorm to eat a family meal.

The only one missing is me.

"Is it Ava?" Emerald squeals. "Ava, I need you. Daisy won't let me talk to this really cute guy at school. She says he's a hot head and a trouble maker and he's not. He's misunderstood. Like uh... the Incredible Hulk."

Daisy has her arms folded. "Emerald is lying, Ava. Don't believe a word she says. It's not that I won't let her talk to that arrogant jerk. It's that I refuse to let *him* talk to her!"

I laugh. "Oh my. The censorship police, are you?"

Daisy nods. "Someone's got to save this airhead from herself. You'd do the same thing."

I don't get to share what I would say or do in this situation because Corrine is waving her arms over Daisy's head in an "abort mission" signal.

"What is it, Corrine?" I ask.

She pushes aside the two youngest and leans in. "Dad's got a girlfriend."

"What? He just told me it's fake news."

"More like the biggest news of all," says Bridget.

"Have you guys met her?" I can't believe I'm missing this huge moment in our family's life.

Bridget swirls her hands up and down in an hourglass shape. "She's hot!"

Corrine nods. "Gorgeous."

"Our Dad is dating a J.Lo lookalike," Daisy confirms.

"No way!"

All four of them nod silently.

"Damn! Forget her looks. Is she nice?" My voice gets fierce. "Is she nice enough for him?"

"Let's put it this way," Bridget says. "She wears Prada."

"She kills at karaoke," adds Daisy.

"Her name's Maxine and she's a VP of a Forbes 500 company in Boston, but she has a second home in Maine so she's here a lot." Corrine rubs her fingers together to indicate she's got a lot of money.

"Who cares?" Emerald pouts. "Can we get back to my Hulk? I mean hunk? His name is Jackson and he's sooo beautiful."

"Okay, wait, Emmie, we'll get to Jackson. First, what's this woman's full name I want to google her."

"Don't google my girlfriend," Dad shouts from the background.

"Oh my, he called her his girlfriend? Why didn't you guys call me? Or text me? I'm in Italy. Not Mars!"

"We hoped you'd be too busy with your own dating life to be concerned about what's going on this side of the Atlantic." Corrine winks suggestively.

I shake my head at them. "You guys come first. Always!"

"Not if you find Mr. Right," Daisy argues. "Did you? Because we haven't heard from you except hello and I'm having fun and I'm learning a lot. *Blah blah blah*. Not exactly forthcoming with info, Ms. Thing."

"Did you call me Ms. Thing? Do I look like a Ms. Thing to you?"

"Whoa! Ava's getting feisty! Must be love." Bridget laughs.

"Or her period," Emerald grumbles.

I roll my eyes at them. "Ok, Emmie, tell me about Jackson."

Daisy sighs loudly. "You're wasting your time."

Emerald ignores Daisy and launches into a full blow-by-blow description of the hottest senior boy at their high school. Daisy rolls her eyes at every overblown adjective.

"And I'm supposed to be the writer in this family," Daisy says when Emerald stops talking.

"Wow!" I say. "He sounds...interesting."

Daisy scowls. "Which part of he's been in two fights and suspended for a week did you not hear?"

"He was supporting our Global Climate Strike Friday. Some kids were making fun of us, and he stepped in."

"He's not even a part of your Youth Sustainability Leadership Group." Daisy pokes her sister. "He was just looking for a fight."

"Ok, you two settle down," Bridget puts a hand on their

GELATO FOREVER

backs. "Let's not make this a big deal. Ava will want to run back here to fix things."

I frown. "Exactly what I was thinking. How are you handling all this, Bridget? Should I cut my trip short?"

All my sisters shake their heads vigorously.

"No!" Emerald sniffs. "I was sharing. Not trying to make you come home. Sorry, Ava."

Daisy raises her eyebrows at Em. "See what you almost did?"

Emerald looks miserable.

"It's okay, Emmie. I want to know about you and your sustainability strike."

"And Jackson?"

I nod. "Him, too." Although I'm with Daisy. I don't want my littlest sister dating some hothead who gets suspended for fighting. I wish I could give her dating advice, but I'm only starting out myself, so I have to leave this up to Bridget and Corrine who have dated enough for all five of us.

Bridget must be reading my mind. "Don't worry about this, girl. I got it."

I nod. "Any other news?"

Preferably news that doesn't involve a member of my family having dating issues I can't help with.

"I won second place in the college writing contest for high school students," Daisy offers.

I clap my hands and raise them above my head in a cheer. "That's fantastic news, Daisy. You guys should have led with that."

"I tried to but this one here..." she points at Emerald, "had to blabber on about that maniac boy."

I frown. Does Daisy sound like she might like this maniac boy more than she's letting on? Or am I so far away I'm not reading the room properly?

Bridget must understand the wheels turning in my head. She nods her head in the background. As if she's saying, "You figured it out."

Shoot, this one is hitting a bit close to home. Is more than one Walker sister liking the same boy in high school? *Not again.*

Of course, I don't say a word. But a part of me wants to take Daisy aside and let her know it's okay to speak up and let her feelings show. That she doesn't have to accept being a wallflower or whatever kids call the ones on the sidelines these days while the more extroverted sister takes center stage.

In my case, Bridget literally took center stage as the lead actress in our school musicals. But from the sound of Emerald's climate change protests, she's taking the stage in her own way. Which I'm beyond proud of.

"Are you listening, Ava?" Daisy leans toward the screen as if she wants to touch me, and I wish I could hug my baby sister so badly.

An ache to be in the same room with them talking and laughing and baking cookies or watching a Netflix series rocks me hard. I've purposefully built up a wall to block out waves of homesickness. But the feelings we try our best to avoid always end up barreling over us and taking us down.

"I'm right here, sweetheart," I tell Daisy as cheerfully as I can manage.

"But what about you?"

"I'm fine."

"Yes, you keep saying that."

Bridget reaches for the tablet. "Let me talk to her alone for a little bit." My three younger sisters make rude noises and wander off. Bridget eyes me fiercely. "Tell me, who he is and what he's done to my sister's heart?"

I laugh awkwardly. "It's no one special." Oh, my lying heart.

Bridget shakes her head until it looks like it'll roll off. "Not buying it, sis."

I give in. I have to tell someone. It might as well be Bridget. She's the person I'm closest to but also the person it's most difficult to tell because I can't tell her the entire truth.

"Tyler Donovan," I whisper as if I'm in the middle of a room of people instead of alone in my cozy warm studio with the red checked tablecloth and embroidered cream comforter.

"I knew it!" Bridget's eyes light up. "Tell me you're finally getting some action."

"You're so crass."

"But honestly."

I laugh feebly. "Yes, we're getting physical. Not the fireworks bombard the sky kind of physical. But sweet and perfect for me."

Bridget sticks her finger in her mouth and pretends to gag. "You're worse than Daisy. She thinks we have to wait for a Prince Charming to sweep us off our feet, although her idea of a prince is slipping fast with Jackson what's his name."

This time I giggle for real.

"Tell me what's wrong?"

"What do you mean?" I ask.

"Tyler is a great guy. I know him well. At least I knew him in high school and he was wonderful. But you're looking miserable. Like you're hiding something. Is he married? Going to die soon? Is he part of a satanic cult? What?"

I scoff. "Nice options."

"Well?"

I bite my lip and stare hard at the screen. A part of me wants to shout it out. Tell Bridget this mess I created. I would if it didn't directly involve her.

I decide I'll give her a portion of the truth. "It's just that he wants to stay in Italy. For about two more years and long distance is out of the question. No matter how I feel about him, this relationship ends when I leave Italy."

"Hmmm," Bridget frowns at me. "Is that it?"

I nod sadly.

"That's not a deal breaker, girl. So put the idea of it ending out of your head and give this your all. There's nothing wrong with falling in love in Italy. While studying abroad. And nothing wrong with falling in love with your high school crush, Tyler Donovan."

I sigh. "It's complicated. But thanks for listening."

"Are you guys done?" Corrine wanders back into the room. "I want to ask Ava something."

"Me, too," Daisy pipes up.

"And me!" Emerald says, popping her head into the middle of the girls.

The rest of the conversation with my sisters covers a wide range of topics with one common thread: not boys or dating or fashion or food. But travel. An idea I put in their heads for good or for worse.

Bridget tells me about her new job as an online content creator for a book publishing company. "I get to combine my two loves, reading and…."

Before she can finish, Corrine pipes up, "Being on her phone!"

I laugh. "Do what you love, right?"

Bridget beams. "I can work from anywhere in the world."

"Oh?" I hold my breath. "Anywhere in particular?" Don't let it be too far away, please.

She shrugs. "No idea. Wherever my heart takes me."

"Oh boy," Daisy says.

"Ditto," I joke.

Corrine tells me she's looking into an internship or work abroad program for her last year at college. "Somewhere I can use my language skills. Preferably Mexico or somewhere in South America."

"I have a friend from Ecuador named Gisela. I'll introduce you online. Maybe she'll know about programs for you."

"I'd love to go to Ecuador!" Corrine gushes.

"Looks like you're chasing away all my beauty queens, Ava," Dad says, coming closer to the screen.

"Sounds like you've found a new beauty queen all your own." I tease him.

He raises his hands up in a helpless gesture. "I can't win here." He's standing in the middle of my four sisters; Daisy with her arms around his waist and Emerald hanging from his neck. He's got one arm around Corrine and another around Bridget. A pang of regret almost suffocates me. For being so far away from my family.

Then Dad says, "Baby, I'm so proud of you for having the courage to travel to a new country and follow your dreams. You are an inspiration to me and your sisters. We'll all be right here when you return."

"Speak for yourself," Bridget says, and Dad puts a hand over her mouth. "Hush before I ground you."

We laugh as we say goodbye. Although I have a lump in my throat making it hard to whisper, "I love you," to them all.

Chapter Thirty-Four

Whatever doubts I was harboring about Tyler and not pursuing a relationship with him fly right out the window as soon as I see his handsome smiling dimpled face in front of the classroom on Monday afternoon.

But before Monday afternoon, I have to get through Monday morning's classes with Chef Marco. My plan to focus entirely on gelato-making gets sidetracked by Gisela and Patrick making googly eyes at each other across me.

As her lab partner, standing right next to her, I can't help but feel Patrick's looks of longing and desire scorching my neck.

"What's the deal with you two?" I whisper to her.

She blushes bright red. "Nothing. Just a holiday romance."

"Really? Do you agree with that? And how do you prevent it from escalating?"

I'm asking for a friend. Ha!

Her face turns even redder, all the way to the roots of her brown hair. "We don't talk about it," she whispers. "It's understood."

GELATO FOREVER

My mouth falls open. "By whom?"

She stares at me. "By everyone who's ever been in a holiday romance." She says it like it's common knowledge. I wonder if that's what Tyler thinks about us. That this is strictly a holiday romance.

Oh my God, and here I am saying I love you to him first and thinking I must tell him my secret and reveal who I really am when everyone but me apparently knows that what happens on vacation stays on vacation.

I'm thinking I'm more innocent and naive than even I suspected when Gisela breaks more news to me. "Patrick wants me to stay over in Germany for a while after our classes have finished. What do you think?"

I blink. I think that's crazy if it's just a holiday romance, but I don't say that. "It depends on how much you like him."

She smiles a smile I know well. I've seen it on my face in mirrors and glass walls when I'm thinking about Tyler.

"Girl, I think you like Patrick a little more than you realize."

"No, it's a holiday...."

"Romance, right I get it. I hope you convince yourself of that before the smile on your face betrays you."

"Back to you, girl."

"It's back *at* you,"

Gisela turns a full-wattage smile on me. "You know exactly what I mean."

"Touché," I respond. Because Gisela is right. I'm trying to convince myself my feelings for Tyler don't mean as much as they really do. And I'm failing.

My heart flutters anxiously as I make my way to Italian class.

Italian phrases pop in and out of my head. "Andrà tutto bene." Or *"Everything's going to be alright."* And my personal favorite, "L'amore vince sempre." The beautiful Italian phrase for "*Love always wins.*"

It's this last one I'm reciting over and over in my head as I walk into the classroom and look down the steps to the front by the podium.

Tyler sees me as soon as I enter. Almost as if he's been watching the doorway waiting for my arrival. The look on his face, expectant and bursting with happiness, melts my heart.

My man. My handsome boyfriend. All my negative thoughts flitter away at the sight of him standing there in the flesh, strong and real.

"Bridget!" He calls out to me as if the rest of the class isn't there.

As soon as I hear my sister's name, the doves of doubt flutter back into my heart waiting for my next move.

I give him a little wave and whisper to myself, "Andrà tutto bene."

I push all doubts out of my head and barrel down the steps to hug Tyler. He grabs me in a fierce bear hug in front of the entire class. I bury my face into his broad chest. Tears leak out my eyes and I turn my head to the side, so I don't completely soak his shirt.

"I'm sorry. I'm making a mess."

He laughs lightly. "It can wash."

Suddenly I'm propelled back to freshman year of high school. I was crying behind the outdoor lockers used by the football team. No one was around and I was ugly crying.

It was before Mom died, but I knew it would not be long before she'd leave me forever. Dad had been talking about transferring her to a hospice and I had to look it up because I didn't know what hospice was.

I'd just read that it was a place for the terminally ill to receive end-of-life care. The phrase "end-of-life" kept repeating in my head like a lighthouse beam circling in my brain.

Each time the words, "end-of-life" circled back around, it pierced the hope I'd been holding onto.

That's when I ran out of school and hid behind those lockers.

I was crying so hard I didn't see who handed me a clean towel from one of the lockers. I buried my face into it and sobbed hard, feeling like my guts were leaking out along with my tears.

A locker door slammed shut and I gulped, "I'm sorry for the mess." I indicated the towel I still held over my face.

The football player answered, "It can wash."

I still hear his voice in my terrible memories of that day. The day I found out what hospice meant. It was this voice.

I lean back out of Tyler's arms now. "It was you, wasn't it?"

"Who was me?"

Then I catch myself. I can't ask him if it was him who gave me the towel that day. Because he gave it to Ava, not Bridget. I shake my head.

I say with utmost seriousness, "It's always been you, hasn't it?"

A smile that could turn devils into angels appears on his face. "I sure hope so."

It's then I realize what a dangerous game I'm playing.

All I have to do is utter three little words. "I am Ava." This entire charade would end, and I could relax and we could see where this relationship can possibly go. Even with the idea of him staying in Italy longer than me.

I stare into the depths of his gold-hazel eyes. I ignore the students filing in and settling into their seats. The three little words are on the tip of my tongue.

Just say them already won't you, Ava!

He reaches out a hand and pushes a curly strand of my afro behind an ear.

"You know, I love your hair," he says. "You look younger and cuter than you ever did before."

"I do?" I croak.

He nods. "Did you want to tell me something, Bridge?"

Someone behind me clears his throat. Papers rustle. Laptops slide open. The clock behind Tyler clicks into its 5 o'clock position.

"We'll talk later, okay?" He runs a hand down the side of my face.

I smile wanly at him. Overcome by feelings of guilt and remorse.

I slide into the nearest empty seat and try to concentrate on our lesson.

But all I can think about is how I'm ruining everything, all chances of real happiness and possibilities with Tyler Donovan because I feel the need to live a lie. Because I didn't feel that I, Ava Walker, was enough. Or had anything to offer him.

When the truth is, Tyler liked me all along. Or could have liked me if I had paid attention.

I am enough, I really am. I must believe that and face up to the truth. Or lose Tyler forever.

Just like I lost Mom.

Chapter Thirty-Five

No one talks about Florence, Italy in rainy November. No photos are shared of the bars and restaurants hunkering down, with festive holiday spreads and fairy lights decorating their walls and bars, as the locals sip espressos instead of Aperol Spritzes.

The carefree summertime decadence has disappeared and everyone is serious and studious and a bit more serene—probably because the tourists have mostly all gone.

The Florentines get their city back for themselves until next spring. I can't tell if they prefer it this way because they behave the same. No matter who comes to visit, the Italians are themselves.

Which I envy as I am still not completely myself with Tyler.

I still think about how Bridget would act or react at times, although that feeling to behave like my sister is decreasing so much that I forget about it most of the time.

I also forget about telling Tyler the truth. The urge I had to tell him after our week apart got buried under the business of day-to-day life.

I'm not the only one who's been busy from morning to night with classes and volunteering. Tyler has ramped up his research by interviewing vendors and food market organizers and is spending a lot of time in the library putting together his research for the first draft of his master's thesis.

But we put everything aside for one weekend to visit Lucca, an ancient artistic walled city known as a foodie paradise. As we drive, Tyler tells me that he's surprised I'm volunteering at the English cemetery as that wasn't something he knew Bridget to be interested in.

His exact words are, "I always thought public service and volunteering was more Ava's interest. You never did that in high school. Ava must have rubbed off on you."

I slink into my seat. My spine seems unable to support any more lies so I say nothing.

He frowns as he switches on the windshield wipers to chase away the cold raindrops outside.

"There's nothing wrong with volunteering if you're thinking of it. I don't mean to discourage you. I admire it honestly. I always admired Ava's spirit."

He's right. Bridget wouldn't be hanging out in a cemetery. For *any* reason.

Tyler leans over and grabs my hand briefly before putting both hands back on the wheel. The weather isn't conducive to hand-holding drives. "You, okay?"

I nod. God, I want to tell him everything. I want to blurt out everything I felt and thought about him since I first laid eyes on him in eighth grade when our different middle schools went on a high school visit day, and I saw him with his friends laughing and sharing his sunny smile with everyone around him.

Even before we started high school together, he was the brightest star I'd ever seen. No boy in my own eighth grade had caught my attention.

But there was Tyler Donovan. Dark burnished skin, toothpaste white smile. Curly short hair. And lean muscled body. Even then he stood out.

And I feel like somehow all the stars aligned for me to be sitting here right now, next to him. To be the one he likes. The one he wants to kiss and hug and love.

Except he thinks it's Bridget he's hugging and kissing and falling in love with. Not me.

Plus! What Gisela said about a holiday romance makes me nervous.

Does Tyler consider us as boyfriend/girlfriend? Or as a holiday romance?

I'll ask him today. Find out once and for all, if we're both feeling the same way.

As for me, I'm 100% in love with him.

Chapter Thirty-Six

"You look worried about something, what's up?" Tyler tucks one of my hands under his jacket and holds it close to his chest.

We're sitting side by side in a cafe close to a real fireplace where logs are crackling and yellow flames dance cheerfully. A stereo plays the Dean Martin song, *Amore*, which sounds cheesy but it's sweet.

I can't believe this is my life right now. We're starring in a scene from a movie.

Ask him, Ava now is the time.

I clear my throat. Before I say a word, two mugs of warm cider with cinnamon sticks appear. We thank the server and sip the delicious spice-infused cider.

"Cider gelato?" I raise a brow at Tyler.

He sweeps a hand outward as if he's saying *why not?*

"I know I may seem obsessed but I want to deliver more than just a new flavor. I want to recreate an experience with my gelato.

Something that will remind people of a beloved time in their lives. Or a moment of joy. I can't do much to change the world with gelato, but I can bring smiles to faces."

"Your eyes are shining," he says. He reaches over and tugs a loose curl of my afro. "Have I told you how much I love sitting next to you, doing nothing at all?"

I scoff. "We're doing something. We're researching."

"Speak for yourself. I only use the idea of 'research' to lure you away from your busy life. How else can I convince you to drop everything and come driving around with me to these quaint towns in the Tuscany Valley?" He has his fingers raised to do air quotes and I bat them down.

"No need to lure me here, silly. I love exploring with you."

Ask him, Ava now is a perfect time.

The Dean Martin tune ends and a Christmas one comes on. It's in Italian but I can tell it's about the holiday season. It's cheerful and bouncy. It's got to be about reindeer and St. Nicholas.

Tyler leans back in his armchair and lets go of my hand to reach down and pick up his mug. My hand feels lost without his warm touch. I tuck it under my jeans-clad leg to keep it warm. Or to stop it from shaking so much.

"Uhm, Tyler..." I start.

He glances over the top of his mug, a slow smile spreading on his red lips. I want to kiss him. Maybe I can kiss him instead of asking awkward questions.

Make us both forget that we're only in Italy by chance together and one of us will be leaving before the other.

"Yes, smooches?"

I giggle/cringe. I wish he would not call me a pet name when I'm about to crash a wrecking ball through this romantic moment.

"I was wondering." I look around the room. Couples huddle together close to the fire and chat softly. Some read the newspaper, some a book, but all are looking peaceful and calm. No one looks as if a raging tornado is going on inside of them.

I swirl the cinnamon stick in my cider and take a big sip. How do people do this? How do they ask the person they like...okay, *love*...whether they love them back, or if it's a temporary thing?

For the first time, I wish I were Bridget sitting here. She'd know what to do. Bridget isn't afraid of anything.

Tyler reaches over and twirls my fingers between his long ones. It's distracting as hell. I pull my hand away. "What's the plan for us?" I blurt it out so fast it sounds like "whatsplanning us?"

He frowns. I see it appear and then disappear instantly. But it was there. Like a goblin ready to jump down, hands on hips demanding me to retract. Abort, step back to a safe space.

"What do you mean?"

I always heard that people who answer a question with a question are trying to buy time to figure out how to answer it.

I take a deep breath and look him in the eye. I'm supposed to be Bridget, right? So, I'll be Bridget. I'll channel Bridget's bravery.

I look him in the eye. "Is this," I fling a finger back and forth between us like it's a windshield wiper gone berserk, "just a hookup?"

That's the word I heard my sisters using. "Or something more serious? You know, a holiday romance because we're both in Italy at the same time? Or...." I can't seem to stop giving the man options so I bite my lips to shut up.

He blinks. "Are you serious?"

At the look on his face, I grab my mug and stick my head into it sucking down the last dregs of cider like a raccoon on a garbage hunt.

"Bridget," he says, taking my free hand and firmly intertwining our fingers. "*I love you*. Don't you know that? All I think about is you. How we can spend more time together. I think about waiting as long as it takes to be with you in every way as a boyfriend, as your man, as your everything."

My heart flips over. It's beating so fast, like a bird flapping its wings trying to escape my chest. I did not expect this answer. I feel a soft smile stretching my lips.

Then he pulls back. "What about you? Is this a holiday romance for you? Am I a temporary fling? Like those guys whom you dated in high school?"

I frown. "What are you talking about? I didn't date anyone in high school." I slap my hand over my mouth.

Shoot! I almost slipped up.

I drop my hand. Regroup. "I mean, I wasn't dating anyone seriously." I want to tell him I only had eyes for him. But that wasn't Bridget's experience.

"You dated your co-stars for three months each year then dropped them as soon as the shows were over. Everyone knew that. The co-leads of your plays would get sad when the play was coming to an end."

"Wow!" I mumble.

I didn't realize Bridget did that. She was popular and pretty and surrounded by boys and girls and even teachers adored her. I didn't know she went through relationships like they were seasonal fruit.

"I've changed," I say softly. Hoping that's good enough for Tyler. I hope Bridget *has* changed.

I'll have to think about her lack of commitment later. Maybe there was a reason Bridget didn't date anyone seriously. Maybe she's as worried as I am about someone we love leaving us.

"Have you?" Tyler asks as lines deepen on his forehead.

I nod swiftly. "Yes."

"Good. Because I trust you. I can see you're different. You're not going to treat my heart carelessly. Or do something reprehensible like lying to me about our love."

I gulp. Shake my head in a guilt-ridden no. I would not do that.

It's only later, as I get ready for bed in my warm studio apartment after he's driven me straight to my door and kissed me soundly, wrapping his arms around me like he never wants to let me go, that I realize, I didn't say I love you too.

I didn't tell Tyler Donovan that I want him to be my boyfriend, my man, my everything.

Chapter Thirty-Seven

The gelato base is key to excellent gelato. You use the freshest ingredients. In the proper ratio.

The problem was that somehow I got it backward. My brain was on vacation when I was measuring out the ratio of ingredients.

Instead of the 40/60, I flipped it and did 60/40 solids to liquid. Which means I ended up with a soft and gooey diabetic disaster.

Chef Marco was not happy. We were in the middle of our mid-semester gelato test and my gooey mess almost broke the pasteurizer machine.

Shame seeped through me. I wanted to run out of the class. Gisela hugged me and rubbed my back. "We all make mistakes," she comforted me.

"But this is a simple step. What is wrong with me?"

My face burned with shame. My hands were raw and blistered from washing the canister under scalding hot water for as long as it took to clean out the sugary mess.

Milk, cream, sugar. 40% sugar. 60% milk and cream. Duh!
How did this happen?
But I had an idea.

"Oh, what a tangled web we weave when first we start to deceive." Mom's voice was stern, her dark brown eyes flashed with disappointment when she first told me that line.

At the time, I was twelve and didn't know it was a famous quote. I thought Mom was witty and clever and dead wrong because lying had its benefits.

For one, if I said I had homework to do at the library, I could get out of helping Mom with watching my baby sisters who were whiny and annoying, and who wanted to "read" my favorite books by scribbling in them with their wet crayons.

I could hang out with Rosalie, my best friend from middle school, who didn't have any siblings so when we went to her home after school, it was quiet and we could watch television without interruptions.

Lying had its benefits. That was for sure.

Until the day I told Mom I was staying after school for a test review and instead went with Rosalie and her mom to Pizza Hut, where, lo and behold, Mom walked in with five-year-old Daisy and four-year-old Emerald who were both crying.

She caught my eye. I was sprawled in relaxation mode in a red booth, laughing, talking, and eating pizza. I was even drinking a forbidden Coca-Cola, enjoying life as an almost only child.

It was the look of hurt and disappointment on Mom's face that made me choke on my bite of pizza. Literally, choke.

I started coughing and spitting bits of chewed-up dough onto the table. Rosalie pounded my back to clear my airwaves and Mom came rushing over to check on me leaving Emerald and Daisy crying at the counter.

It was a total family meltdown. Mom was holding back her own tears and fighting to be polite to Rosalie and her mom who watched in horror as I hiccuped "I'm sorry," over and over to Mom while my two baby sisters bawled down the restaurant and we had to leave without any pizza.

Everyone else at home hated me, well, Bridget and Corrine because they'd been waiting on the pizza.

I never thought about the difference between Black and white families. To me, at twelve, it was all the same.

Rosalie's mom was way more lenient on her than Mom and Dad were on us, but I figured it was because she was an only child, so she got away with saying and doing things we could never get away with saying and doing in our home.

It was Rosalie who encouraged me to tell a little lie. She called it a "white lie." I thought a white lie was what white people said and that as long as I was saying a white lie, it wasn't bad because I wasn't white.

That was my irrational logic to justify deceiving Mom back then. I was twelve and the world was unfair. Some people got all their parents' attention while I got one-fifth of my parents' love and attention.

"But Mom, I didn't say a *black* lie." That was my excuse.

She slapped me. A real honest-to-goodness slap across my arm. I was shocked.

So was Mom. She got up and ran out of the room, slamming her bedroom door behind her.

It was Dad who sat me down and explained real life to me. He told me I had hurt Mom by lying to her. But I also embarrassed her in front of everyone.

"We live in a white city, sweetie. We inhabit a white neighborhood, church, and school. I'm not saying it's true, but Mom and I feel as if we have to be on point in everything we do because we're constantly being looked at and judged as a Black family."

I shook my head. "What do you mean?" But I knew what he meant. And the idea that I had embarrassed my mother by lying to her and hanging out with my friend and her mother instead of helping out at home, or at least telling Mom the truth made me get defensive.

"I don't think you're right, Daddy. Nobody cares we're 'Black.'" I did air quotes for the word Black and he raised his eyebrows.

"I care. Your Mom cares. And so should you, missy."

The next day, I found three large books sitting on my bedside table. My punishment for lying to my parents was to read these books. I groaned as I picked up the books and read the titles.

The Autobiography of Malcolm X.

A Call to Conscience: The Landmark Speeches of Dr. Martin Luther King, Jr.

Brown Girl Dreaming.

It was the last book I read from cover to cover as soon as I opened it. I didn't even move from my bed.

Before I got to the reverend's famous, *I Have a Dream* speech or Malcolm X's anthems for living as a Black person, it was *Brown Girl Dreaming* that made me walk into my Mom's bedroom, tears rolling down my face and beg for her forgiveness.

I promised I would not lie again.

My parents had given me a life blessed with endless opportunities. My dream had been a selfish one. It was a desire to be loved first and foremost by my mother. Not regulated to second, third, fourth, and then fifth, after each new daughter was born.

Brown Girl Dreaming changed how I saw the world as a dark-skinned girl in America. It helped me appreciate my life and my parents and sisters and everything I was blessed to have.

I didn't realize it at the time, but that book made me embrace my power to change the world, well, my little corner of it. I went from wanting to be an only child, to seeking out ways to help others who may not have all the advantages I had.

They say books can change your life and they are right. Books can do that.

But there's no book to help me now.

Because once again, I'm paying a hefty price for lying to someone I love.

At the end of our gelato mid-semester test, Chef Marco gave me a big fat F.

He shook his head with disappointment. A mirror of how my mother had looked at me years ago in Pizza Hut.

"I don't know what's on your mind, Ava Walker," he said. "But fix it. Or you will not receive your course certificate and you will not be able to participate in the Gelato Festival."

"Ok," I said, softly. "I'll fix it. I promise."

I could fix the gelato base formula and get it right forever more. But I couldn't fix the Tyler problem without losing him forever.

Chapter Thirty-Eight

"What's going on with you Ava?" Gisela pours me an extra large glass of wine from the bottle of Pinot Grigio we ordered for what was supposed to be our post-exam celebration, but which is now an Ava Walker pity party.

"Yes, how can you fail the test? You're like the best gelato maker of all of us." Patrick sips his wine and frowns at me.

"I was gutted, Ava," Matilda speaks up. "You're my inspiration."

"Me? You're *my* inspiration, Matilda."

"Aww, sweet as." Kiwi speech for "nice."

"I'm worried about you," another student pipes up.

"She'll be alright." Matilda pats my hand. "Won't you?"

I nod miserably. "Thanks, guys. I appreciate all your efforts to cheer me up. This is my fault. I messed up because my mind is elsewhere."

"On a tall, dark handsome someone?" Gisela smirks at me.

"You better snap out of it. Only a few more weeks before the Christmas Gelato Festival."

"I know." I slide my head down onto my arms, hiding my face with my mass of curly hair.

"What's wrong, mate?" Matilda leans forward to peek into my half-covered face.

I groan. "I lied to Tyler."

It's amazing how the truth will fly out your mouth when your stomach cannot contain the lie any longer.

"About what? Anything serious?" Gisela pulls me up gently off the table and leans me back against my chair.

I cannot hide from these folks. We've been through so much together. Days and weeks of anxiety at incurring Chef Marco's wrath and endless critiquing of each other's work can bring even the strangest group of people together.

"We're here for you Ava, just tell us and we'll help you straighten it out." Gisela's kind words bring tears to my eyes.

"I wish you could help. But I have to do it. The problem is when he finds out the truth it'll be over and I don't want it to be over. I love him," The last part comes out in a wail and everyone looks at each other with wide eyes.

"Bugger!" Matilda claps her hands. "More wine."

Gisela refills my glass and pushes it toward me.

I pick it up and take a guilt-ridden gulp of the delicious fruity drink of the gods. "I don't deserve wine. I don't deserve anything good. I'm going to hurt Tyler when he finds out I lied to him for months."

"*Pssssshhhh!*" Matilda smacks a hand on the table hard enough to make the glasses jump. "Listen up, Girlie, I'm sorry to say that if you love this man, this won't be the only time you hurt him. We hurt the people we love. Even if we don't plan to or mean to or want to. It happens. You say you're sorry and you try harder. Pash and makeup. Everything will be good as gold."

"Pash?" Gisela swivels toward Matilda. "What does that mean?"

Patrick leans over and kisses Gisela. "It means kiss. Obviously."

Gisela blushes hard.

I frown. "I promised my mom I would not lie. And I feel as if I'm hurting her too, not just Tyler. Like I broke this big promise to my mother."

The table quiets down. I feel bad I'm spoiling their celebration. I half rise from my seat, ready to slip on my jacket and head out.

"Where are you going, love?" Matilda asks. "Wanna head outside for a smoke?"

I almost laugh at sweet dear Matilda. She's older than my mom would be if she were still alive. Yet she feels like a friend. "No, mate, I don't smoke."

Matilda snorts. "I know that. It's an excuse for fresh air. Although I'll be smoking, so not sure how fresh it'll be."

"You're not going anywhere," Gisela insists, pushing me back down in my seat. "Snacks are arriving soon."

I sigh. "Fine."

"So, Ava, what's this big lie you told Tyler?" Patrick fiddles with a napkin on the table. Passing it to me to make my favorite animal shapes.

I reshape the napkin into a rabbit with floppy ears and a tail. "I told him I'm my sister Bridget. He doesn't know that I'm me, Ava."

If I wasn't feeling so sad, I'd laugh at the look on everyone's face. They're all frowning in the same way, heads cocked to one side, eyes puzzled and confused.

I clear my throat. "It's kind of a long story. But Tyler knew me and my sister Bridget in high school. I was a different person back then because of my mom being sick and dying and Bridget was more fun and popular. When I ran into Tyler on our flight to Italy, he thought I was Bridget. I look different now, too. From six years ago when we last saw each other. A different hairstyle, different style in clothes, a different look altogether. When he called me Bridget, I went along with it because it was easier than telling him I was Ava, the quiet girl who secretly adored him but pushed him and everyone else away."

Wow, I can't seem to shut up now that I'm speaking about this out loud to someone other than myself. Or maybe the wine has unsealed my lips. Whatever. The faces of my classmates look as confused as ever.

"And why would you want to pretend to be Bridget now? This is years later. Everybody is a new person six years out of high school. It's the basic logic of the universe." Patrick says in his German accent.

"Plus," Gisela adds, "you're fabulous. No offense to your sister but I'm sure you're exactly who he wants. Not her."

I hang my head. "We may never find out. I screwed this up badly. I don't know how to tell him the truth now. This lie has gone on so long."

"Course you can do it. It's a piece of piss." Matilda pats my hand again as she downs a fresh glass of wine.

"I assume you mean it'll be easy?" Gisela laughs. "I swear you New Zealanders make English difficult for us second language speakers."

Everyone around the table laughs and Matilda says she's ready to teach us all Kiwi lingo.

Our snacks arrive and people dive in eating and drinking and sharing their slang words from around the world.

I glance at my watch. Tomorrow is Thanksgiving in the States and I wish with all my heart I could be spending it with my family.

Making a supersized turkey, pumpkin pies with marshmallows, homemade rolls, and cranberry sauce.

And not because I believe in what the traditional holiday stands for. But because I want to be close to people who'll love me no matter what. Even when I mess up and tell a dumb lie that gets out of hand.

At the end of our pseudo celebration, I say goodbye and head out to walk home alone on the cold November night.

Tyler is spending the evening in his school's library. Our Italian classes were canceled from today until next Monday because his university recognizes the American Thanksgiving holiday, something Gelato University does not.

I arrive home. Despite its cheery colors and comfy quilts and blankets on the couch and bed, the studio feels quieter and emptier with the idea that tomorrow is Thanksgiving and I'm here in Florence alone without the noise and fuss of my sisters and Dad.

Bridget told me Dad invited his new female friend to dinner, which is a big deal and I'm missing out. I close my eyes and plop down on my bed, still garbed in a coat, boots, and scarf.

"Mom, what should I do?" I whisper. "Please send me a sign, or something to let me know how to fix this mess."

If I close my eyes tightly I can almost feel her next to me, patting my curly hair, smiling with her crinkly brown eyes, and opening her arms wide to hug me close.

My phone buzzes. I pull it out of my coat pocket and see it's Tyler calling, not texting as I expected. Which means I must gather myself together to sound cheery and okay.

"Hello?"

"How'd it go, baby?" Tyler's voice is unusually upbeat.

"Did you kick butt on the exam? Dumb question, I know you did. What flavor did you make? Can you start bringing some home as yet? I mean you passed the exam right so you must know how to make gelato that won't kill me! Plus there's someone else who wants to eat it."

My mind races. "Someone else?"

"Guess what?"

"What?"

"My best friend Ajax is here!"

"From *Greece?*"

"Yup. That crazy dude hopped on a flight and showed up."

I hear loud laughing in the background. "When do I get to eat gelato with you, Bridget?" A deep accented voice shouts from somewhere near Tyler's phone. "I've heard so much about you. This guy can't shut up."

"You need to shut up before I punch you again," Tyler says to his friend in a hopefully fake menacing voice.

I would join in the laughter pouring from the phone except now I'm anxious.

My stomach is roiling like the Atlantic Ocean on a windy day. I can see it from our home in Maine. I wish I were seeing it now instead of sitting here wondering what to say.

I must lie to two people. Tyler *and* his best friend.

"Oh," I stall. "I didn't know he was coming."

"Me either," Tyler says. "I told him I had the entire week off from school and teaching. He said his olive harvest is done and he wanted me to come over and celebrate the supreme quality and quantity of his precious olive oil."

A rough voice yells, "But he said no because he doesn't want to leave Bridget. So, here I am!"

"Right, that part is true." Tyler sounds like he's smiling at the other end of the phone.

I'd heard about Ajax, Tyler's best friend from Harvard. Ajax lives on an island in Greece. He studied business at Harvard and is now running his family's olive oil business. Tyler and I talked about visiting Ajax in Greece as it's so close to Italy. A dream that obviously won't happen once he finds out I'm not Bridget.

"Wow!" I respond, my head in a daze.

"Yes, babe I can't wait for you to meet him. Although we're going to make him jealous. He's on the lookout for Ms. Right. And can't find her."

"Facts," Ajax snorts loudly in the background. "You got any available sisters, Bridget?"

I gulp. My face feels like it's on fire. If Tyler could see me now, he'd know something was up.

I sit on my bed staring into space.

"You still there, honey?"

"Yes," I whisper thinking, how can I treat Tyler so horribly when I love him so much?

"I'm here."

The question is, for how much longer?

Chapter Thirty-Nine

I awake on Thanksgiving morning to the usual sounds of water rushing through pipes and Italian news playing softly on radios through the thick stone walls.

Back home we'd be getting up extra early to season the big turkey, make stuffing, and prep the pie crusts.

One of my sisters would make pancakes and waffles and another would fry up slices of bacon. I would put the glass jar of thick maple syrup next to the stove to warm up so it would flow smoothly.

Thanksgiving breakfasts were even nicer than dinners because it was just us: Me, Bridget, Corrine, Daisy, and Emerald. No aunts, uncles, and cousins arriving from Boston yet.

We'd cuddle together on the couch in cozy pj's and blankets laughing and commenting on the large colorful balloons sailing by in the Macy's Day parade on the widescreen television.

Today, however, my first Thanksgiving alone is dismal. And I don't mean it because I'm far from home. Or because I miss my family, although I do.

It's awful because I'm carrying around this big secret that seems to get bigger and heavier every day.

My thoughts juggle between breaking up with Tyler and leaving Italy, hopefully with my gelato certificate in hand, or confessing the truth and hoping he forgives me. Highly unlikely.

Ajax's arrival feels like a sign I should tell Tyler the truth. As if him having his best friend by his side will make it better. He will have someone to confide in who will hopefully beg him to consider my side of the story.

Which, by the way, is *what*?

What could possibly be serious enough to warrant a lie about my identity for *months*?!

No wonder I failed my gelato mid-term. It's karma. The gods hate me. I hate me. And soon, Tyler will hate me too.

Unless I find a way to explain it as something that got out of hand, and was hard to reel in because I liked him so much. Surely, he could understand that. Especially the part about me liking him so much.

I look at my reflection in the mirror as I dress.

"He will, won't he?"

My reflection frowns back at me. "Would you?"

I think about that. How would I feel if I found out Tyler was covering up some big secret from me? Something on par with me hiding my identity.

These thoughts are stirring up a storm in my mind as I finish dressing. I slip on my cutest warm sweater, tie a pretty head scarf in my hair, and switch my pj bottoms for yoga pants and boots.

In the mirror, I look ready to face the chilly Tuscany day. The wind blowing down from the hills surrounding Florence can be a little brutal at times.

But then I'm from Maine. This is a piece of cake compared to our weekly snowstorms and blizzards. Our snarly snowplows sound like monsters trampling the roads late at night.

Florence is much sweeter, with its church bells clanging and opera music floating from high windows, as I walk through the narrow cobblestone streets, the sharp scent of roasting chestnuts and espressos mixing in the air outside cafes.

As soon as I walk into the classroom, I'm greeted with shouts of "Happy Thanksgiving," from my mates.

I manage a smile as they all gather around me.

Apparently, I'm the only one who failed the exam. My stats have gone from the top of the class to the very bottom. It's humiliating. Chef Marco has posted the class rank for us all to see. In blue letters on the screen: *"Ava Walker number 12, Grade Zero."*

I bow my head and slide into my seat next to Gisela.

She reaches over and places a warm arm around my shoulders.

"It's the curse of the Roman gods," she sighs. "Italy is...about amore. You fell in love. No one can blame you for failing a test if your love is in trouble."

I swallow a lump in my throat. "It didn't have to be in trouble, though, that's the problem. But thank you...I'm glad you're here. You remind me of my sisters."

Gisela gives me a dazzling smile. "Me too," she says. "I'm glad I'm here with you. We can be...spirit sisters instead."

I grin. "Spirit sisters." We shake hands and touch pinkies. It's teenage high school stuff but it feels nice and I wonder for a minute if I'm recreating my high school days because I didn't live mine. In fact, I've blacked out most of those four years.

Chef Marco clears his throat as he walks over to our table.

"Ava, I'd like you to work with Gisela today." He wags his eyebrows down in a deep V like a villain. "Pay attention to how she prepares the base, take notes, focus."

"Um...I'm sorry...about my gelato...it was...a mistake," I falter. My words are stuck so far down my throat that I feel like I'm dragging them up one by one with a pole.

His head gives a tiny shake, like stop talking.

I press my lips shut.

"Gelato is more than a dessert. It's art. It's our history. It's Italian as much as our grapes and olives. Our Michelangelo and Dante. It's our soul. *Never* is it a mistake. Okay? You did not make a mistake. You just did not *make* gelato. Your life is your choice. Your choice yesterday was not to make gelato. Sometimes we believe we are failures because we choose not to do something we should do. Yesterday for you it was gelato. Today is a new day. Choose wisely. Choose to do something you *should* do."

He raps his knuckles on the tabletop and swaggers off toward Matilda's table where we can hear him congratulating her for being number one in our class.

I'm happy for Matilda. She works hard and came from so far away to start a brand new career at age 60. She deserves it.

But Chef Marco's words echo in my head. "Choose to do something you should do." If I were looking for signs, that advice is as clear as it comes.

"Gisela!"

"Yes?"

"I'm going to tell Tyler today. I've made up my mind. I'll tell him everything. I mean it." Just saying I'm going to do it and knowing I will today feels freeing.

Gisela smiles. "You got this. Now let's make some fantastic gelato. Here, take a bite of my chocolate." She unwraps a piece of her precious cargo and we munch on it together, our heads close as we measure the base ratio carefully.

One of Mom's favorite sayings pops into my head. *When you do the right thing, good things happen.*

I've no more doubts. I'm telling Tyler tonight.

Chapter Forty

Tyler and I have plans to celebrate Thanksgiving at a cute restaurant near my apartment, right on the Arno Riverbanks.

Now Ajax or Jax, as Tyler calls him—although if my name was *Ajax* after the famous Greek warrior, I'd want everyone to know it—is joining us so it'll be three instead of two. I hope I can get Tyler alone to talk to him.

I invited Gisela and Patrick, but they have plans to stay up all night and pick out stuff to buy online for Black Friday, which has become an event in Italy too.

I teased them about their shared love of consumerism and they both said thank you so they're perfect for each other.

I hurry home running multiple scenarios in my head of how to get Tyler away from Ajax to have a one-on-one that could end in tears (mine) or relief (mine, again), or total destruction (mine, for sure).

Before I reach my street, I get a text message from Bridget.
Where are you?

She probably wants us to do a Facetime call while they're cooking. I text back, *I'm almost home I'll call you.*

Then a text comes in from Tyler.

Our restaurant is closed! (sad emoji face). Jax and I will come by your place in a few minutes if that's ok. We can regroup and make other plans.

I give it a thumbs up and walk faster. I hope I can squeeze in a quick call before we head to a restaurant. My stomach growls noisily. I was saving my appetite for the big bash we'd planned but now it may be just gyros and fries.

As I reach the top of my little road, there's still enough light in the darkening sky to see a figure perched on the concrete steps in front of my door.

The person is huddled in a furry cloak and her hair is braided in loops around her head. A hand flies to my mouth.

"Bridget!" I yell it so loudly windows pop open. "Is that you?"

I run up the last few yards and throw my arms around my sister before she can finish unfolding herself and stand up properly. I want to pinch her over and over to make sure she's real.

"What are you doing here?" I lean back and stare at her.

"*Girl,* we weren't leaving you alone for the holidays! We drew straws, and I won." She grins broadly at me, her cheeks puffing up, making her eyes squinch into slits.

"I can't believe you're here. I can't believe it."

"Believe it. Emerald almost had a breakdown trying to keep it a secret. We wanted to surprise you."

I'm digging out my keys and my hand freezes. I look up at Bridget, the muscles in my face working hard to maintain some semblance of normalcy.

"What's wrong?"

I shake my head. "Let's get inside." I insert the key and get ready to turn the lock when a voice calls out from behind us. "Bridget?"

"Yes?" My sister spins around.

I turn slowly, feeling time slow down into microseconds. *Dear*

God, this can't be happening. No way. My breath sticks in my lungs. I can't breathe properly. My hands shake. My heart pumps too fast. I feel lightheaded as if I might collapse right here on my front steps.

Tyler Donovan is standing there. Staring at me, then at the real Bridget, then at me again.

"Bridget?" Tyler speaks again, but this time his voice is unsure. He takes a step toward me. I shrink back. "What's going on here?"

A tall man stands next to Tyler. Big and broad and burly. Looking like he could pick up the road and bend it in half. A Greek god who's come down to Earth to play with us humans.

The Greek god puts a hand on Tyler's shoulder. "Dude, you ok?"

At the same time, Bridget turns to me, "Ava, what's going on?"

Tyler and I stare into each other's eyes. I can't speak. Everything I'd plan to say is meaningless now.

All I can do is stand there and witness the enormity of my lie dawn in his eyes.

He blinks.

A pain I've never known stabs me in my gut. I grab my stomach it feels so visceral and real.

I've felt sadness yes, grief, yes. But not this.

If I ever doubted my love for Tyler Donovan, all doubt is eviscerated. I am truly, madly in love with him. I know this because right now I feel as if the world has tipped over on its side and can't be righted again.

This is the pain of knowing you've hurt someone you love deeply. This is the pain on the other end of betrayal.

This is the pain of cowardice.

Plain and simple. I, Ava Walker, was a coward and now I must watch the man I love suffer.

Chapter Forty-One

"You're *not* Bridget?" It's Ajax asking. The only one of us brave enough to speak.

"I'm Bridget," my sister says biting her lip, not sure if she should fess up or not. Her glances over to me are filled with confusion.

When no one else speaks, Bridget continues to clear up the matter. "This is Ava, my older sister. Who are you?"

"I'm Ajax. From Greece. I'm his best friend." He tips a thumb as large as a tree branch in Tyler's direction. "But call me Jax."

"Oh," Bridget says. Then slowly, "It's nice to meet you. Can I call you Ajax? I've never met anyone with that name before." I can tell she's trying to buy me time to recover my senses.

"If you don't mind," she adds.

He shakes her head. "Not at all."

I stand there numbly. Watching the scene unfold as if I'm a bystander. Instead of the catalyst.

"Should we give them a minute, Ajax?" Bridget speaks slowly

GELATO FOREVER

again as if this entire scene is in slow motion. "Let's go grab a coffee?"

The large hairy bear head nods vigorously. "Yes, let's go." He reaches out to help her down the steps. They hustle off leaving me, Tyler, and Bridget's carry-on suitcase on the steps.

I watch them heading down the road and I want to tell them the Gelato Bar's still open and serves great cappuccinos, but I don't dare say a word.

Tyler looks down at his shoes. I look up at the sky. A breeze swooshes up the road, blowing aside debris in the gutters.

"I can explain." My voice sounds low and pitiful.

He shakes his head. "What's to explain, *Ava?*" He stresses my name as if it's a virus to be aware of.

I wring my hands. "I'm sorry." A deep shame fills me. It reminds me of the time my mom caught me in Pizza Hut. "I'm really sorry, Tyler."

"You already said that." He swipes a hand over his face. "So, let me get this straight. *You*...are Ava Walker? *You*....are the girl from my class that I've been talking about? And *you*...pretended it wasn't you? Why would you do that? Why did you lie to me?"

I'm so shaken I can't find any words to explain it to him.

The puzzled expression on his face is replaced with disgust.

"You made a fool out of me this whole time we've been together. Since the plane ride. I can't believe it! You must have been laughing at me. Is this some kind of high school revenge you and Bridget played on me? Trick Tyler into falling in love and throw it in his face? Did I do something terrible to you or her back in high school for you to do...*this*?" His voice rises until he's shouting at me. Then drops at the end, sad and defeated.

He takes a deep breath and keeps going. "I told you this is the one thing I cannot accept. That is the deal breaker. Lies, deception, dishonesty." He sweeps his arms outward. "You knew that!"

"I wanted to tell you." I cry out, finally finding my voice. "Can you come inside, please? I'll tell you everything."

His gold eyes look like death stars under the streetlamps. "Everything? There are more lies?"

I shake my head no. "Not *more* lies. Kind of tentacles of the same one."

"Like?"

I shrink into my jacket. His voice is colder than the wind.

"I pretended to be Bridget because I thought it would be easier than explaining I was Ava, the girl you said ignored you in school." I huff out a breath.

He looks at me like I'm nuts.

"I know it was a dumb move, but you kept calling me Bridget."

"Oh, so it's *my* fault?"

"No, not at all. I don't mean that. Just that you seemed so happy being with Bridget. I didn't know how to burst the bubble of our romance."

"You let me believe I was falling for your sister instead. That's your idea of romance? What else did you lie to me about? You might as well tell me everything, so I know what's what, and stop thinking I've been living in a dream."

"Tyler, it was real. Everything was real. I promise. Everything I said was real. I was planning to tell you the truth tonight. I swear."

"What. Else. Did. You. Lie. About?"

Tyler's voice shakes with contained anger.

I gulp. "I'm volunteering at the English Cemetery twice a week. You were right, Bridget wouldn't do that, so I didn't tell you about it. Also," my voice breaks and a sob escapes my throat, "I flunked my mid-term exam. I may not get my gelato certificate."

His eyes open wide. A bit of the old Tyler peeps through full of concern. Then it disappears.

His lips set in a grim line. I hear myself confessing that I'm a liar and a failure. *Great combination, Ava. Who'll want to be with you now?*

"Is that it?"

I nod, my heart miserable at the look on his face. It's like a shield has slipped down and covered up all the sweetness and kindness of Tyler Donovan and left a furious replica in its place.

"I'm sorry...so sorry...I hope...you...can forgive...me. It was a dumb thing to do. I..."

His hazel eyes get even more steely. "I better go find Ajax and head back home. Tonight is done. And so are we. I don't want to see you again...Bridget...Ava... whoever you are. The joke's on me. You win."

He turns on his heels and marches down the street.

All the air goes out of me and I collapse on the cold hard steps. A piece of me feels as if it's been torn away for good as I watch Tyler Donovan disappear into the tunnel at the end of the road.

Chapter Forty-Two

Maybe people just leave you no matter how much you love them. No matter how much you try. Maybe that's how the world works. Dad lost Mom and he was an amazing husband.

My sobs come harder. From somewhere deep down. A place I've never allowed myself to venture.

Tears for me and Tyler. Tears for Dad. Tears for the girl I was and could have been in high school, the girl Tyler noticed and liked and believed in. Before Mom died.

That girl never got to grow up. Instead, she's so afraid a guy wouldn't like her for herself that she pretends to be her sister.

I don't deserve a guy like Tyler. He knows who he is, and what he wants and wasn't afraid to speak up about his fears and his boundaries.

And I smashed all those boundaries. I stepped on his fears. Made promises to him that I wouldn't keep.

My body shakes with the incredible gut-punch feeling of knowing I hurt him.

My nose stuffs up with snot and I can't breathe. I feel as if I'm drowning in the tears leaking from my eyes.

"I'm sorry Mom," I whisper. "I wanted to make you proud. I tried to be strong. For Dad and my sisters... to make sure I didn't bring shame to our family. Because that is what you taught me. Now, look at this mess I created."

I sniff loudly trying to suck up some air to breathe through my stuffed-up nostrils.

Nothing feels right. My heart pinches inside my chest. My toes are frozen cold. My fingers curl into tight fists clenched by my sides. They want to pound the cement steps.

How long can I sit here hoping Tyler will change his mind and come running up the hill, to say he forgives me and let's start over and this time it'll be real and good and honest and forever?

How long can I wish on the dark starless sky for a miracle to reverse time and give me a new start?

I'm not new to the feeling of loss. The forever kind of loss.

Only this time, I'm not sure I can bear it.

Chapter Forty-Three

An Italian voice next to me is soft and soothing. "Tutto bene cara?"

I almost don't hear her over the rasping sound of my breath.

I look up, knowing I must be a terrible fright with black mascara stains on my cheeks and my afro curls damp with tears.

Windows slide open letting out precious heat. Heads pop out. All asking the same thing.

"You okay, dear?" Musical Italian voices remind me I'm not alone in this neighborhood.

Signor Moretti slips out of his front door and runs across the cobbled street to hand me a wilted flower. He pats my head awkwardly. "Va bene."

I give him a teary smile. I dash a hand across my eyes to wipe away the wet trails of tears.

Then Signora Rossi comes out and sits on the steps next to me. She slides a warm pastry into my hands.

My stomach growls. I'd forgotten I was hungry. I take a bite of the sweet chocolate cream pastry and feel my shoulders drop.

I sigh my thanks to her. "*Deliziosa.*"

She pats me as if I'm a small child.

Another neighbor appears, dragging a long shawl behind her. She's *tsking*, but she wraps the shawl around my shoulders.

"*L'amore tornerà.*" She speaks slowly. I understand she's telling me love will come back. I squeeze her hand.

More neighbors appear. Some with flowers, some with food. Nick leans out his window from upstairs, telling me he heard it all and that although he adores me, I was definitely in the wrong and I should make it up to that hot American man. "And by the way, happy Thanksgiving, sweetie."

"You too," I tell him before he slides down his window.

I shouldn't be surprised that half the block is here with me. They've been making me feel like a part of the neighborhood family since I arrived.

I sit up and take in all the worried eyes and concerned faces. I pat down my curls and properly wipe my eyes with an old-fashioned handkerchief, embroidered with initials that someone hands me.

"Grazie, grazie," I tell them one by one. "Thank you for being here with me."

Sometimes the reasons for giving thanks are not the reasons you expect. Opportunities for gratitude can be right in front of your face if you open your eyes and heart.

Someone brings out a bottle of Madeira, the sweet wine from Portugal. Glasses are poured and shouts of "Salud" sound into the air.

I am halfway through a glass and listening to my neighbors tell me their own stories of lost love when Bridget walks up.

"Are you serious?" she asks. "A block party? Ava, you really know how to live."

I introduce my sister to everyone, and they all shake hands or hug her. Bridget sits on the step by my feet as we toast "Salud" with my Italian family. It's too cold to stay outside for long so we finish our drinks and say goodbye to everyone.

Once inside, Bridget throws herself across my bed and sighs. "Damn, I'm exhausted. But I need to hear what drama is going on here. Apparently, my arrival was badly timed."

I shake my head. "Never. It had to happen."

"Yes, you have a lot of explaining to do."

"Tomorrow," I whisper, sinking down on the bed beside her, thankful there's no school tomorrow, no obligations, nothing to do except figure out this mess and welcome my sister to Florence.

Bridget nudges my arm with her shoulder. "That guy Ajax."

"Yes?"

She waggles her eyebrows about in a crazy way. "He is HOT!"

I groan. "No! He's Tyler's best friend."

She shrugs. "Who cares? He's dynamite! And he's smart! If you like hearing about olives and harvests and the purity of olive oil and that kind of stuff."

I laugh. It sounds hollow and strained and it hurts my insides. I rest my head on Bridget's shoulder. "I'm glad you're here."

Chapter Forty-Four

As soon as I awake, the horrible sinking feeling of my and Tyler's break up hits me fresh and I don't have the will to get up.

If Bridget wasn't here yelling at me to move my butt, I'd spend all day in bed.

"How do you expect to mend fences if you don't gather the nails?" She asks hands on her hips, quoting our mother.

A laugh barks out of me unexpectedly.

"Gotcha." She plops down on the bed next to me and snuggles close like we used to do when we were five and six and shared a room, but she always ended up in my bed because she was scared of the large bullfrogs that appeared on warm Maine summer evenings. She feared they would hop into our open windows, and we'd have to kiss them like in the fairy tale.

"You gotta fix this, sis, how else can I get with Ajax before he leaves town?"

"Wait," I say, pushing her away. "You want me to make up with Tyler just so you can hook up with his friend?"

She shrugs her slim shoulders as she jumps up pulling covers with her. "At least *I'm* honest."

She gives me a side eye that makes me hang my head. "I know. I'm a terrible person. Tyler will never forgive me. I don't want to think about it."

Bridget clicks her teeth. "Yes, he will. If he really likes you he will realize it was a...." She looks at me. "It was a *what* the f? I still don't understand it."

I hustle across the cold floorboards to the bathroom giving her a mini version of what unfolded between me and Tyler starting with the plane ride.

"That was dumb," Bridget says when I wrap it up with me being afraid to tell him the truth.

"I know," I wail. "It was a dumb never-ending lie. At the end of the day, we were not meant to be okay, can we drop it? Please!"

Bridget gives a loud "hmmm" sound. I can tell my little sister's brain is whirling with ideas of how to spin this nasty lie into a chocolate chip gelato.

That's her talent. Her specialty. Advertising. Marketing. Branding. Making something sell.

But there's nothing she can do to turn chicken shit into chicken salad.

It turns out Bridget's idea of mending fences is to first stop off at the Galleria della Academia museum to see Michelangelo's masterpiece the David, for which she bought tickets online a week ago.

She waves her phone around in front of my face. "We have to go!"

I mope around making tea. Outside the sky is gray and rain is forecast for the entire afternoon. I can't think of a worse idea than standing in line with tourists. Even to see one of the world's greatest pieces of art ever created.

"I don't feel like going out," I say honestly. "Can't we order pizza and watch movies?"

Don't be selfish, Ava, I tell myself. Get ready and show your sister a good time. She's come from far away.

"Nooooo way! We can't miss the *David*," Bridget says, jumping around the studio. She's already put on a shimmery sweater over leggings and her makeup is on point.

"Fine," I grumble.

"Right. And while we do that you can explain this mess to me in detail, leaving nothing out, because what you said just now makes no sense."

I grab a pair of old sweats and a tired-looking jersey and head to the bathroom. Bridget cuts me off before I get there. "You aren't wearing that."

I look around at the pile of clothes she's dumped out on the loveseat. My own clothes are thrown in the closet. I don't have the energy to pick out an outfit.

"What do you want me to wear? It's cold outside and rainy and wet and I'm not in the mood to be fashionable."

In two seconds Bridget has plucked an entire outfit from my closet. Black jeans, a sexy pink fuzzy cropped sweater, and tall boots plus a silky Italian scarf to tie around my neck or hair or maybe my waist. Who cares?

When I emerge from the bathroom, showered, dressed, and with a dab of lipstick and eyeshadow on my face, I feel a little better.

Bridget grabs my hands and spins me around. "Wow! No wonder he thought you were me!"

I crack a smile. "Funny."

"No, for real. You're a fox, Ava Walker. A stone-cold fox and you better own it."

"Thanks." I give her a real smile as we head out the door. "I'm glad you're here. Truly. Sorry for being a 'drip,' as Mom used to say."

Bridget laughed. "I remember that. She'd say, 'Don't be a drip, you'll end up a puddle.'"

We laugh at the memory as I lock the door and we head down the cobbled street. Fat raindrops splash on our heads. We wrestle with our umbrellas until they're both raised high, colorful as flags against the dreary sky.

I bet we're both thinking the same thing. If Mom were here, she'd fix everything right up. She always knew what to say or do to make everything better.

And if that failed, she'd drag out the ice cream maker.

"Hey Bridge, let's stop for a gelato first, okay?" I tug on my sister's hand.

She winks at me. "Absolutely. Because no matter what..." She stops and swings my hand in the air. We glance at each other from under our umbrellas and say simultaneously, "We'll always have gelato."

She grins at me. "Another of Mom's sayings."

"Yup."

To most people, gelato is just a lovely sweet dessert. A special treat.

To me, it was a lifeline. And apparently, it still is.

Chapter Forty-Five

"No, I'm not texting Tyler to ask him what he and Ajax are doing tonight," I say firmly. Bridget doesn't hear me.

She's stroking the garment bag slung over the back of the chair next to her.

We're finally seated in a restaurant, cozy and warm inside after trudging through the rain puddles on a day full of museum viewing and boutique shopping.

Not that I had a bad time. But it was difficult to concentrate on Bridget's queries about which dress looked better when my mind was stuck on the image of Tyler's stricken face last night when he saw Bridget standing next to me.

"I can wear my new dress," Bridget sighs. "If you text them."

She holds up her phone and leans toward me. "Come on, sis, smile or the family will be asking a lot of questions about why you look like you lost your best friend."

She clicks our photo and sends it to the family group chat.

"I kind of did," I say, glancing through the menu, although I already know I'm ordering the Margherita pizza as my first plate and pesto pasta as my second with a carafe of pinot grigio to wash it all down. Apparently, I'm not one of those people who lose their appetite with heartbreak.

A server appears and deposits baskets of bread, a bowl of olives, and a large bottle of sparkling water. Bridget stares at the goodies, eyes wide before diving in.

"Tyler Donovan did become my best friend, not counting you guys, of course." I break off a chunk of bread and lean forward to dip it in the plate of olive oil that Bridget is hogging on her side of the table.

"Of course," Bridget says airily. "Did you make any other friends though? What about that girl from Ecuador you told us about?"

I nod. "Yes, we're all friends, the entire class. It's like being on a reality show where you bond over a common goal."

"A gelato reality show," Bridget muses. "I can see that! A sweet romance show." She laughs out loud.

"That could be a thing," I say. "Except for how long it takes to freeze the stuff."

"More time for smooching with contestants while you wait."

"Right. I see you have a one-track mind."

"Love comes first," Bridget says seriously. She has always been open about her many boyfriends and love connections. She had them lining up to take her out.

But I've never seen her be serious about anyone. It was always easy come, easy go, for Bridget—she being the one to leave the poor dudes scratching their heads and wondering what went wrong.

"Another reason I don't want you going out with Ajax," I tell her. "You know you'll break his heart and then Tyler will never ever speak to me again." I try to forget the part where he says he never wants to speak to me now.

"Ah, phooey! Ajax has *playa* stamped all over him. He'll probably break *my* heart." She gives me a wicked grin. "But I'm willing to risk it. Did you see that guy's body? Built like a mack truck. A Greek god. A..."

"Oh, I saw it. Still, no!"

She sits back and sulks while dipping pieces of focaccia into the delicious olive oil.

"Do you know Ajax has an olive oil farm?" she asks.

"It's an olive grove. But yes, Tyler told me." I stop talking. A pang goes through me saying his name out loud.

Bridget doesn't notice. She's busy waving her fingers in the air. "Imagine all those real homegrown olives making real homegrown olive oil." The reverence in her tone makes me look up and push thoughts of Tyler Donovan out of my head.

"You never got this excited about olive oil before." I frown.

She looks off into the distance. "He showed me pictures of him and his family and friends harvesting the olives. Did you know if you shake the olive trees hard, like hold the tree and shake the heck out of it, the olives tumble into nets on the ground?"

I actually did *not* know that. I continue staring at her. Bridget didn't do farms or dirt or trees or anything outdoorsy. She was 100% a theater nerd who sang, danced, and acted her way through life. And put it all on social media.

"He explained it to me," she says defensively as if reading my mind.

"You were only gone for ten minutes."

She shrugs. "He's compelling, what can I say? He had me at 'olives.'" She does the air quotes and I roll my eyes at her.

"Sometimes I don't know if you're serious or joking. This is one of those times. But honestly, he's only here for a week, and you're only here for...." I stop and look at her, "For how long?"

She smiles sweetly, "As long as you need me."

I almost spit out the water I'm sipping. "We can't leave Daisy and Emerald by themselves!"

"Oh hush, you're such a mother hen. Fine, I'm here for one week, too. When Ajax leaves, I'll leave."

I lean back and raise an eyebrow at her. "You'd better be going back to Maine."

"Duh!"

Our meal arrives and we forget about the guys and share pizzas the size of wagon wheels, fresh-cut pasta, and wine and talk nonstop about all I've missed back home.

I'm as hungry for information and gossip and theories about Dad and his new girlfriend as I am for the food.

By the time we've finished eating and drinking and chatting the rain has stopped and a purple dusk has settled in around the small city that feels like home to me.

As we stroll around the piazzas, stopping to admire Florence's abundance of churches, a question pops into my head that has long bothered me about my sister.

"Why do you treat your dates as if they're disposable?" I ask bluntly.

She comes to a halt right in front of the oversized statute of Neptune, her iPhone held high to snap his photo.

"What do you mean?" Her voice sounds hurt like I've hit a nerve.

"You act as if you don't give a damn about them."

She frowns. "I do not. I don't think Tyler Donovan is disposable. I think you guys need to work things out. You were happy when you were seeing him. You should have seen your face on the screen. It was all lit up. Every single time."

I look away. "Yeah, well that's done."

"Doesn't have to be." Bridget snaps a few pics of Hercules and continues walking.

"By the way, this is amazing." She spins around in a circle in the middle of the Piazza della Signoria. "I can see why you love Florence."

"I walk by here every day."

"Do you ever get tired of looking at them?" She points at the art.

I shake my head. "Never! They've become like friends, Perseus

GELATO FOREVER

with his Medusa head, Hercules in mid-struggle with the centaur, even the fake David statue...I love them all. I feel so alive here. I know that sounds cliche, but it's true."

"Glad you found a place to be *yourself*." She says snidely. I ignore her. She can be a pain even though I love her.

We end up walking along the Arno River to the farthest bridge, then cross over and walk back up the other side trying to walk off the exorbitant number of calories we've ingested.

As we get closer to my apartment, Bridget blurts, "Are you texting Tyler or not? If not for yourself, do it for your beloved sister." She gives me huge puppy dog eyes and tosses her braids over her shoulder.

"I like your hair," I say changing the subject. While I keep mine natural, Bridget experiments with all kinds of looks and styles.

I never know what to expect when she heads off to the beauty salon. She could return looking like anyone from Princess Leia to Beyoncé.

"Don't change the subject," Bridget huffs.

When I don't answer, she asks, "You up for another gelato before we go home?"

"Always!"

Stopping off at the Gelato Bar on my corner turns into a sit-down affair. We order the works—whipped cream and thin wafers on top of our gelato flavors, three each.

"I hope you can get into that dress tonight," I remark as we slide spoonfuls of the rich, smooth, and airy desserts into our mouths.

She raises her eyebrows. "Why? Are we going somewhere fun?"

I smile. "I did text someone. But it wasn't Tyler."

As we finish our delicious treats I tell Bridget about my class's favorite karaoke hang-out spot.

"We're all going there tonight. You can meet them and have a night out. Italian style. Lots of locals and Americans, as well."

"You think Tyler and Ajax will be there?" she asks innocently.

I grimace. "I hope not."

When she doesn't say a word, I remind her, "He said he doesn't want anything to do with me again. I'm going to respect that. Plus, I need to concentrate on my gelato class. And the Gelato Festival in two weeks. December 8th is a big day for us. I still don't know what I'll be making and it's arriving sooner than I expected."

"Okay, okay, I won't say another word." Bridget slides two fingers across her lips to show she's zipping her mouth shut.

Then she immediately opens it again. "But Ava, you deserve to be happy. You've carried our family through the worst of times and now you need to live your life to the fullest. We all agreed on that. Corrine, Daisy, Emerald, and me."

"I *am* living my life. Exactly how I want to live it."

Bridget shakes her head as I pay the bill. "Are you though?"

Chapter Forty-Six

Of course, I'm not. If I had a choice, I'd be with Tyler. We'd be exploring the wintry Tuscany countryside. Sipping hot cider and espressos and discussing food in all its permutations.

I need to forget about Tyler Donovan, as difficult as that is, and concentrate on showing Bridget a great time.

After a long hot bath with lavender oils, I sit patiently while she does my makeup because she begged me to do it.

Afterward, I zip myself into a flowy jumpsuit and wrap the gorgeous red coat around me. I have to admit I look pretty good.

Or as Bridget puts it, "One sexy mama." She pats my curls into place and sighs. "Tyler won't be able to resist you tonight. *If he's there.*"

The way she says it makes me look at her twice. "Is there something you know that I don't know?"

She gives me a wide-eyed look. "No."

"Liar."

"Same!" She sticks out a tongue at me.

"You're shameless."

She smiles. "I am!"

The club is pumping. Probably because it's Black Friday, the day after Thanksgiving, the day the holiday season officially begins in the U.S. And maybe in Italy too.

When we get inside the karaoke room, I glance around from one table to another looking for Gisela, Patrick, Matilda, and the others.

"This place is packed!" Bridget remarks.

"Hmmm."

I tiptoe and press one hand on Bridget's shoulder for balance as my eyes roam across the room. A sea of colorful lights, swirling and flashing and strobing in time with the music, makes it difficult to make out anyone. My heart beats in an erratic unsettling pattern.

Bridget fans herself. "Damn, this place is as hot as a July 4th BBQ."

She's right. Sweat beads on my forehead from the moist, hot air. The smell of spilled wine and beer permeates the room. It's far louder, and more crowded than ever.

"I don't see them," I say, dropping back onto the balls of my feet. "Let's walk around." I pull out my phone to text Gisela as we walk when we're blocked by a large figure in front of us.

"Ajax!" my sister squeals.

I glance up anxiously. My heart beats triple time as I swallow hard. Tyler is not with him, is he? I whip around to see if he's behind me.

"Where's your boy?" Bridget shouts at Ajax, loud enough for half the room to hear.

My leg shakes uncontrollably. If I see Tyler I won't know what to do. Should I ignore him, or try to be friendly? Or maybe act as if nothing happened. Although that would be dumb.

I should have prepared myself better for this moment.

Suddenly, the lights and noise, and smells overtake me and I feel my heart racing too fast.

I gasp for air and come up empty. My hands begin to shake. I bury them between my thighs. I try to take gulps of air. More gulps. My heart tightens. What the hell is happening to me?

The room blurs and spins. "I have to get out of here," I gasp, hoping Bridget hears me.

She doesn't. She's giving Ajax the third degree, flinging her arms about, her mouth forming words I cannot hear because of the loud buzzing in my head.

I'm going to collapse right here. I look toward the arched opening that leads to the hallway and the bar and the big red front door. No way I'm going to make it there.

"Are you okay?" A soft voice sounds in my ear.

I shake my head violently back and forth. I can't speak. I just want to get out of here. I feel as if I'm falling into a giant black hole.

A hand circles my shoulders, presses me close, and guides me away. The hand feels familiar and strange at the same time. I glance up under my eyelashes thinking it's him, Tyler.

"It's me, Patrick, let's go outside." I let him lead me to the arched entry to the other room, through the dark hallway, past the crowded bar, and finally outside through the blessed red door.

I lean forward, hands pressing on my thighs, and try to inhale the cold air into my lungs. It ends up making me cough. Patrick hauls me back up and lets me lean against him.

When I finally feel cold air filling my lungs, I slow down my breathing as best as I can.

I sag against Patrick, and he hugs me. "It's okay," he says., "I think you were having a panic attack. I get those sometimes."

"You do?" I ask, thinking I know nothing about my classmates. Not enough anyway.

"Yes, I go to a therapist about it. It's much better, but still...." He shakes his head, "Very scary."

I nod. "Tell me about it."

He was still holding me when the red door bursts open.

"What happened?" Bridget comes pelting over. "Are you okay?"

Ajax is on her heels, and right behind them is Tyler Donovan in the flesh. The cause of my anxiety.

I glance up under the circle of Patrick's protective hold on me.

Tyler's eyes travel the length of my body cradled by Patrick's arm. I push against Patrick hard but he doesn't budge. He's actually holding me up, so I don't collapse but Tyler doesn't realize that.

A bright red anger flashes in his eyes. *Does he think I'm holding onto another man just one day after he broke up with me?*

The answer is clear in his face. His gold eyes glitter with anger. His shoulders stiffen and pull back as if straining to get away from me.

He reaches for the door, hesitates, and looks at me over his shoulder. "I should have guessed your name wasn't the only thing you were lying about."

I gasp. "Wait! This is Patrick, my friend."

But the red door slams shut behind Tyler.

My heart which was beating so fast a few minutes ago plummets like a roller coaster down the deep end. But this time it's not coming back up.

Ajax and Bridget are staring at me. Like I've done something horribly wrong.

"You want me to go talk to him, Ava? Tell him you were feeling ill?" Patrick asks kindly.

I have two immediate thoughts. One, Patrick is a good guy and I'm glad he and Gisela are talking about a future. The second is that there's no coming back from this. Tyler won't believe me. But maybe he'll listen to Ajax. All I have to do is explain it to his best friend and hope Ajax will speak on my behalf.

I shake my head at Patrick. "It won't help. But thanks."

"What's going on?" Bridget asks, confusedly. "Who's this?"

Ajax crosses his arms on his broad chest. "That's what I'd like to know. You're playing games with my friend?"

"Her?" Bridget squeaks.

"Me?" I stutter.

"No, sir." Patrick holds up his hands like he's in a Western and Ajax is the large cowboy seeking answers.

"I think you've got some explaining to do," Bridget says, raising an eyebrow at me and looking between me and Patrick.

I open my mouth to speak, but at that moment, the door opens and this time it's Gisela. She rushes past the giant Greek guy and my indignant sister.

"Oh my God, Ava, Patrick, are you guys, okay? Matilda said she saw you almost fainting. Patrick rushed over to help but I could barely make it through the crowds."

Patrick checks to make sure I can stand on my own, then turns towards his girlfriend. He wraps both his arms around her and looks upward at Ajax. "This one is with me."

Bridget throws up her hands. "What's going on here?"

Ajax's face is red. "Worse than a soap opera."

"I had a panic attack. Patrick was helping me. We're friends, classmates." No one hears me because Bridget is arguing with Ajax about how it's all his fault. "You promised you'd fix things!" she wails. "It looks like you've made it worse."

He shakes his big head, dark curls tumbling in every direction. "Maybe it's your sister who did that all by herself."

I can't let him yell at Bridget anymore. I raise my voice. "I keep trying to tell you guys...I was having a panic attack. Patrick is my classmate. He was only helping me. Nothing is going on with him or anyone else."

"Why doesn't Tyler know who Patrick is, if he's just a friend?" Ajax asks. "That sounds fishy."

My shoulders slump. "I know. It's all my fault. I was so worried Tyler would hear my classmates calling me Ava and not

Bridget that I kept them apart. Tyler never got to meet Patrick or Gisela or any of my classmates. I kept them separate to maintain the big lie."

Ajax shifts and moves toward the red door. "I should never have brought my boy here for your sister to hurt him again."

Bridget's jaw drops open. "But...she just explained!"

Ajax stares her down and speaks firmly. "I'm not sure what shenanigans you and your sister have stirred up, but we want no part in it. We won't stand for any nonsense!" His gaze doesn't waver from her, as if I'm not standing there at all.

As for me, my heart aches as if it's truly breaking in two. The sharp stabbing pain of this reality I created is dragging down Bridget along with me.

I had envisioned tonight so differently—a chance to show my sister the fun nightlife of Florence while I buried my pain about Tyler for the evening.

I never imagined I'd make everything worse, not only for me but also for Bridget who's obviously catching feelings for the Greek giant.

Standing in the shadows of the sidewalk, people streaming by laughing and swaying, the smell of beer clinging to them, I just want to get out of here.

"Come on...Bridget, let's go." I speak up loud enough to get her attention.

Without uttering a single sound, she strides up to me, and the disappointment that radiates from her eyes is palpable. My heart sinks further into my chest.

She links her arm with mine and we step off the sidewalk to walk in the street. When we cross over the Ponte Vecchio bridge and turn to go up the road toward my apartment, the lights of the Gelato Bar wink at us.

Neither one of us looks in its direction. We bypass it straight.

Not even gelato can help tonight.

Chapter Forty-Seven

I always thought I could handle anything life threw at me.
 I mean I handled...am still handling...losing my mother as a young teen. When I needed her the most.
Nietzsche said, "What doesn't kill you makes you stronger." Or something like that. Well, I thought I was the epitome of that saying.

I am strong. I am invincible.

Until tonight.

The cover I've kept locked down on all my emotions has been blown off. Handling these feelings is the last thing I can do right now.

"What's wrong with you, sis?" Bridget sighs, taking off her coat and hanging it up in my closet. "How could you treat Tyler like that?"

She eyes me as I slump against the headboard fully clothed.

I slide down on top of the embroidered comforter. A loud pounding fills my ears like I'm underwater and pressure is building.

Am I having another panic attack? Dread fills me up.

"You should take off your new coat, sis. No need to ruin your beautiful clothes."

"You mean on top of everything else I've ruined?" I say miserably.

She sighs. "I didn't say that. But okay, yeah."

She pads over to the kitchenette and fills the electric kettle with water. She pulls down two mugs from the cupboard and plucks two tea bags from the box on the counter.

While she's waiting for the kettle to boil, she comes over and takes my coat from me, and hangs it up.

"You don't have to do all this," I say, gesturing with one hand at the tea being poured into mugs, the biscuits she's putting out on a plate, and the chair she's pulling over next to me to put everything on. "I'm not sick."

Bridget ignores me.

"Fine." I'm too exhausted to argue with her. I'm more tired than I've ever felt in my life, even more than being jet lagged, more than when I spent nights holding Emerald and Daisy while they cried themselves to sleep, more than when I sat up in Mom's hospital room while Dad went home to take care of the younger kids.

As Matilda would say, "I'm gutted."

Bridget plops down on the floor in her pj's, legs crisscrossed in front of her and her head leaning back against the bed.

She sips her tea and munches on a biscuit.

After a while, I pick up my mug and drink some of the tea. It's delicious and exactly how I like it. A full teaspoon of honey and a squeeze of lime.

"Thanks, Bridge," I say gently, patting her braids with my free hand.

She nods silently. We sit like that for a few minutes, the only sound in the room is the hot steam radiating through the pipes on this cold night.

GELATO FOREVER

Bridget turns around and puts her mug on the floor. She presses her hands together in front of her as if she's praying.

"Do you realize how amazing you are Ava?"

"What?" I stutter, almost dropping tea on the bed.

She shakes her head up and down firmly. Braids swing over her shoulder like a black cape.

"You are." She presses her hands to her lips, then drops them onto her lap.

"The thing is you don't have a clue that you're one of the most amazing people in this world. I bet Tyler recognized it."

"No, he really thought I was you."

"But we're nothing alike."

"I know that. But..."

"What?"

"I don't even know who I *am*!"

There! I said it aloud. The thing I've been hiding from everyone, especially Tyler. The reason this whole fiasco occurred.

"What are you saying to me?"

I slide my mug onto the floor. Press my fingers to my eyes. It doesn't help. Hot tears leak through.

"I impersonated you because...I don't know how to be anyone... except an older sister and...well, a substitute mother."

Not that I was a substitute mom, but I tried.

"I knew I couldn't be like Mom. She was incredible. She was the amazing person, not me."

Bridget gasps and determination fills her eyes. "But you stepped up! Kept us all from falling apart! Ava, I was there. I was thirteen, you were fourteen. I saw what you did. I was glad to let you take charge."

Two rivers of tears flow down my cheeks.

"I should have helped more but I was so afraid." She reaches up and grasps my hands in hers. We cling to each other like we're in a lifeboat.

"I was so sad. I didn't want to be at home. That's why I did all those extracurricular activities. And had so many friends. Being home was depressing, but I see now how unfair that was to you."

I drop her hands. "Unfair! Mom's death was unfair. She was taken away from you Bridget."

"And from you too."

I sit back. "Yeah, me too."

We've never talked about the weeks and months following Mom's death. This is a conversation we've never had.

"I think I was so worried about you guys I forgot about myself. Mom used to tell me to put myself first. I never knew what she meant. But now I can see it. I lost myself along the way."

Bridget nods. "I assumed you were being yourself taking care of us all. But that was selfish of me. You were just a freshman in high school. Taking care of a large family almost single-handedly wasn't what you signed up for."

"Someone had to do it. I don't regret it. The problem is that now I'm not sure who I am. So, I portrayed you. They say fake it until you make it. That's what I was doing. Pretending to be you while I figured out who I am, and what I want. Do you know I'd never even kissed a boy…a man."

Bridget's eyes open wide. "You're kidding me!"

"Well," I feel red hot blood flooding my face, "I have *now*."

Bridget gives a muted smile. "It's safe to say you at least knew you wanted Tyler Donovan."

"Since I was in eighth grade!"

Bridget squeals and claps a hand over her mouth.

For a split second, I see what life would have been like if Mom had not died. I see me and Bridget talking about Tyler in school, and me confessing I liked him and her teasing me and pushing me to talk to him.

Although back then I was fearless. I was running for student government president as a freshman. I was someone to reckon with. I probably would have bravely walked up and said whatever I wanted to Tyler Donovan. He'd have been the nervous one, not me!

"What are you giggling about?" Bridget asks peering closely at me.

"What I was like before Mom died."

"Tell me about that girl," Bridget says, leaning her head back so our eyes find each other. "Who was...is...Ava Walker?"

I shake my head. "It doesn't matter. It was a long time ago."

Bridget ignores me. "Did she like gelato? Did she always want to go to Italy? Would she have dated the star footballer and president of the debate club...and uhm whatever else he did?"

"He led justice walks. Argued against book censorship before the school board and got into Harvard on a full scholarship."

Bridget smirks. "Oh, you were a full-fledged Tyler Donovan groupie."

"I was...still am."

Her lips droop downward. "I'm sorry you didn't get to figure out who you are for the last ten years. I'm truly sorry. You made life better for us all. I hope you know that."

I nod reverently. "I'm glad to hear that, sis. It was what I wanted. I would do it again."

She holds my hand under the covers. "Isn't that who you are though? The kind of person who does what's necessary because *someone has to do it*."

"Like John McClain in *Die Hard*? Is that me? *Yippee-ki-yay*."

She rises and turns towards me. "No. I'm serious. You do know who you are. You're the person who gets shit done."

I frown. In my mind I'm hearing the many times I shut down my voice to be able to do something for my sisters. Ignored callings, ruled out ideas, passed over possibilities.

"You know what I think?"

"No, Bridge, tell me."

"I think you're scared to let Tyler discover the real you. Because you're afraid he won't like you. Not because you're not good enough. But because you're a whole lot better than he could dream."

I'm shocked by her words. Is that how my sisters really see me? As some kind of Wonder Woman?

"If things had gone differently for us, Tyler would have been an Ava Walker groupie. Because you'd have crushed it in high school. As a leader, a fellow justice advocate, as anything you'd have put your mind to."

"Thanks for the vote of confidence." I squeeze her hand. "Although it's too late for me to try and make amends. I deceived him. He'll never forgive me. I doubt I'll ever forgive myself."

I let go of Bridget's hand and drop my face into my hands. "I miss him so much!" I cry.

Bridget rubs circles on my back. It makes me cry harder. "I really liked him. He...took me to Verona. We sat in front of Juliet's balcony...watched lovers come and go. It was the most romantic thing..."

I hit the mattress with a soft fist. "I'll never feel like that with anyone else. We could talk or not and it was fine. We rode around Tuscany to all these adorable villages... tried everything...food, gelato...we even went to my first wine festival."

I take a gulp of air and let the tears fall all over my hands, the bed, and my sister's lap. She keeps rubbing my back. Other than Mom, Bridget is the first person to comfort me while I cry. It makes the tears come harder.

"Tell me everything," she whispers. "He sounds perfect for you."

"He is...was," I cry. "From the very beginning on the plane. He's goofy, you know. *And* smart. I've never been happy like I was with him. It's a different kind of happiness than being with family."

Bridget nods her head against mine. "Yeah, I get it. He's your person."

"Right," I hiccup. "Tyler Donovan was my person."

As I say those words, I realize it's true. I may not know much about love or relationships, but I know that feeling doesn't come along often.

It's like Dad losing Mom. It's taken him ten years to find someone special to date.

If it were easy to get over your true love and move on, there'd be no love songs.

"We were meant to be. But I ruined everything. I've lost him forever."

I curl up into a tight ball under the covers.

Bridget's voice shakes, "Hush, Ava. It'll be okay."

But she doesn't sound convinced.

And I, for one, know she's wrong.

Chapter Forty-Eight

The sun is blazing through the windows when Bridget and I crawl out from the bed, hair messy, cheeks stained with smudged mascara and tears.

The image staring back at me in the mirror is a stranger. A woman I've never met. One who's been through the wringer and more.

"God, we look awful," Bridget croaks. "If this is what true love looks like I want no part of it." She gives a strained laugh as she stumbles toward the bathroom.

But strangely enough, I'm not feeling the same way I did last night. It's as if someone reset my internal clock and new blood is coursing through my veins.

I quickly shower and put on PINK sweatpants and a cropped hoodie. I'm in the middle of dragging furry-topped boots on my feet when Bridget emerges from the shower, wrapped in a towel.

She eyes my clothed figure and raises an eyebrow. "Are we going somewhere this morning, sis?"

I give her the biggest smile I can muster. It falters around the edges, but I'm determined.

"Yes. We're going to fix this mess."

"*Ooooh! What!*" Bridget squeals loudly. She bounces on her feet as she looks madly around the room.

"What are you looking for?" I ask.

"Not what. Who. I'm looking to see where the dejected, heartbroken Ava Walker went. And who this imposter is."

"Hah!"

"No seriously, girl, what's up? Last night it was 'I can't fix this,' and today it's 'let's go fix this mess,' so what happened?"

"Tyler Donovan is my person. It's that simple. You said it yourself last night."

Bridget tugs on a pair of jeans, belts a silvery long-sleeved sweater on top, and ties her braids into a high knot making her look as regal as a Nubian princess.

"That still doesn't explain the switcheroo," she says.

I pour out two cups of coffee and hand one to Bridget. "We'll get espressos when we hit the corner. Drink this for now."

She shakes her head, her braids staying as perfectly aligned as a real crown. "I never say no to coffee," she grins, accepting the cup.

"The truth is...I woke up thinking...how can I give up on my person so easily. I can't let him go without trying. I'm done with being a coward. I'm stepping up. If he says no, then so be it. But I'm going to try. And you're going to help me."

"He doesn't want to talk to you again." Bridget points out the obvious.

"That's why we have to think outside the box."

I don't say that I've thought about what to say and do all morning. Since I awoke before the first light and laid in bed running scenarios through my mind.

To show Tyler I'm sorry. And get him to understand I love him deeply. And will do everything in my power to never betray his trust again.

Bridget dresses and quickly gulps down her cup of coffee, then she rubs her hands together. "Let's do this."

I smile at my sister. "Thank you for being here with me," I say, meaning it. "I'd never be able to do this without you."

"Yeah yeah yeah." She says it as if it's no big deal, but the glow in her eyes begs to differ.

We end up finding seats in the corner of the Gelato Bar and ordering espressos, and croissants. Bridget adds mimosas to our order at the last minute.

"With premium prosecco," she says to the server.

"No!" I say shocked. "We need to concentrate."

"We're in Italy!" she exclaims. "I'm ordering damn prosecco for breakfast."

"Lush!"

"Prude!"

I give up and take out my phone.

"What're you doing? Are you going to text him and apologize?"

"No. If I thought it was that easy, I'd have done it already. I'm...here, look at this." I show her the photo of me and Tyler by the giant heart in Verona.

Bridget grabs my phone. "OMG! You guys look like a perfect match."

"Our first trip together. Someone snapped our photo on his phone and he forwarded it to me that night."

I sit back as Bridget slides through all my photos of my trips with Tyler.

There's one of me and Tyler at the wine festival. One of us dancing. A selfie of me sitting on his lap. Another selfie of us on the Ponte Vecchio bridge during sunset.

"Ooooh! What's this one?"

I peer over her shoulder as images appear, singing and dancing on a small stage, faces aglow, lips moving in sync to the song blaring out of my phone.

Before I can respond, Bridget swings shocked eyes on me. "Were you on a stage singing? Ava for real? When?"

I stare at the man I love, the boy I knew so long ago, and it feels as if the entire world has stopped spinning. How could I have been so stupid to not see what is so clear in front of my eyes?

Bridget doesn't say anything as I hold the phone, watching me and Tyler perform for the crowd as if we were meant to be together. I never watched the video even when Gisela first sent it that night. I was too embarrassed.

But now. The way Tyler is looking at me, the gleam in his eyes, the dimples on his cheeks popping out whenever he touches my arm, or my waist, or just leans over near me in mid-song. It's the first time I'm seeing myself the way Tyler must have seen me.

I touch my shining face on the tiny screen. "I look beautiful," I whisper.

"You *are* beautiful. And that right there is a man in love with you, Ava Walker. I've never been in love, but I know the look."

My eyes drift from the phone screen to Bridget's face. She has the same brown eyes as Mom, tilted up at the corners, and squinty when they smile or laugh.

"You have to help me apologize to him. You have to. He's the one for me. I don't want anyone else."

Bridget nods solemnly. "We will figure it out. Don't worry."

But I am worried. I am worried I have made the biggest mistake of my life.

Bridget hands me back my phone and takes a long sip of her prosecco and orange juice. She hands me my own flute.

I inhale the bubbles and let the cold sparkling wine slide down my throat, stinging it sweetly.

"You're a bad influence, Bridget Walker," I tell my sister after drinking half my flute.

She shrugs. "When in Rome..."

"Or Florence."

"Exactly. Okay, what's our plan to get your man back."

I chew thoughtfully on the flaky croissant. "I need to *show* him how I feel. The time for telling him anything is long gone."

"Hmmm," she nods. "Normally I'd suggest we create...a montage of your photos and post it on social media..."

I shake my head. "No way. That's like blackmail...or manipulative..." At Bridget's frown, I backtrack. "It's just not me. Or Tyler."

She shrugs, "Well, I have no clue. I've never been in love."

I stare at her. "*Ever?* You've dated over..." I can't count it in my head. "A lot of guys. You're on *so* many dating apps."

She gives me a point-blank stare. "Falling in love is not my thing."

"*Okaaaayyyy,*" I drawl out the word. "What is your thing?"

She shrugs. "Having a good time. I'm about the fun and games. Once it starts to get serious, I'm outta there like a reality show star."

I choke on the piece of croissant in my mouth. After I manage to swallow it, I grumble at her, "You're no help to me right now."

Bridget orders another round of mimosas. The server tells her it's *less* expensive to order the entire bottle of prosecco, so she does.

For the next couple of hours, Bridget and I huddle in our corner, on adorable pink and white chairs, drinking prosecco and eating everything from croissants, to mini Sicilian éclairs, and then finally toast and cheese sandwiches to absorb the alcohol.

If I wasn't so brokenhearted over Tyler, I'd say this was the best time we've ever had together.

Bridget gives me a play-by-play of how she contacted Ajax

yesterday to convince him to bring Tyler to the karaoke night and how they'd been texting each other a few rude messages late last night and early this morning.

"What do you mean rude messages?" I worriedly ask.

"It started off nicely. He wanted to know if we got home safely last night."

"And?"

"And then it went south from there."

I twirl my hand in the air like hurry up and speak. "Meaning?"

She says exasperatedly, "He didn't ask for nude selfies if that's what you're thinking."

My mouth drops open. "I am *not* thinking that!"

"Oh, okay," she says grouchily. "He said beautiful women cause men's downfall. Then he mentioned all these seductive women who tried to bring down Odysseus. And compared them to you. And implied me, too, by association. It was a thing."

I groan. "He's not going to help my case with Tyler. He's probably poisoning Tyler's ear right now. Telling him I'm a seductive temptress who's out to ruin him."

Bridget barks a laugh. "You? A seductive temptress!"

I frown and cross my arms on my chest. "Can we get back on topic, please? I need to come up with a way to show Tyler how I feel about him."

We mull over possibilities.

"Boom box playing his favorite song," Bridget suggests half-jokingly.

"*Nah!*"

"Whisk him away on a romantic trip for two?" I ask.

"*Hmmm, maybe,*" Bridget leans her head to her right shoulder, then to her left, like she's working out kinks.

"Call up his brother and try to get them to mend their broken relationship?" I already told her about Tyler's destroyed relationship to explain his distrust of liars and his refusal to forgive me.

"With that snake?" Bridget asks. "No way. You can't convince

Everly to apologize to Tyler. Everly thinks he's too good for apologies."

I throw up my hands. "Then what?"

Bridget finishes her glass of prosecco. She's stopped disguising it with orange juice and we're ingesting the bottle of sparkling wine slowly but surely.

"I'm afraid that only you know the answer." She burps.

"Excuse you."

She waves a hand in the air and then uses it to cover up another imminent burp.

"You've got this Ava. If anyone can figure this out, it's you. Do you know how many projects you saved me and our sisters on during the years? Hundreds! Science projects, research papers, art homework, and creative writing tasks. You even helped to write raps for Corrine's Music History class, remember?"

My mind swirls with memories. "How is that relevant?"

Bridget leans forward and stares into my eyes. "You're a genius at fixing things. Coming up with clever solutions. Isn't that what you're always telling us?" She mimics my stern voice saying, "*Solutions, not problems.*"

I giggle. "That's not how I sound."

"Anyway," Bridget continues, "It's why you're so good at creating gelato flavors. Creativity and execution are your forte. Trust yourself!"

Chapter Forty-Nine

Bridget suggests we Facetime with the family on Saturday night since they'll all be there. Corrine is home from college for the Thanksgiving weekend.

Daisy's chubby cheeks are the first thing I see and I almost cry. "I miss you pumpkin," I tell her.

She and Emerald are yelling over each other asking if I was surprised when Bridget showed up.

I nod vigorously. "You have no idea how surprised I was."

Bridget snickers in the background. I turn towards her. "Hush."

She silences her mouth like a zipper.

"Tell us about your Thanksgiving," I say to my sisters. "I want all the details."

One by one they give me the low down on Dad's friend, Maxine, who came to Thanksgiving dinner and brought with her two huge pies she made herself.

"They weren't like yours," Daisy says quickly. "But they were okay."

Emerald scoffs. "Please! Daisy ate most of them. She said they're better than yours, Ava."

"Shut up, tattletale."

"You shut up."

I laugh at seeing and hearing my two beautiful sisters fighting amongst themselves. I reach out to grasp Bridget's hand.

If she weren't here with me, I'd be terribly homesick.

Bridget leans forward and claps her hands together to get everyone's attention. "You guys, we need to give Ava a reminder of all the different projects she's helped us with over the years."

Three frowns fill the screen.

"What do you mean?" Corrine asks.

Emerald raises a hand high. "Ooooh, I know."

"You don't have to raise your hand, Emmie, but go ahead," Bridget says.

"Last year, Ava helped me design a mosaic mermaid for art class. We went to the art supply store, picked out the colorful glass pieces, drew the mermaid, and...created her on the canvas thingie. I got an A+."

"Suck up!" Daisy sticks out her tongue at her sister's back.

Emerald's face falls. "I remember that project," I jump in fast. "I loved doing that with you."

Emerald sniffs. "I hope you come back so we can make more mosaic mermaids."

"Me, too, sweetie."

"Anyone else?" Bridget asks.

"Why are you asking us this?" Corrine demands. "We all know Ava is instrumental in helping us with every single thing."

"Right, but apparently Ava doesn't know it."

"What?" Three shocked voices on the other end of the call echo each other.

The next thing I know, they're clamoring to tell me about homework I helped with.

Art projects, dance routines (with Bridget), science projects (late nights with Emerald), polls and surveys for a statistics class

(Bridget in college so she wouldn't fail her math requirement), playwriting (that was Daisy), and even learning Spanish on an app to help Corrine practice so she'd qualify for a scholarship to a gifted language camp.

My head is spinning with my sisters' accolades and thank yous. I can feel my face beaming with appreciation and gratitude.

"Why is this reminder important at this time?" Corrine questions Bridget.

Before Bridget can reveal the ulterior purpose is to give me the backbone to win over a man, which would be humiliating, I interject with the truth. "I miss you all so much. It's good to hear what I mean to you. How I helped you all."

I'm not lying to them. It makes my missing out on a lot in high school well worth it.

Plus, if my sisters felt my love through my creativity and hard work on their projects—I mean a mosaic mermaid, seriously!—then I can come up with a way to show Tyler how much he means to me too.

Mom said, "Life is in the details."

Maybe love is too.

Maybe love is in the details of the foundation and blossoming of your relationship and you must pay attention and nurture it as you would anything else you're trying to grow.

The only question punching holes of doubt in my brand-new outlook is, *am I too late*?

Has Tyler Donovan written me off completely and moved on?

Chapter Fifty

"Have you figured out what you're making for the Gelato Festival?" Gisela flips pages in her recipe notebook, her frown deepening as I shake my head no.

"You have two more weeks!"

"I know. But I've got other things on my mind right now."

She nods sympathetically. Everyone in our class knows what went down on Thanksgiving weekend.

They know Tyler discovered my lie and broke up with me. They know about my panic attack at the club. I've thanked Patrick over and over for saving me.

Now, Gisela wants me to focus on our class and get my project started.

But it's hard. My mind is filled with memories of me and Tyler. My first kiss. And how can I forget the way his warm hard body felt when it held mine?

"You've come so far. And worked so hard. You can't stop now!" Gisela's urgent encouragement resounds in my mind.

"I won't," I promise.

Chef Marco walks by and stops at our table. "Ah ha! I see you're busy." He looks pointedly down at my closed recipe book and my apron folded next to it.

I smile weakly as he passes by and force myself to snap out of my Tyler daydreams. I slide open my recipe book.

What can I create for the Gelato Festival?
How can I show Tyler Donovan how much he means to me?
What can I create?
How can I show him I'm sorry?

The two questions swirl around and around like ingredients to a tantalizing gelato. One that...I sit up straight.

"Oh, my goodness!"

"What?" Gisela whispers. "What is it?"

I turn to her petite form, covered from head to toe in an industrial apron, a sweet smile tugging at her lips, eyes eager to help me.

"Do you think...I can make...um...a gelato with..." I stop and think. "Ginger snaps?"

"Ginger snaps," Gisela repeats slowly. "What is that?"

"A cookie. It's delicious. Tyler's favorite snack." I don't know why we're both whispering. As if we're creating a recipe for disaster instead of love.

"And with espresso? His favorite drink."

Gisela perks up. "Cookies and espresso?"

"Right...and...." I stare out into space, my mind is far away in a plane in the sky. What was it Tyler said was his favorite thing ever? Black sapote? But no...it had black sapote in it. It was...." I snap my fingers.

"Brownies."

"*What?*" Gisela squeals.

I stand up. Grab my recipe book and my pen. "He adores brownies. Rich, chocolatey brownies. I'm going to create a gelato for Tyler with the flavors he loves the most. Espresso, ginger snaps, and brownie...but, how will I blend all those strong flavors into one?"

"Sounds impossible."

I shake my head. "I've got to try."

"What about the competition? If you go with such a risky choice, you may lose everything. Fail the class. Not get your certificate as a Master Gelato maker *and* lose the internship and the prize money to open your own store back home. You can't take such a risk, Ava."

I look down at the gleaming steel tabletop. "I know it's risky." I turn toward my friend. "But the most important thing is letting Tyler Donovan know I love him. He's the man for me. Nothing else matters if he isn't with me to share it. I'll just have to hope the gelato is amazing."

As I say the words, my heart knows they're right. For once my mind and my heart are in sync.

Gisela sighs. "I understand. Love *before* gelato."

I laugh a self-imploding laugh. "You're wrong my friend. Gelato *is* love, that's why we do this."

Gisela's face breaks out into a big smile. "It is, isn't it?" She glances over at Patrick, and of course, he's looking back at her at the same time because those two have figured out the secret. *Lean into love*. Not away from it.

The difference between having an idea and executing it is a lot! Think backbreaking, soul-crushing hours of trial and error.

The next two weeks are a slow and tedious process of measuring, cooking, straining, blending, and freezing ingredients to try and produce the right blend of my three-flavor ingredients.

The only time I'm not in the Gelato Lab is when I head over to the English Cemetery to spend three hours twice a week tutoring Roma pre-teens in English.

I carry along tubs of gelato to share with them because our class is producing a lot of desserts as they gear up for the competition. Being with the kids is my only chance to forget about my romantic problems and focus on other people. I appreciate it more than they know.

The custodian says one of my ideas is working brilliantly. I'd asked Bridget to set up social media accounts for the English Cemetery to showcase the famous people buried there and highlight the need to pay workers to take care of the cemetery.

Thank God for Bridget's job that allows her to work remotely. She extended her trip until after December 8th, the day of the Gelato Festival and the lighting of the Duomo's giant Christmas tree.

She stops by the lab regularly to bring me lunch in between her sightseeing trips around Florence and her daily jaunts by train to Rome, Siena, and Venice. She's caught the travel bug more than me.

Her bags of goodies were always appreciated. Bridget would sit on a stool and watch me work while regaling me with stories about her and Ajax's texting banter.

I can't tell if they're enemies or friends or what. But I listen in case she mentions Tyler, though she almost never does.

I've dropped out of Tyler's Italian class. I tried to go back on the first Monday after our disastrous weekend, but as soon as I walked in and saw him my heart began racing and I felt faint. I quickly exited the building.

No way I was enduring a repeat performance of the karaoke club panic attack. Best to concentrate on creating my gelato, which I'm calling *"Ti amo Tyler"* so there is no doubt about what the gelato represents.

One night, back in my apartment, as I'm scrubbing off the sugar and milk stains from my skin, Bridget asks why I'm going so hard on this project that she calls "Get Tyler Back."

I told her I hated that name, but she playfully replied we shouldn't "sugarcoat" the plan. Call it what it is.

Now, watching me, she says, "Why are you killing yourself over this? I'm sure whatever you make he'll like. You already said you don't care if you win the prize, you just want him to know how you feel about him."

I wipe my arms with an old soft towel and consider her question. It's true, I'm going all out. I'm throwing everything I have into this creation. "It's Michelangelo's fault," I say cryptically.

Bridget bursts out laughing. "I get it. You want to create a gelato worthy of the *David*?" She hugs herself laughing at me. She knows me so well.

I wait for her to stop killing herself with joy at my expense and say without an ounce of amusement. "Yes, I do. I want to create like these artistic geniuses we're surrounded by. I'm giving it my all—my heart, my passion, and every fiber of my being. Anything less would be an insult to them, and to *Florence*."

She shakes her head. "I hope they're all worth it."

"*I'm* worth it."

Bridget lets out a whoop. "Say that louder for the folks in the back, please."

I grin at her. "It's not in the bag, you know. He may reject my efforts."

"He might." She shrugs. "But think about what you'd be gaining."

Chapter Fifty-One

It's Bridget's last words that hound me through the long days and evenings in the lab.

What if Tyler rejects my gelato as a peace offering? What if I lose him for good? What is there still to gain?

Other than a delicious specially-designed gelato flavor. Honestly, I don't think I could ever eat it because I'd be reminded of Tyler and how I foolishly lost him by being afraid to be myself.

On the last evening before the Gelato Festival, I'm not the only one in our lab working late. Matilda is there, along with Patrick and Gisela and Lisle, and a few others.

"It's down to the nitty gritty now," someone says.

Nervous laughter wafts through the room. We're all putting the finishing touches on our masterpieces.

I've gotten my espresso mixed sublimely with my ginger snap cookie flavor, but the brownie is troubling. It's too rich in some batches. Too subtle in others. Crumbly and disgusting in most.

"Damn!" I smack the tub of gooey gelato on the table. "I can't get this right."

Matilda is the only one left in the lab, perfecting her kiwi "down under" special. I've tasted it during one of her test runs and it's excellent. Fruity, creamy, light as air, and flavorful. Everything Chef Marco taught us to aim for.

"What's wrong, Ava?" Matilda leaves her side of the room and hustles over to mine on her thick, strong legs.

I drop my head in my hands. "It's no good. I can't get the brownie taste and texture to work with the other ingredients."

Matilda dips a spoon into my container and licks it clean. "You're suffocating your ginger snap flavor."

"I know," I sigh.

"Do you need the brownie in it? Your espresso has a strong flavor. It can carry the mix."

"Take out the brownie, right? It's what I think too, but I want it to be right for him. He loves brownies. We shared one on the plane. I want to create an experience. To help him remember how we started, where we came from." My voice goes up in a wail.

"Some things are not meant to go together. It's like forcing somebody to love you." Her eyes are wise as she looks at me. "Trust me," she says in a soft voice. "Try the gelato without the brownies. Then see what happens."

She puts down the spoon in the sink and walks away.

I slump against the table. All this work and I still can't get it right.

"Thanks, Matilda," I say as she packs up to leave. It's after nine o'clock. I'm exhausted. Too many sleepless nights. Lack of food. And, I'm missing Tyler so much that there's a constant ache in my chest.

I'm wondering what he's doing. If he's seeing anyone already. If he's forgotten about me. Has he put me out of his mind?

My phone buzzes. It's Bridget asking if I'm okay.

I'm ok. I'll be home soon. Just one more time.

I did it. I got Ajax to agree to bring Tyler to the tree lighting and then lead him over to the Gelato Festival.

What do you mean lead him? Against his will!

No. Let Ajax handle it.
Do you think he'll come through for me? He kind of hates me.
He doesn't hate you. He'll do it. For me, even if not for you.

I decide not to ask what that means. I text back my thanks and turn to make a brand new batch of gelato with my perfected espresso and gingersnap base which is difficult enough as it is. I put aside the brownies and press on.

The hope I've been harboring is deflating. First, I must get rid of the beloved brownies. Next, I don't know if Tyler will even show up.

He'd promised me he wouldn't miss this event months ago when we first talked about it.

He knows the prize money would enable me to open my own business back home. And he knows I long to earn the coveted internship with an Italian gelateria to gain more experience.

But I'm willing to sacrifice those wins to make a gelato to win his heart. He's my inspiration. His love and friendship mean more to me than anything.

I'm not giving up. I believe in my *Ti amo Tyler* gelato.

Chapter Fifty-Two

Please let him come. Please let him come.

Those words hum through my head as I stand dizzy, but excited with my classmates in the large truck set up in the middle of Piazza della Repubblica.

All the gelato for the Firenze Gelato Festival is made on-site in large trucks containing freezers and mixers.

Bridget and I arrived this morning. I'm wearing a new, long white chef's coat, with my name, Ava Walker, stitched in red embroidery on my left shoulder. I have a little white chef hat for my afro.

Chef Marco gifted us all these coats and hats yesterday and I'm honored to put mine on. It means I've passed the class with my espresso gingersnap gelato flavor, but now is the real test.

Eighteen gelato masters from around the world are here today, having won in their own countries.

I, along with eight of my classmates, have entered the student category. We're competing with other gelato students from around Italy.

We heard the students at a culinary institute near Genoa are the ones to beat. Last year the top gelato master hailed from Genoa.

"But we represent Firenze, Florence, the birthplace of gelato during Renaissance times. We must do more than represent! We must excel today!" That was the pep talk from Chef Marco this morning before he let us loose in the freezer truck to recreate the flavors we made for the final test in his class. The flavors that got us selected to be here right now.

The piazza is awash in the colors of the rainbow, from the pink and blue of the judge's tables to the blue and yellow striped tents of the stands for the gelato makers.

Bunting in pastel colors—pinks, greens, blues, and yellows—flutter in the breeze. The entire piazza looks like a postcard of a summer day instead of the winter's day we're having.

The pungent scents of burnt sugar, coffee, dark chocolate, and lemons fill the air, making my nose twitch with anticipation.

Quirky and brightly colored gelato carts line up around the festival grounds, their freezer boxes perched on bicycles or wooden stands. Cheerily painted images of cones and scoops of gelato decorate their sides.

Visitors can buy their gelato from the vendors. But almost everyone is here to taste the creations of the gelato masters and students in the competition.

A large white stand is set up with the words, "Gelato Card" in giant letters on top. It's where the public can purchase their gelato cards to go around and try out all the flavors.

Judging is divided 50/50 between a panel of experts and the public so we get to welcome the visitors to our stands and tell them a little bit about our gelato, to win their votes. It's understood that each creation has its own unique story. I'm not sure I want to share the story of my gelato with hundreds of strangers.

I can only hope my gelato speaks for itself. But just in case, I've written down a few ideas on an index card. I brainstormed with Bridget last night. We came up with:

"*Ti amo Tyler* is a wake-up call (espresso) to be brave and different (ginger snaps). Doesn't everyone want to be in love? Try a scoop of Ti amo Tyler!"

Bridget says that it sounds and tastes perfect. But I want to add to it. That's why this morning I got up extra early to prepare something I hope will elevate my gelato and my presentation to Tyler.

"Are you nervous?" Bridget asks as I set up my spot behind the counter where I'll be handing out cones or cups of gelato to whoever wants to taste mine.

"Yes."

"What about your secret ingredient? Is it going to work you think? You really want to try it *here* for the first time?"

I nod. "Yes."

"Okay," Bridget throws her arms around me, and we hug tightly. "You'll make magic. I just know it. I can't wait for Tyler to taste it and forgive you so we can move on."

"Me too," I whisper. "I haven't told anyone the new plan yet. I hope it'll work out."

"It will sis, it will. It's a brilliant idea."

I want to say, "I hope so," or "Maybe," but a growing feeling inside of me, like I'm getting behind the wheel of a race car and heading for the starting line is filling me up.

I've never known if I was competitive before. But heck, I was running for student president at fourteen, that girl is in me.

I can feel my competitive genes inching forward now with the adrenaline.

I shake my head to get rid of any doubts trying to sabotage me.

"I got this," I tell Bridget.

She rewards me with a big smile. "You do! Now let me go find those knuckleheads in the crowd."

I glance at my phone. "My gelato will be ready in an hour give or take. Don't come back too early with them."

"Trust me even if we get here a little early there's plenty to do...and eat!" She wiggles her eyebrows at me. I laugh as she disappears into the crowd.

I turn to Matilda next to me. "You ready?"

She grins. "'Born ready,' as you Americans say."

I turn to my other side. "Gisela, what about you? Do you need any help?" She's busy grating chocolate for the topping she'll sprinkle on her delicious rich dark chocolate gelato from her country's original cocoa.

She gives a tiny smile looking out at the crowd that is growing even larger. People are swarming around the gelato stands, cones in hand, looking to see what we have to offer.

As students, we got to go last in the trucks so our gelato is still freezing.

"What about you, Ava?" Matilda asks, a kind look in her eyes. "Do you need any help?"

Normally, I'd say no. But I'm trying to be a different, braver woman and there's nothing braver than admitting when you need help and accepting it when it's offered.

"Actually, I'd love a little help," I tell Matilda. "When my gelato is finished freezing, I need to add something and I've never done it before."

Matilda's eyes open wide.

Gisela's head snaps up from her grater. "What is it? How can you change it now?"

I shake my head. "I'm not changing it. I'm...enhancing it...making it better...I hope."

"Of course, we'll help you," Matilda says.

"Yes, me too," Gisela smiles. "My chocolate sprinkles are ready so I have time."

Patrick, who decided *not* to compete, but is providing support to us all, especially to his girlfriend, slides over and hugs Gisela. "What are we planning over here? You all sound like you're planning a coup to wipe out the gelato masters."

I say nervously. "You'll see."

Chapter Fifty-Three

Finally, the timer sounds for our freezing units and we each scrape our gelato mixture from the paddles into stainless steel canisters.

I scoop up a tiny bit on a spoon to taste it. Truthfully, it's the best gelato I've ever made.

The texture is smooth and creamy. The espresso flavor is the highlight with the gingersnap cookie flavor leaving a subtle and mysterious aftertaste, a technique I picked up from the winemakers at the festival in Panzano.

If I didn't know what was in it myself, I wouldn't be able to figure it out. I only hope that Tyler can.

When we've all finished scraping our gelato into our individual canisters, Matilda and Gisela come over to my workspace and help me with my creation.

They each divide up the new ingredient I brought from home. We're allowed to bring in our extra toppings. They don't have to be made right here.

One chef has brought hibiscus flowers he's adding to his

gelato. Another chef drizzles honey in stripes across his gelato, which he's naming Tiger Stripes.

Matilda, Gisela, and I work carefully to introduce my special ingredient to the gelato, scoop by careful scoop.

We're like seamstresses in a factory line, handing off the part we did to the next person to add their own part.

When we're done, we slide my creations into the huge stand-up freezer for a half hour while we clean up and carry canisters of gelato to the stands designated for us under the tent.

In half an hour, we return to the truck and pull out the trays with my gelato.

"This looks amazing," Gisela's voice is full of admiration. "How'd you think of it?"

Matilda's cheeks are bright red from going back and forth and up and down the truck steps.

"I am so proud of you. You didn't give up. This should win a prize."

"I don't care about winning. But thanks. I hope Tyler appreciates it."

Gisela laughs, "If he doesn't, I'll be here to eat it up." She eyes my dessert greedily.

Matilda shoves her shoulder. "What about me? I'll beat you to it."

I stand back and admire our handiwork.

"It looks awesome. Thank you both so much."

"Hey, what's going on? You need to get behind the counters and hand out gelato. And don't forget to tell the patrons the inspiration behind your masterpieces. Their votes count for 50%." Chef Marco strides toward our little group.

He stops talking and stares.

My heart thuds loudly against my chest. He could kick me out for making something different, although technically, it's still the same gelato. I hold my breath as he looks it over.

After a long minute of poking, tasting, and eyeballing it, an unprofessional whistle escapes his teeth.

"Ava, you would make Buontalenti proud." He turns toward me, his face a bright red, lips stretching from one side of his face to the other.

"It's okay?"

"Are you kidding? It's a masterpiece."

"It's my *David*," I whisper.

He must have heard me because he says, "Museum worthy for sure. This is a winner if I say so myself. What's it called?"

"*Ti amo Tyler.*"

He shakes his head with laughter. "You definitely have Italian blood. *Amore* conquers all. Even gelato!" He walks off and I can hear him laughing even after he leaves the truck.

"Come on, gals," Patrick pokes his head into the truck. "We've got customers!"

I gather up my gelato and hustle out behind Matilda and Gisela. We set up ourselves behind the high counter, protecting our creations from dust and soot and anything in the air that could destroy it.

When my first customer presents me with their card, I pull out my gelato creation and hand it over. "It's called *Ti amo Tyler*," I tell them. But nothing else.

No one seems to hear me anyway as they all gasp or whistle or clap or show their appreciation in some way.

If I weren't so busy meeting customer demands, I'd be blushing hard.

"Hey Ava, don't forget to save some for your boyfriend!" Gisela shouts across the stand where customers are busy eating her Ecuadorian Epiphany gelato. She changed the name from Zamora. Naming gelato is a whole experience all by itself. I know now why the judges like to hear the stories behind the creations.

Gisela proudly tells her patrons the chocolate she used is the highest premium chocolate from her country sourced from the rarest cacao on earth.

I glance over to Matilda further down the counter, dishing

out her kiwi, white chocolate, and sour cream gelato, a combination I never imagined could exist until she created it.

As the crowd surges several times over the next hour, I pace myself, giving out a small portion to each patron as instructed.

I find myself smiling at each and every person who tells me they've never seen or tasted anything like what I've made.

Suddenly, Patrick comes running over to our stand holding up his phone. "Guys, you won't believe what's trending on the Gelato Festival's social media site. It's going crazy!"

"What?" We yell out.

Patrick lowers the phone, looks at me, and says, "The hashtag #*Who's Tyler?*"

Chapter Fifty-Four

"What if he sees it?" I gasp. "This could ruin everything."

Gisela leans over, patting my shoulder with her gloved hand. "You've created a masterpiece for him. He'll be honored."

Matilda speaks up. "If he's mean about it, you don't want him anyway."

"That's exactly what I tell my sisters," I stammer. "Never thought I'd be on the receiving end of those words."

She squares her shoulders and turns back to a customer with a big smile. "Welcome to Kiwiland."

Gisela giggles.

Patrick laughs. "Kiwiland! Ha! Back home we'd call you all 'Depps.'"

"As in Johnny?" Gisela teases him.

"As in kooky," he retorts.

"Okay, thanks for warning me."

"Don't you dare change your gelato name, Ava. Don't you dare!"

"Mind reader," I mutter at Matilda.

"We're here to win this thing for Florence. For Chef Marco. For every one of us. Your gelato is kicking butt." Matilda digs deep into her canister to scoop out her dwindling supply, so her words are muffled. But I get the message.

I check my phone to see if Bridget has messaged me, but nothing. What's taking her so long? The Christmas elves could have lit up ten trees by now.

More customers line up for a taste of my gelato. I'm running low on supplies. At least the judges got theirs already.

As I hand over each cup, almost everyone asks, "Who's Tyler?" Then, they take a selfie with my gelato and post it on the festival page. Each time I glance down at my phone I notice the hashtag trend has grown. Like a dragon with a hundred heads.

Another half hour later, as my gelato is dwindling to nothing, Bridget still hasn't arrived with Tyler and Ajax. I'm ready to give up.

"Hey, excuse me, can we get some service, please?"

I almost think, *how rude,* when I hear a snort I know well.

I swing around. Bridget is standing there, looking happy with the tall, debonair Ajax next to her in a black leather jacket, motorcycle boots, and dark sunglasses. He looks more like a movie star than any real movie star.

From my peripheral vision, I see Matilda press a hand to her chest and hear her whisper, "Oh my vision!"

My eyes quickly swerve from Ajax to the tall, handsome man next to him. I'd recognize his cocoa-dark skin, curly hair, and golden hazel eyes anywhere. His cream sweater and hunter-green duffle coat, with the hood up, make him look like a Black Robin Hood.

It doesn't matter how old we are now, he still looks like the cute boy I first saw in the eighth grade on that long-ago school trip.

He was the boy I wanted to meet back then. He's the man I want now.

A memory of the smile we shared in eighth grade before I climbed back on my school bus, morphs into the welcome hugs we shared at the beginning of ninth grade when we saw each other six months later.

That memory is replaced by Tyler bending over to help me when he found me crying outside the school the day Dad decided to move Mom to hospice care.

That memory switches to Tyler saying he's sorry for my loss and offering all his notebooks and assignment sheets so I wouldn't fall too far behind.

A memory of Tyler doing some of my homework and turning it in for me resurrects itself from the abyss of my memory bank.

My brain is suddenly flooded with the moments we'd shared that he mentioned, but which I'd locked away. Because those memories are all a part of the horrible dark period in my life, the after-effects of losing my mother.

I see Tyler's smiling face saying "hello" to me in every class we had together over the years. He sat next to me in every one of them. Even though I ignored him. He never gave up on being a friend to me.

Life-changing events may have ripped me apart since ninth grade, but the one constant in high school was Tyler Donovan. And I'm only realizing that now.

Mom called it. When I confessed to her my crush and asked her how to know if a boy likes me. She told me, as she stroked my arm, a slight smile playing at the corners of her lips, "When a boy likes you, he'll let you know it. Look for the signs. They'll be right there."

The memory slideshow occurs in a split second. I clasp my hands over my mouth to stop sobs threatening to escape. Because Mom was right. The signs were there, back in high school. The signs were here during the past few months.

Bridget clears her throat. "Um, Ava...you got something for us?"

I raise up my freezer, pull out the entire canister, and place my gelato surprise in three separate cups. I lean forward and hand them over.

One to my sister. One to Ajax. And lastly, one to Tyler Donovan. Our eyes lock for a second before his own slide away.

This is not the time to play shy, Ava. This is not the time to hold back. Mom's voice echoes in my ear. She's never let me down.

I straighten up and face Tyler. When I speak, it's to everyone gathered around, but my eyes are for him only.

"I've named my gelato *Ti amo Tyler* because on my plane ride over to Italy, a man named Tyler offered me gingersnap cookies to calm my nervous stomach. It was my first time flying and I was terrified."

Laughter rings out from the folks gathering around.

"After eating an entire box of his precious ginger snap cookies, we proceeded to drink a gallon of espresso between us, and much to the dismay of our fellow passengers trying to sleep, Tyler and I talked nonstop for ten hours."

More laughter reverberates through the crowd. Our student stand is surrounded by more patrons than the stands of the master contestants. Phones are held high recording my confession for the world to see, which makes me nervous, but I blast on.

"Weeks later, after we'd eaten our fair share of gelato throughout this beautiful country, Tyler confessed that his favorite food in the world is brownies and he wished someone would find a way to put brownies in gelato or gelato in brownies."

The crowd makes *oohing* and *aahing* sounds, clearly recognizing where this story is headed.

"We checked many gelaterias and were saddened to find that no such brownie gelato existed. So...I...created it for him."

Loud clapping echoes around us. But I'm not finished. I hold up a hand.

"When the man you adore with all your heart loves gingersnap cookies, espresso, and brownies, you must find a way to combine them into the best dessert on this planet—an artisanal gelato called *Ti amo Tyler*."

I hold up a cup to show everyone the freshly baked brownie sliced in two and filled with espresso gingersnap gelato, adorned with a thin layer of sliced almonds pressed into the brownie sides to highlight the brown concoction. "This is my gelato sandwich," I grin. "In honor of my love for this man, Tyler."

The crowd cheers, claps, whistles, and stomps their feet.

I look directly into Tyler's eyes. "You are the only one for me. Please forgive me, I promise I will respect our bond and do my utmost best never to deceive you again. Can I please have a second chance?"

Deafening shouts erupt around me. I almost put my hands on my ears. Some people are screaming, "Forgive her, Tyler!" But they're snapping photos of Ajax.

"Not *this* one!" Bridget growls at the crowd grabbing Ajax's massive arms. She points at Tyler, who's looking dumbfounded.

After the clapping stops and the whistling ceases and people begin drifting away, I'm still looking at Tyler, who hasn't moved since the whole confession started.

The ball is most definitely in his court. What will he do?

Part of me expects him to rush up here, catch me in his arms, smother me with kisses and say he misses me, and he loves me back.

But the way he's staring as if in shock, not moving toward me, not moving at all, I realize those scenarios only happen in the movies.

This is real life. When he doesn't say a word, I feel my knees weakening. Someone comes to stand next to me, but I can't see through the tears blurring my eyes.

"It's okay honey, you did it. You're brave and resourceful and I wish I had a daughter just like you. I'd be the proudest kiwi mama bear in the world."

I fall into Matilda's arms and somehow, they feel like my own mother's arms.

By the time I manage to wipe away the tears, Tyler Donovan is gone. He said before he never wanted to see me again and now, he's made it clear. Nothing I do will convince him otherwise.

To make matters worse, he didn't eat a single bite of the dessert I created for him.

His cup is sitting on top of the counter, a melting mess of gelato and brownie, a balled-up napkin next to it as if the holder was squeezing it tightly to contain his anger.

Chapter Fifty-Five

"Well, that's that," Bridget says, laying back on my pillow, her arms bent behind her head, her pajama-clad legs stretched out on top of my bed.

On her stomach rests my wooden plaque and gold star certificate I was awarded for *Best Student Gelato*.

The excitement of winning is far overshadowed by Tyler's rejection.

Not even when Chef Marco gave a speech about how I arrived on the first day of glass and dropped his bowls and he thought, oh no, this student won't make it through the course, not even then did I join in the celebration.

I don't want to be a party pooper, but I couldn't possibly go out with Bridget and the class to celebrate tonight.

Matilda suggested we go all head home, rest up, and regroup tomorrow night instead. So, that's the plan.

I can feel Bridget's eyes on my back as I pad around the apartment straightening it up, placing clothes on hangers, folding laundry, stacking dishes into cupboards, all the things I ignored during the past two weeks while I worked on making the best gelato I could for Tyler.

In the end, I did make a supreme dessert. Better than I expected based on the reviews I received.

The public overwhelmingly loved my gelato-filled brownies.

The judges said I was inventive and that's what they're looking for in a winner.

"You will take gelato to the next level," one of the judges said as she handed me the certificate.

"One day in the future you'll look back on today and be happy about it," Bridget says firmly. "You came to Italy to accomplish a goal. You've surpassed that goal. You should be extremely proud of yourself. *We* are all proud of you."

She means the family. Bridget insisted we call them when we got back to the apartment and tell them the good news. I forced a cheerful smile as they shouted and jumped up and down exclaiming about my amazing gelato brownie.

"Does this mean you're staying another three months in Italy, baby?" Dad asked. "Doing the internship with the gelateria?"

I nodded, not trusting myself to speak.

"You happy about that, sweetie? Dad asked, a frown growing on his face at my lack of enthusiasm.

I nodded again. Bridget took over and said I was overwhelmed and tired and we'd catch up again tomorrow.

Now, I'm busy cleaning while she lays back and fiddles with my wooden plaque.

"I don't know what's wrong with him, sis. He seemed like he was in shock more than anything else. Ajax texted me that they went straight home and Tyler's being unusually quiet."

"Great," I mutter. "I made it worse."

Bridget doesn't try to convince me otherwise. She opens her laptop and sets it on a pillow. "Let's watch some Netflix. The new season of *Outer Banks* is out, and I could use a little treasure-hunting excitement with JJ, my fave bad boy."

I roll my eyes at her. "What, you're tired of Ajax already?"

"Ha! He's no bad boy. He's a Harvard graduate-slash businessman. He just looks like a bad boy."

"Meaning?"

Bridget shrugs. "Meaning we're friends. Just friends. He's looking for Ms. Right. I'm looking for Mr. Right Now."

I crawl into the bed and get comfy to watch the show. "Fine, at least you both know what you want."

"Yup," Bridget says as she presses play. "Now, not another word about real-life men. Let's focus on JJ and John B and Pope and ..."

"Do they all have to look so...*raggedy*?"

"You're such a kook."

"And you're such a Pogue."

We end up watching two full episodes, eating popcorn I microwaved, and shouting at the characters for their dumb moves.

After Bridget falls asleep, I lay awake staring at the ceiling for a long time. Trying hard to come to terms with Tyler and me being done for good.

By the time I drift off, I think I've convinced myself I can handle life tomorrow, no matter what it throws at me.

Chapter Fifty-Six

I open my eyes to Bridget standing over me waving her phone in the air. "Ava, wake up, wake up!"

"What the heck? Is the apartment on fire?"

"We gotta get ready. Hurry up!"

I groggily pull the covers up over my head. "I need more sleep!" I wail. "Leave me alone." Based on the lack of light in the room, it's not even 7 o'clock.

But Bridget isn't having it. "Listen to this. I got a text from Ajax."

"So, go talk to your *friend*."

"But it's about you! Tyler wants to see you."

Boom! I pop up so fast that my head hits the back of the headboard. "Ouch!" I rub the spot on my head while frowning at Bridget.

"What does he want? I can't handle being taken through the wringer again."

Bridget dances around the room. "They've invited us both on

a road trip. They're coming to pick us up in an hour if we want to go. Ajax says we'd *better* want to."

And you say he isn't a bad boy. That sounds like a bad boy threat."

"Oh please, Ajax is a pussy cat."

"Cats have claws."

"Okay, he's a fluffy Australian shepherd puppy trying to herd us together."

I sniff. "Bad analogy. There's nothing fluffy about Ajax."

Bridget grins wickedly. "How do you know?"

"Ugh!" I throw up my hands and get out of the deliciously warm bed.

"I'm only doing this for you, okay? I'm done with Tyler Donovan. I shot my shot and got knocked down. From now on I'm concentrating on perfecting my culinary skills and inventing new gelato desserts."

"Yeah yeah yeah."

"I'm serious. I made up my mind last night after watching John B get shot at a hundred times. I'm done getting shot down."

Bridget smiles sweetly. "Just get dressed. So glad you hung up all those clothes last night."

"Hrrrmph," I grumble.

The car they've rented is larger than the little minis Tyler usually rents for us. This one has four doors and a full backseat.

When the guys pull up in front of the Gelato Bar, Ajax pops out of the front passenger seat and opens the door to the back.

Before I can slide in, he grabs Bridget, pulls her in next to him in the back, and shuts the door.

Rude!

I'm left standing on the curb next to the empty front passenger seat.

"You're pitiful," I mumble to Ajax as I slide into the seat and tuck my legs in. I refuse to look over at Tyler. "Just say you're dying to sit next to my sister."

His booming laugh echoes around the car. "I'm in love with your sister."

Bridget covers his mouth with her hand. "Shut up."

Out of habit Tyler and I exchange glances, but I quickly avert my eyes to stare out the window as we rumble past the Piazza de' Pitti, and toward the Porta Romana, the massive 13th-century southern gate that leads out of Florence.

In the back seat, Ajax and Bridget are chattering away running through topics like podcast hosts.

"Ehm..." Tyler clears his throat. "Ajax is leaving in a few days."

So, *that's* why we're on this road trip. To show Ajax a bit of Italy before he leaves.

All I say is, "Bridget, too." I don't trust my mouth to say anymore or else I may break down or worse, confess my undying love for him again and look like a fool.

We follow the road leading north towards Bologna. The same route we took on our first trip. Winter has changed the view. Instead of vineyards brimming with grapes waiting to be picked, fields of naked gnarled trees greet us.

When Tyler takes the road toward Verona, I gasp audibly.

His eyes swing toward me. "Are you okay?"

I'm thinking, is this a joke? But I don't say it out loud.

Bridget leans forward and pats my shoulder. I swallow hard. Why are they doing this to me?

I get the impression Tyler wants to say something. But it's probably something like, *let's be friends*, or congratulate me on winning, which would be ironic, and I can't deal with that right now.

The tension in the front of the car contrasts weirdly with the happy bantering in the back. If I didn't know better, I'd believe Bridget was falling hard for Ajax. And vice versa.

Chapter Fifty-Seven

Tyler turns off the highway and drives into the beautiful romantic city of the ill-fated Romeo & Juliet.

Ill-fated indeed. Like me and Tyler Donovan.

"We're here," he says.

Bridget and Ajax cheer from the back. When Tyler parks the car, they tumble out laughing and teasing each other like playful puppies.

I can see what Bridget meant. Ajax's looks don't match his personality at all.

He's a goofy fun nerd instead of the cool sophisticated man he appears to be. This says a lot about Tyler, too, since Ajax is his best friend.

When we're all standing on the sidewalk, Ajax pulls Bridget to the wall overlooking the river and they lean over to admire the view of Verona from there.

Tyler and I did the exact same thing just a couple of months ago. I huddle down into my coat, blinking fast to cover up the tears threatening to fall.

"Are you cold?" Tyler's voice is close. I glance up into the hazel eyes I know well. I shake my head no. I still don't trust myself to speak.

I want to get today over with, go back to my apartment, and tuck myself under the covers to sleep for a long, long time.

After selfies and one group photo, we follow Tyler along the riverbank to the center of Verona and down the alley straight to the courtyard of Juliet's house.

Bridget exclaims, "It's just like in the movie, *Letters to Juliet!*"

She skips over to the wall in the courtyard of the Capulet home where declarations of love, heartbreak, and hope are scrawled in notes taped across the massive stone edifice.

I watch silently as my sister and Ajax read messages out loud to each other.

Tyler has disappeared, so I perch on an ancient bench, blowing on my cold fingers.

From somewhere in her backpack, Bridget produces a pen and a notebook and tears out a page.

She sits next to me and writes on the paper while pressing on the notebook. When she's done, she folds it in half and sticks it on the wall using tape from a tape dispenser someone has left on the bottom ledge.

"There, I did it," she says, sounding like she scaled a mountain.

Ajax follows suit, scribbling madly. He tapes his note to the wall right next to Bridget's.

For the first time today, I perk up. I wonder if their messages have anything to do with each other.

Wouldn't life be easier if we could write our innermost feelings for someone in a note and tape it to a wall for them to find?

"Sorry, that took me so long. I'm ready."

I swing my head around to see Tyler strolling toward us fiddling with something in his hand.

I wish I could say to him, "Guess what? These two idiots

wrote love notes to each other but pasted them on a wall instead of confessing what they feel."

And Tyler would roll his eyes, and say something funny like, "They probably just wrote, 'You're the peanut butter to my jelly.'"

And I'd laugh and we'd cuddle, all smug in our coupledom.

"Did you hear me?" Tyler's speaking. He's reaching out a hand to me and I stare at it like it's a snake.

"What?" I lean backward.

"Will you please take my hand?"

I look over at Bridget, her arms wrapped around Ajax's tree trunk body. She's nodding her head. "Go," she whispers.

I get up slowly, taking Tyler's hand in my cold one. His hand is warm as usual as if he has a raging fire coursing through his veins.

He leads me over to Juliet's balcony. We're standing in the exact same spot that we'd stood at back in September checking out the locks on the gate.

"Ava Walker," he says, his voice firm.

"Yes?" I force my gaze to stay on him even though I'm afraid of getting emotional.

"Uhm…Ava," He stops and tilts my chin up so I can look into his eyes. "You have no idea how happy I am to say your name. *Ava*."

My mind is blank. "What's going on?" I ask frantically.

Bridget yells, "Give a brother a break. He's probably nervous."

This time Ajax puts a hand over *her* mouth.

I turn back to Tyler. In his hands is one of those tourist padlocks you can buy from the Romeo and Juliet kiosk.

"Yesterday…your gift to me in front of everyone…the brownie gelato…I was stunned. Speechless. No one has ever said those kinds of words to me, or ever done anything like that for me. It… was hard to process, especially since I believed you liked someone else…"

"But that's Patrick…he's…"

"I know. Your sister explained. *Twice!*"

My fingers grasp his hand like it's a life raft. "What are you saying now?" My heart stomps against my chest ready to break out.

He kneels in front of the balcony. Holds up a big red lock and turns it around. In red pen, a crooked heart is drawn, and in the middle are the words:

"Ava & Tyler forever"

"I love you, Ava Walker. I always did and I always will. Since high school."

"What?"

"He says he loves you," Bridget shouts, yanking Ajax's hand from her mouth.

I ignore her. My eyes are on Tyler Donovan kneeling before me. "You do?"

He nods slowly. Dimples flash as he smiles at me. There's a glow in his eyes I've never seen before. A warm, peaceful, happy light. Like he's completed a difficult challenge.

"I can't believe this is happening," I stammer. "I thought I lost you. I thought…." Before I can say another word, Tyler stands up and pulls me into his arms.

He lifts me off the ground. Our mouths find each other in a desperate kiss. "I missed you," I say into his mouth.

He responds by kissing me harder, pressing me as close as we can become, our hearts aligned and beating as one.

"Finally!" Bridget claps her hands.

Ajax brays a loud donkey sound. "We did it."

"Forget them," Tyler whispers as his lips move over my face, kissing me everywhere, my forehead, eyes, nose, both cheeks, and back to my lips again. Pulling all my breath into his own body so my knees weaken, and my poor heart feels as if it will burst with joy this time.

When he releases me, he says, "We're not finished."

"There's more?"

He holds up the padlock. "Let's lock this up!"

I nod vigorously. "Absolutely."

Tyler and I find space for our red padlock on the gated door below Juliet's balcony and slip it in place.

Together we close the lock. Tyler picks up my fingers and kisses them. "To us, Ava Walker. To us forever."

I hold his hand to my heart and repeat his words. "To us, Tyler Donovan. To us forever."

It is hard to describe the love I've felt for him since I was a teenage girl.

People say you can't know so young, but I did. We both knew. Love is a gift.

As Shakespeare shows us with his classic tale, no walls, real or imaginary, can keep out love. Not if you stay open-hearted, believe in yourself, and believe you are worthy of true love as you are, *exactly* as you are.

"Can we go get something to eat!" Bridget wails in the background.

"I know the perfect place." I give a last look at our lock and turn toward the archway leading us out of the courtyard.

As we walk quickly against the wind, toward the famous gelato shop Tyler and I discovered, Tyler asks, "You got any more of the *Ti amo Tyler* gelato at home? I didn't get to taste mine."

I shake my head and smile. "I can make more any time you want."

"Right," he says. "Because if nothing else, we'll always have gelato."

"Don't push it."

He laughs, kissing my hand as we hurry into the shop. A warm blast of heat embraces us. Along with the gorgeous sight of gelato being dished up into bowls.

Time to get down to business. I rub my hands together. What flavor am I having today?

Chapter Fifty-Eight

Our class celebration party is scheduled for Saturday the night before Bridget and Ajax both leave Florence to go their separate ways.

Him to his Greek island of olive groves and her to our family home in Maine.

There's an abundance of joy in the air, but a definite aura of sadness, too. I'm going to miss Bridget a lot. Having a sister here made Florence feel a lot more like my real home, and not just an adopted city.

But I have so much to look forward to. Since this is my first Christmas away from my family, Tyler and I are going to visit Ajax in Greece! Ajax says to prepare for a big fat Greek Christmas, which sounds...well, amazing.

So, Saturday night is happy and a little bit sad, too.

We've chosen the karaoke bar again! Duh!

When we arrive, my classmates have already dragged two tables together to fit us all.

They know I'm bringing Bridget, but they're shocked to see me and Tyler walk hand in hand toward them.

A round of applause greets us and we bow like a king and queen.

"We're here for a major re-do," Ajax says after he's been introduced to everyone.

"You mean 'do over,' right?" Bridget teases him.

He shrugs. "Just bring on the beer."

"You're singing a duet with me," Bridget tells him. "Keep the vocal cords clean."

"Yes, ma'am," the poor guy says, caving into her bossiness.

My classmates tease me and Tyler about finally making up after the whole *Ti amo Tyler* reveal.

"That was some story," Matilda chirps. "And what a win!"

"Thanks, I'm sorry I was out of it that night," I say.

"No worries, mate."

"Hold up," Tyler shouts above the noisy chatter and music. "You won!?"

I nod my head. "You didn't know?"

His face contorts into a sea of emotions. "Why didn't you tell me?"

"I thought you knew."

He shakes his head. "No. I didn't want to ask you because I figured you lost, and it was my fault. You mean you're staying longer than Christmas?"

"I'm staying for another three months, at least, it depends on how the internship goes. Maybe longer."

"Woo hoo! That is incredible." He stands up. "Everybody, my girl won! She's a gelato master. She's the Queen of Gelato."

He sits back down, grabs my face between his hands, and kisses me soundly. I've never felt so adored.

"So, wait," he pulls back. "*Ti amo Tyler* is an official gelato now? Officially?"

My classmates howl at him, "Yes!"

"And Matilda here won second prize. She also gets an internship with a gelateria."

Matilda raises her glass of beer high. "To my Kiwiland special!"

I'm thrilled Matilda will stay in Florence. She's become like family to me over the past couple of months.

A server comes by and Tyler orders pitchers of beer and wine for everyone. He special orders me an Aperol Spritz.

"We have a lot to celebrate tonight," he says. "I can't believe you're staying here longer. Although we'd have made it work long distance. I wasn't letting you out of my life."

I press my forehead on his. "I'm happy to hear you say that. I'm not letting anything get between us either."

When the DJ calls for singers, Bridget grabs Ajax's hand and drags him over to the stage. Tyler and I exchange looks.

In my head, I'm saying to him, "Remember when we were up there?"

And from the glint of happiness in his eyes, I can tell he's saying back to me, "I'll never forget the night of our first kiss."

The great thing about being in love is the telepathy you develop with your partner. It seems like part of the package. To understand them without words.

"Hey, you two, come join us," Ajax and Bridget bodily haul us out of our chairs and escort us to the stage area.

"Only if I get to pick the song," I say.

"Fine," Bridget answers.

Tyler and I look at each other.

"Are you thinking what I'm thinking?" I shout.

"Of course, I am."

He leans over to the DJ and the next thing I know we're hearing the opening beats of the Black Eyed Peas song that started our relationship.

Bridget grabs the mic and belts out Fergie's opening line in her clear perfect voice.

Ajax's eyebrows shoot right up into his dark unruly curls. "

Holy crap. She's incredible!" The way he's looking at her, something tells me Bridget hasn't seen the last of Ajax.

The song pumps up the crowd big time.

Tyler raps fast and furious while we all sing the chorus.

Everyone in the club is singing along, dancing, and having a ball while my voice is hoarse from shouting "*Let's get it started in here*!"

I couldn't have picked a better anthem. My life is getting started right here. In Italy. And I'm so ready for it.

L'amore vince sempre.

Do you want to see where Ava and Tyler are six months from now? Grab their free bonus story today!

To read Book 2, Bridget and Ajax's story, you can order **Olives Forever, now**!

PLEASE LEAVE A REVIEW

If you enjoyed this book I would be very grateful if you could spend a few minutes leaving a review. Indie authors depend on our readers to get the word out! It can be as short as you like. Thank you!

Lynn's Newsletter

Join my Newsletter to receive free bonus chapters, books, and tons of information about the Walker sisters' trips abroad, including gelato schools and the best gelaterias in Italy!

I'll keep you posted on when to expect my new books. I look forward to hearing from you.

It's free to sign up.
www.lynnjosephbooks.com

Also by Lynn Joseph

Olives Forever

Sangria Forever

Paris Forever

Princess Abroad

Lime to My Coconut

The Color of My Words

Flowers in the Sky

Acknowledgments

Writing this book was a grand adventure that started way back when my son Jared was 16 and we traveled to Florence, Italy on a mini-European tour. Jared and I wandered the cobblestone streets, eating gelato three times per day. It was our thing!

Four years later, I returned with my son Brandt when he was 16, and we explored Florence even more, eating gelato from the same shops. I have since spent many months in Florence, living as a local with my daily aperitivo, singing karaoke, and visiting the English Cemetery. I never get tired of the art, the architecture, and of course, the gelato.

A heartfelt thank you to all who have believed in me as a writer, including Linda Camacho, Baz Dreisinger, the entire Joseph clan, and many more!

I'd like to thank my sons, Jared Scott and Brandt Scott. You are the heart and joy of my life always. Brandt, thank you for your wisdom and humor as we developed the character arcs and plot lines for this book on our long drives to and from Quebec City.

Thank you to your wife, Meredith Scott, who patiently reviewed every word and provided stellar feedback to help me create a better story. And thank you to Jared's wife, Monet Scott, for her unwavering enthusiasm and willingness to help get the word out to the public. I love my family.

Of course, thank you to Eva Martinez for being my Day One. I'm grateful to have you and Moni in my corner always.

And lastly, to Cursey, my "partner in crime"— for trying all the gelato I made, and for giving up so many events to stay by my side while I worked hard to get our new venture off and running!

About the Author

Lynn Joseph is from Trinidad & Tobago. She's the author of the award-winning, *The Color of My Words* and *Flowers in the Sky* (HarperCollins). When she's not writing, she can be found on a beach somewhere in the world. Or binge-watching *Hart of Dixie* and *The Vampire Diaries*. Lynn lives in the charming Ferry Village in South Portland, Maine, and in Tobago, where she's known as the Mermaid Queen. Join her journey of love, food, and romantic destinations!

Visit www.lynnjosephbooks.com

Copyright © 2023 by Black Mermaid Press, LLC

All rights reserved.

No part of this book may be reproduced in any form or by any electronic or mechanical means, including information storage and retrieval systems, without written permission from the author, except for the use of brief quotations in a book review.

This is a work of fiction. Names, characters, businesses, places, events, locales, and incidents are either the products of the author's imagination or used in a fictitious manner. Any resemblance to actual persons, living or dead, or actual events is purely coincidental.

Cover Design by Yosbe Design

Interior art by Annalize McLean, PhD

Cover Photo by YuriArcursPeopleimages - Freepik.com